The Whaler, Fortune

A novel written by Wyatt Michael

THE WHALER, FORTUNE
FIRST EDITION © 2012 - Wyatt Michael
ALL RIGHTS RESERVED
SECOND EDITION © 2014 - Wyatt Michael
ALL RIGHTS RESERVED
ISBN-13 978-0692260920
ISBN-10 0692260927

Book Cover Art and Design by Wyatt Michael
© 2012 – Wyatt Michael
ALL RIGHTS RESERVED

ALISTAIR'S STORY BOOKS
PRINTED IN THE U.S.A.
SECOND EDITION

For Heather Baby

for loving my stories and
for saying, "You should make this into a novel!"

Contents

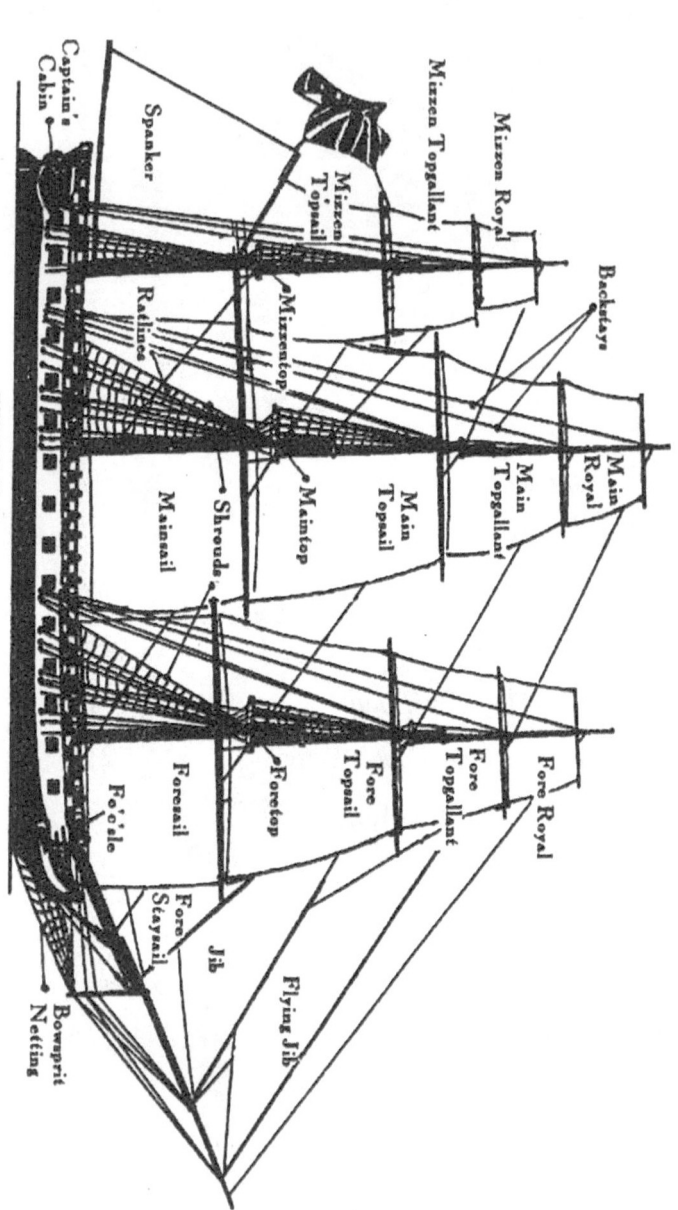

Captain's Cabin
Spanker
Mizzen Topsail
Mizzen Topgallant
Mizzen Royal
Mizzentop
Reefline
Shrouds
Mainsail
Maintop
Main Topsail
Main Topgallant
Main Royal
Backstays
Foresail
Foretop
Fore Topsail
Fore Topgallant
Fore Royal
Fo'c'sle
Fore Staysail
Jib
Flying Jib
Bowsprit
Netting

Preface

In beginning the drama of The Whaler Fortune I would like to say a few words to the reader. During this age of sail much went into getting the tall ships to sea. It was important to me to resurrect the procedures taken by these nautical masters who accomplished unimaginable feats in those times with nothing more than the power of the wind. This story follows that closely at times to allow the reader to get a small glimpse into the lives of those men, the complexities of operating a great floating beast, and should not be taken in chapter one as the projected feel or style of the remainder of the book. It is not at all written to only those who find sea stories thrilling, but is intended for general readers of Adventure / Thriller / Horror. I myself find and I know many other readers like me will find this lost information to be fascinating and as far as I can tell, no one has ever penned it to parchment like this.

The research and study for this book was truly epic and spanned two years of time and in retrospect, am quite pleased with myself in deciding to climb that discouraging and threatening mountain.

For readers of the paperback edition, I would suggest keeping internet access handy for searching the various terms used. Jump into that reference if you find yourself wondering what just happened.

For your pleasure and necessity, there is a diagram of a whaleship's sails that you will find most helpful. E-readers and online users can start with the links listed below. There are many diagrams and nautical glossaries online if needed.

I encourage you, if you ever had the opportunity, to visit the maritime museums along the Northeastern coasts of the United States to which very few long-living artifacts of this whaling history are on stunning display.

Now brace yourself for a rocking and pitching ride into the unknown where there is no escape and nowhere to go if you try.

~ Wyatt Michael

http://mysite.du.edu/~ttyler/ploughboy/whalingbarkbot.htm

http://snakeladylibrarian.files.wordpress.com/2008/06/pirateshiip1.jpg

http://www.macyplace.com/FirstFury/Supplementary/Image_alice.gif

http://www.wanttaja.com/navlinks/MAST.GIF

For He shall give His angels charge over thee,
to keep thee in all thy ways
Psalms 91:11

Chapter 1
Farewells

oseph walked through the dirty streets of Saint Giles District in London, England, on the cold morning of April the Second, Seventeen Hundred Eighty-Six. The place where his feet carried him was run down with poverty and the poor diminished there. It was a far cry from Windsor Castle or Buckingham House, the lush residences of King George the Third, or his Weymouth, Dorset holiday resort and it was everyone's desire to see it washed away by some divine tidal wave. That place had lost its former glory, being uninhabited by people, with the inevitabilities of all life; ashes to ashes and dust to dust - and Saint Giles was no exception. Built from a leper colony hundreds of years before, it had not come so far from its contagious beginnings and he felt that it was to remain forever in the Dark Ages - along with all those who laid themselves down in its hopeless nights. Upon looking at it, one with any familiarity with mankind could see that in the years to come much evil would transpire there by the ways of those beings if The Lord himself were to tarry. If one were to have a list of them, it would wrap around the earth a dozen times and only the angels would find the ages to read it. It was a sad and unfortunate business and Joseph was unfortunate enough to be having his life there at the time.

He was young in the span of it, being nearly thirty-four years old, never married, and dressed warm with a thin black coat and floppy hat. He traveled with a large scuffed wooden case against his back, slung over one shoulder and a heavy canvas sack in his hand. He was solemn and somewhat tired as he made his way onward up the street to a corner building with a stair rising from the alleyway. It was a place he knew but had not seen in some time although he had not been so far away. He would have returned much sooner, but the preservation of extinction kept him hidden from the things that he held closest to his heart. He stopped in the street and gazed upon a small window that overlooked him. It was lonely and even appeared saddened by the colors that it reflected; much like the ones that Joseph himself imagined were naming themselves after him. He smiled that bereft half-smile between the thin brown sideburns that grew to the corners of his mouth, the one that had taken permanent residence upon his character, and then continued to climb the stair to the solitary door at the solitary landing. It was a day that he wished would never come, but over the course of the last two years, knew that it probably would.

As he came to the second floor of the rental

corridor, away from the sounds of the waking world and the heavy smell of gin and urine, he set his canvas sack against the wall and knocked.   He pressed his face closer to the rugged door when he spoke.

"Mother…it is I, Joseph."

It was opened to him and a woman in her late sixties stood smiling. She was dressed warm in very plain clothes and appeared poor, but her face was pleasant and shining. She was relatively short in stature in comparison to others and her sweet green eyes that sat within her rosy cheeks made anyone who looked upon her immediately assuaged. Under a triangular black headkerchief-taffeta, she wore her dark hair in tight pinned curls and it kept her ears warm in the chill of the room.

"Joseph! Come in, son!"

He entered and they embraced in the old doorway.

"It has been some time, my dear…too much," she said with a very heartfelt smile and a pause. "Come," she quickly urged, "I have made us tea which will warm you right."

He took up his sack and set his things on the floor at the entrance to the tiny flat. Only a few wooden chairs and a table sat in the center of the room of the woman's home. They, like everything else, were old and had seen many years of use with as many years of travel; much more than one would expect from objects designed to stay still and firmly planted. The small but comfortable kitchen lay only fifteen feet from the door and nothing much else existed within, save a room where she slept. Joseph rested at the table and his mother immediately placed out tea in a humble set and settled at a place beside him. He took a sip and she was right - it did warm him. He gave her a smile that was overshadowed by sorrow and because of it she waited for him to speak.

"I'm going to try to take up as hand of a whaleship, Mother," he said softly while looking into her eyes. The woman's countenance changed from a beaming smile to one grave. There was a moment of silence. "There isn't any other thing I can do to earn enough money for us. It is what I must do."

"Joseph, I was getting used to having you around in the hope that we would soon find the time to spend together," she replied softly with much sorrow. "You said you wouldn't do that type of work again."

Joseph looked down to the table and breathed in slowly. "Because of my experience and the payment, I really have but no choice in any matter. I am drowning here and cannot raise my head above the surface," he said, grieved, and then looked up at her. "If there was any hope left for us to have anything more in life then I need to change it."

"But I'm happy with what I have. Why can't you be? You've spent enough time away and its time you can't have back...and for what? You've only lost time with those whom you love in seeking something more; something better. What is better has been in front of you all along, Joseph."

"It is not enough," he answered with his eyes downward. "I don't want it for you or for me, this driving burden to survive with all the memories of better times and things that were in place without need of desperate pursuit."

"Those were different times, Joseph," she said

softly. "Things are not the same now as they were then. I've accepted that. This is my home now and I have accepted that as well. I have made it my own, but you...you have not lain down your head in all these years. You have not acknowledged or recognized a home. You must do this and have peace. You are still a young man with your life ahead of you. Do not take thought for my happiness in such a way. I am old and the flowering years of my life have been spent...and they were spent well. My dreams are of you. And my hopes are for *your* well-being and *your* happiness."

"My happiness is bound to this. I cannot stop what I feel and my peace is the peace of someday living a better life; one that reflects what I've known. I must go. It is what I must do not only for you, but for myself. This will be the last time."

She became deeply saddened by the news. He reached into his inside coat pocket and pulled out a folded poster and a small handful of paper money. In another pocket, he uncovered a small coin bag that was packed full and set it in front of her.

"This is all I have. I want you to have it."

"No, Joseph, I cannot."

"It will last you a long time," he implored her.

Tears formed in her eyes as she looked down to the table and then back to him.

"With the money I'll earn when I return we'll be able to leave this place and start anew, back home in the country."

"But Joseph, it's so perilous!"

"God will protect me," he answered earnestly. His face became much more somber.

It was something that he truly believed and she could see it as she looked into his face. It brought a sense of security and comfort into her soul and she smiled again, softly, from his words. He unfolded the creased parchment and laid it open on the table, facing her.

It read:

~ *WANTED* ~

Strong Healthy Men to hold the Distinguished Positions of hands aboard the Great Whalers of the Sea ~ Men seeking Adventure and Glory of the High Seas should arrive early at the Greenland Dock, Rotherhithe, to set Sail ~ Comparable Wages and Promotion granted to those who desire to Earn ~ Experience preferred but not Necessary.

"I'll try to get aboard ship at the Greenland Dock to day, if possible. I expect I shall return no earlier than two years' time," he said as he looked into her face with an equal sadness. "Mother, this is our only hope for a new life." He placed his hand over hers as it rested upon the table, took his tea again, and finished it. "Will you be all right?" he said, hoping to see her in usual resilient optimism.

"I have Mary and Liza. They will be near as always when I have need of friends," she answered with a reassuring smile.

Joseph nodded with some shadow of comfort upon his face. He looked down to the table and her eyes remained fixed upon him.

"You have turned out to be a fine man, Joseph; one I am content to call my son…no matter what the arrangement. We only wish, out of our own self-indulgence, that we could ignore necessity… but it is never so." She paused a moment of reflection and her heart was heavy with the things that weighed on a woman of her age who had been down the choppy road that she knew. The thought that pressed her most could no longer be quelled and she spoke. "Your father would be more than proud to see you now."

He looked downwards again and the words stung his heart. They made him both melancholy and cheered, although only one was fleeting. The room became quiet again and there was not even the benefit of a clock on a wall that could remind them. It seemed no words could further comfort either one and Joseph interrupted the muted presence of the tiny space.

"I'm sure I must go now to find my way."

He stood and took his mother's hand as she rose. He walked to the door, leaving all of the items on the table, including the poster ad for sailors. They tightly embraced and both shed a few parting tears.

"Things will be better," he said. "I will write you and have the post delivered at times possible from sea."

"You shall be in my prayers continually. I love you, Joseph."

Joseph stepped back and held her by the arms. With a tear running down his face and that smile, bereft of true spirit, he said, "I shall return."

He picked up his wooden case and pulled the strap over his head. The canvas sack was sure to follow and he unlocked the door and stepped into the hall, stopping at the stair to turn again and take one last look at her.

"I love *you*, Mother."

She quickly wiped the tears from her face and smiled as she nodded to him and he traveled on, away from her sight; exiting the building to the street while wiping the tear that tried to make its way down his own cheek.

Many people began to stir on foot, including several loose dogs that went about scrounging for a breakfast. The area was dirty and unsightly. The buildings that looked down upon the ghosts of men were not ancient, but nevertheless, their wisdom would most wholly be ignored. The troublemakers were still too drunk to be up so early - eight-thirty in the morning, but their destructive gods were already in the markets and squares, ready to do business. Ahead, three blocks on a perpendicular street, many horse-drawn carriages and carts rolled by taking the parishioners along the arrows that pointed them in the directions that had been predestinated and the unbelievers to a more forlorn passing.

He made his way to the main street and passed through the crowds of merchants and salespersons. Many dry goods advanced upon carts as Joseph weaved in and around the people who had stopped for them. He made his way to a carriage positioned at the curb and halted to speak to its worn and seasoned driver who was seated atop.

"Sir! What's to be demanded for transit to the Greenland Dock of Rotherhithe?"

The gentleman looked Joseph up and down and considered the distance of the place along with the appearance of the nearly tattered traveler. He was not normally an empathetic man, but to day was a little more sunny than usual and he must have felt it in his soul.

"Fuppence," he replied in a coarse voice.

"Seein' as how I'm goin' only one way, that'll do, sir, if I may be afforded."

Joseph reached into the shallow pocket of his coat and pulled out two coins - one he kept hidden in his palm and the other was one groat. He extended his arm and gave the four pence to the driver who quickly looked it over.

"Climb aboard then."

"Many thanks, sir," Joseph said, taking hold of the door.

The driver nodded and whipped the horse while

Joseph seated himself inside. He opened his hand and looked upon the half-shilling that he had concealed for a moment and slid it into his pocket; the only bit of money he had. It seemed now that there was no turning back and that all his decisions had been forever finalized; chiseled into stone. He could not help but to feel that he had fallen from the kettle into the fire. At the thought of it, he almost wanted to leap from the door and run away in fear, but he did not - for now at this point in his life, there was no place left to go.

The carriage led them away into the bustling traffic of the noisy streets of London. Joseph peered through the carriage door window and gazed upon the skyline of the city, to the smoke of pipes and the distant frames of dark warehouses. He leaned back into the seat and rubbed his hand over the soft leather interior as if to say goodbye to comforts. He kept his eyes fixed on the windows to take in what he saw even though he was unhappy with how he had fared in the city. His thoughts always returned to his childhood; to a place where the world was much different – a world of peace. His lip turned downwards as a marker of troubled reflection mingled with remorse. It was not for him. None of it was. At times, he had felt that he had slipped through the fingers of God and was lost far down below in a mixture of darkness; a coagulate of muddled sound and blindness. At others, he felt there was no one else *but* him and that every word was carefully regarded by the Master with care. It was times like these that he held on to and they would lift him from the spiritual mire and set his feet on solid ground. It was just that sometimes it seemed they did not come and visit him enough.

The carriage made its way through the city quickly and some fifteen minutes later came to the River Thames where it crossed north to south on London Bridge, bearing east to Rotherhithe. The church spires that stood along the way filled Joseph with a sense of hope as he made his way into the canyon-like streets of Bermondsey.

Thereupon twenty-five minutes' time, Joseph discovered the fields around the Mill Pond as he approached his stop. Upon it, the morning birds were more comfortable in their routine and their cheerful songs made it painfully obvious. He rubbed his hands together nervously while the large horse-drawn carts of goods flowed past going to and fro - all stacked with the crates, tubs, casks, and barrels of development.

The carriage drew near the Greenland Dock which sat a few miles outside of London city and it was glorious to behold. It was an enclosed dock of ten acres of water from the Thames which could accommodate one hundred twenty tall ships at busiest times without mooring. At the head, on the western end, the Russell family mansion sat facing the eighty-five ships or so at berth. On three sides of the dock, running from the mansion to the river, were double-lines of leafy and hearty trees that acted as compelling and persuasive windbreaks. The place stirred with the loading and unloading of ships and it was a powerful sound that seemed to rise to the highest elements of the sky. Crewmen and laborers were everywhere like an intensely concentrated city of ants upon an exposed fallen honeycomb trying to accomplish the impossible on a race against the setting of the sun. The carriage halted and the brake was applied. Joseph stepped out carrying his luggage and raised his hand to the driver.

"God bless you, sir!" he shouted over the great commotion.

The driver nodded again with a small feeling of gladness for imparting fairness to his sojourner because of the man's humble traits, released the brake, and whistled to the horse that carried him off.

Joseph turned and stood looking upon a sight not often seen.

Barrels and casks of all sizes were being rolled up and down over gangways to their storage. Men lifted crates high into the air with tackle fixed upon the ships' yards to lower them into their holds. The shouting of orders could be heard across the water from all corners. The place seemed chaotic, but was well organized and coordinated. The need to be rushed was still present even though there was still enough room in the dock for more ships to occupy when they arrived. Vessels of all types were being serviced and Joseph saw among them fishers, merchants, and whalers lined up as soldiers fully turned out and ready for their orders of battle. He carefully stepped into the bustle of the western side and weaved in and out between the diversified parade of workers, looking for an opportunity. He listened as he went and the medley of languages among those there brought on the feeling that he had stepped out of the carriage into another dimension; that he had quickly arrived on some distant and foreign continent unnaturally where he was an unidentified and unnamed species. Several of the ships' hulls were being cleaned and repaired and the sounds of hammering both near and far echoed over. He recognized a whaleship ahead by the whaleboats on her davits and made his way towards her. The tea and cotton stored in the holds of the merchant ships were waggoned off past him and onwards he discovered tables with accountants and ship owners striking off numbers. Also among them were recruiters looking to the men who passed nearby to raise a crew to man the ships on which they would be making a profit. Joseph then came across a man walking towards him, dressed as a rugged sailor would be and smoking a pipe.

"Pardon, sir," Joseph quickly injected, "can you tell me which of these whaleships sets her course to the South Atlantic?"

The man, who was a Frenchman, responded in English with a heavy native accent. "This one's here and there are ze Greenland whalers. There beyond ze merchants is ze Whaler, Fortune. She makes her course South."

"Obliged," Joseph responded with a nod. "Merci."

The Frenchman turned away into the current of traveling men alongside the crates of potatoes, cabbage and sugar, and carts laden with enormous casks of whale oil.

Joseph continued and saw her - the Fortune. She was a 110-foot barque-rigged ship from jib-boom to stern with three masts holding sixteen sails total; along her sides hung five whaleboats with two spares on the skids. The hull was painted frigate fashion, meaning that gun ports were painted on to fool pirates into believing she was heavily armed. On the bow, she carried a figurehead: a carving of a bare-breasted woman with wings. In her right hand under her arm, she held a ship's rudder and in her left, in the same fashion, a ship's wheel - and there being carved another wheel within the wheel.

The barque was being fitted out with many goods including salted pork, flour, salted beef, cabbage, potatoes, limes, and rum (which was to be mixed with stagnant fresh water casks for suitable drinking). Also, for the captain and his officers, was loaded several cases of butter and sugar for their indulgence.

Joseph drew near and at the base of a gangplank, a man sat at a table writing with pen and ink. He was an aged gentleman with white hair and beard, dressed very well and warm, wearing small spectacles and a black top hat of fine beaver fur. Many men with all types of luggage and supplies were very busily going past him. Joseph took a deep breath and approached him and set his sack to the ground at the foot of his table.

"A good morning to you, sir. Does this barque be the Fortune?" asked Joseph.

"It is," said he.

"Sir, would it be to sail to the southern seas and return hither?"

"It shall," replied the gentleman.

"Sir, I am interested in immediate work aboard her."

The distinguished man removed his spectacles, placed his elbow onto the table, and studied the new prospect, looking him up and down.

"Are you aware, sir, that she be a whaler and requires much more integrity from all hands aboard than the merchants be?" said the man.

Joseph opened his mouth to answer, but was interrupted.

"Seeing how a whaleman must not tremble in the face of the great beasts who would stove a boat in his teeth, reducing it to mere matchsticks on a whim?!...willing to spill the monster's blood in his stride, riding him out upon his fury until the seas be red with it?!"

"I am, sir," responded Joseph.

"How well be it with you that the prospect of the voyage be no less than two or more years before the mast and then and only then shall ye be paid for your labors from the take of her at port?" said the man as his eyebrows raised up.

"It suits me well enough, sir."

"Be ye an able-bodied seaman in good health capable of the lifting requirements, climbing of rigging, and doing all manner of strenuous labors aboard a whaler to take whales from the grounds of the Atlantic and around the horn to the Pacific?" said the gentleman. "...And at the ready to depart on a moment's notice?"

"I am," replied Joseph.

"Do you carry any experience, young sir?" he asked as his eyes remained fixed upon him.

"Aye, two years in the merchant service under Captain Rillerby in '84 and two years prior aboard the Whaler, Verdes, under Captain Tailor," Joseph stated.

"And your take aboard the Verdes?"

"About fifteen-thousand barrels in her hold, sir," answered Joseph.

The man at the table set down his pen and gave Joseph a more thorough look over.

"Would ye be agreeable, man, to a 125th Lay of the profits," said the gentleman, "and that amount being subject to debts accrued by use of the East London Whaling Company's provisions aboard ship?"

"Aye, sir."

"Whom do I address, sir, and to what whereabouts be ye from?" asked the man.

Joseph extended his hand to shake which in return the man obliged, remaining in his seat.

"Joseph Michael from Saint Giles, sir."

"Mister Whittier I am…part owner of the Fortune, shareholder and representative of the East London Whaling Company."

"Very good, sir," Joseph said, smiling for the first time since their meeting.

"Well then, if you, sir, do swear an oath under God that these statements be true," Mister Whittier said quickly, "then sign here upon this contract of service."

The old man then prepared a form that he took from a leather bound case and set a pen aside. Joseph took it up, dipped into the ink, and wrote his name upon the line at the bottom.

"Excellent!" Mister Whittier exclaimed. "You may freely board and make preparations for your service aboard her. You sail under a man of integrity, Captain Henry Grey. She strikes sail to day at precisely two o'clock PM. May God be with you."

Then immediately Mister Whittier returned to his paperwork at the table and paid Joseph no mind.

"Thank you, sir," Joseph responded with a serious face.

He turned to his left and looked up at the Fortune's tall masts and rigging. He stepped onto the gangplank that rose to the bulwarks and ascended to the weather deck with the familiar feelings of numbness mingled with hope.

Upon the entrance of the Greenland Dock, two men jumped from the back of an empty cart as it flowed with the incoming traffic. They were dressed much the same way as Joseph, appearing to be poor in shoddy clothing and carrying sacks over their arms. They walked towards the dock and as they went, one man followed behind the other to pass comfortably through the onslaught. The man who followed behind the other raised his right sleeve carefully to his elbow and exposed his forearm. The skin on the inside had a large round black spot and was infected. He scratched it and quickly pulled down his clothing to keep it concealed.

Upon the Fortune, there were many workmen aboard making preparations for a long voyage at sea. Nothing was left unattended or overlooked. Joseph saw an old man with a boy assisting him going over a checklist and counting off stowage. Men were raising crates of lumber and rope onto the deck by hoisting from the blocks in the rigging. All along the yards above and standing upon the tops were rope and canvas repairmen who meticulously inspected the ship's integrity. Below his feet, Joseph could hear and feel a commotion in the lower deck and hold. There was a small army of workers on shore as well whose focus in life was to get the supplies aboard safely.

On the main deck of the Fortune at the bows, lay the ship's bell and aft the bell the windlass, which was turned by handspikes to raise the anchors. Abaft the windlass was the hatch to the forecastle. The forecastle, called the 'foc's'le', was the crew's sleeping quarters and where there personal belongings were stored. Standing over the forecastle hatch was a small wood shed with vertical swinging doors for protection against hard weather. Centered between the fore and main masts was the ship's tryworks - a red brick kiln under a wood roof-deck ceiling raised on stilts wherein there were two large 250-gallon iron kettle pots for cooking whale blubber. Trying out the blubber for the oil was how it earned its name.

Around the base of this was a foot-high framework called the goose pen, which was filled with seawater. The trypots were laid upon checkerboard-type brickwork so water could flow underneath to keep the ship from catching fire. Abaft the tryworks, forward the main mast, lay the main hatch that made a large opening to the lower deck and hold. Abaft the main hatch on the quarterdeck, lay the after hatch. This also made an access to the lower deck and hold. Above the after hatch were the skids - a raised wooden platform, a roof-deck, like the one over the tryworks, which held two spare whaleboats. Abaft the mizzen mast, centered on the deck, was the skylight, which was a wood framework that let light vertically into the cabin below. Directly aft of the skylight at the stern, the back of the ship, was the ship's wheel upon the tiller, which turned the rudder. On each side of the wheel at the stern were two deckhouses. On the starboard (right) side of the wheel was the galley (kitchen) and on the larboard (left) side of the wheel was a storage cabin for cooperage tools. Here also was the entrance to the companion stairs that led to the captain's quarters and cabin. Both rooms were connected by a roof-deck that ran overhead the wheel and formed a shelter for the helmsman called the hurricane house.

Joseph made his way past several men to the forecastle hatch, placed his things at the entrance on the sole (the floor) and descended, carrying them down with him. As he went, he heard two men speaking to one another below.

Joseph landed on the lower deck by ladder in the forecastle where it was a little darker, the only inlet of light being through the hatch above. There, sitting alone on a chest at the waist of a bottom bunk was a man. The room was cramped and along the sides of it, bunks were arranged in a double-tier. There were sacks similar to Joseph's hanging from many of the top bunks. Along an empty wall were hooks where cotton raincoats and rain hats were stored as well as a few lanterns. At the base of the bottom bunks, laid end to end, were sea chests for storage, which were lashed to the floor. The man stared silently at Joseph and remained motionless. His face was unshaven and his hair was black and unkempt. He was thin but fit and held a flask of rum in his hand. He appeared to be somewhere about forty years old. Joseph looked around, but did not see any other person in the room.

"A good morning, sir. I'm Joseph. You'll be a-whaling on this voyage?"

The strange-looking man held his stare for a moment longer without movement and then suddenly, like a switch thrown, smiled oddly and replied.

"Aye. I do go a-whaling on this here voyage."

The man's eyes followed Joseph closely as he found a chest among them that was suitable and settled his possessions inside. There were not enough chests for all hands and were shared between them. Joseph rose and walked to the exit ladder, giving the stranger a short nod before he ascended onto the main deck. The man's eyes continued to follow as he silently kept his smile.

As Joseph stepped out onto the main deck, he gazed over the bulwarks at the water of the Thames and to the other ships at port. Turning to his other side, he looked to the busy workmen ashore. He then noticed again Mister Whittier who was speaking to the two men who had arrived shortly after he did - one being he with the skin infection. Joseph stood and looked straight up to the mast hoops on the fore and main masts which stood one hundred ten feet into the sky from the weather deck. A small melancholy smile grew upon his face as he remembered his time spent alone up there at sea on other ships. Deciding to return to land for his last hours at the dock, Joseph headed down the gangplank. As he went, the two men passed by, carrying their sacks over their backs aboard the Fortune and they nodded to one another on the passing.

Joseph walked on along the dock and made his

way closer to the River Thames as he watched the merchants unloading their cargo. Barrels of tobacco stood in rows in crowded holding zone areas that were stacked high among the heaps of giant chains. From the Greenland whalers came bundles of whalebone called baleen, stacked upon moving carts. Several of the ships in the dock were hove down on their sides by their masts and tied off to heaving posts ashore. Ship carpenters and caulkers, having the keels exposed, filled the seams with hot pitch, then pine sheathing, and finally covered them with copper plates.

Not far from the excitement of the dock, Joseph found a comfortable spot out of harm's way under the outer line of trees. He sat down on solid ground with his back against one of them a final time before going to sea. He pulled his hat down over his eyes with a peace not given to many who faced such a formidable undertaking and dozed off.

Awakened by someone pulling on his coat, Joseph raised the brim of his hat to see a little girl extending an apple to him in her hand. Two hours had passed and he did not realize he had been so tired. He felt that he would have slept half the day away and missed the Fortune's departure if it had not been for her. Being hungry, he took it and gave her a smile. She returned the smile and a woman wearing a red dress and large-brimmed hat called her.

"Come, Cecelia!"

Joseph waved as she ran away and rose to his feet. He took a bite and hurried off to a large crowd of people who had now gathered aboard the Fortune to see her off.

He climbed the gangway to the main deck of the ship as the ceremonies of departure were underway. There stood among them women (the wives or sisters of some men), children, the owners, friends, relatives, and others concerned with the investment the Fortune held for them. Those who were not to depart on the voyage were dressed very well in suits and top hats, the women in fine hats and dresses; everyone being fitted for cold weather. Joseph, with a soft and sad smile, passed through them and descended into the forecastle at the nose of the ship.

Large groups of men who had no one aboard to bid them farewell were chatting and laughing below. They sat upon the chests and lay in their chosen bunks. The screeching and strumming sounds of a violin and mandolin were mingled with the noise as the men prepared themselves for the labor of departure.

One gentleman who stood among them came near and extended a handshake to Joseph who lingered near the base of the ladder. He was a generally happy man it seemed and his demeanor was inviting to one who was alone in a room full of people. Joseph shook his hand with a smile as the thirty-something stranger was first to introduce himself.

"I'm John Morgan from the New England state, Rhode Island."

"Oh, an American?! I'm Joseph Michael from Saint Giles, London. Good to meet you. What has brought you to Great Britain? 'Tis a long way from home is it not?"

"There's an exorbitant amount of work to be done

in that country," he said with a laugh. "I guess it is an accurate summary for all of 'em for that matter, but mighty overpowering for a new world. It's better for me to leave it to others who would rather burn themselves away trying to manage it like a char cloth lit at four corners."

Joseph laughed with the consideration that he had found another who lived by something he almost held in holy observance. "There are scarcely more things that are as true, indeed," he responded.

"I have no objections about a life of hard work, but some things are hardly the things worth dying for."

Joseph looked upon him with a nod and then spoke from that still small voice.

"When a man accepts that *one* path that God has prepared for him, he will rest in a peace that surpasses understanding; whether it is to die or to live a little more...but if only we could have an effective opinion in the matter," he said with a small smile and facetious expression.

John looked at Joseph with raised eyebrows and then followed it with a thoughtful squint. "You believe that? That we will find genuine peace with accepting what God has put into our laps?...no matter what the demand?" he said with a very sincere impression.

"I do," answered Joseph, "and know it to be true, but it will be the life-long trial of a man to surrender to it and God's longsuffering to allow it."

"I will consider your words, Joseph. You seem to hold much instruction that would not hurt my practice."

"Nor mine," Joseph said again with the small smile that would reveal a distant broken heart.

"What will we do, Joseph? It appears you and I set sail across the long reaches of vast ocean – the long arm of man."

"The arm of The Lord is much longer and reaches much further," Joseph said with an encouraging nod.

John smiled very big and at that moment, decided he would come to really enjoy his time spent with his new friend whom he had met a world away.

"The future is uncertain, yes, but we must not fear in knowing that it is He who holds the future," said Joseph.

"I will remember it, my friend," John replied and he meant every word.

The two glanced around at their new home, at the other men, and knew that they were the ones who would be their only companions for a very long time. Joseph was comforted by the presence of John and for some reason he did not understand, maybe a bond of psyche, knew they would be close friends.

"Well, I'll certainly be to welcome the warmth of the tropical seas when they be on us," John said in a hopeful attitude.

"The same for me. The bitter cold of England's winters has not only taken their cruel tax on me, but on all whom I've left behind," Joseph responded.

John Morgan smiled. "But the price we pay to see them," he said.

A half-smile grew on Joseph's face and with a nod he spoke. "Aye, we do that."

At that moment, the ship's bell rang out, signifying five minutes until departure. All hands in the forecastle clambered to the main deck. The sailors began to hug the women and children as some of the women fought their tears. Men trailed out one by one from the forecastle and lined themselves along the bulwarks to see off the guests - especially the women.

The First Mate, James Fletcher, an experienced seaman who fit the figure of a man to be aged in his late forties with nearly black, brown hair and thick eyebrows, wearing a short-brimmed cap, stood at the gangplank and called out in a deep voice to all persons ashore.

"All hands aboard ship! All hands aboard! The Whaler, Fortune, takes to her course in the South Seas! All hands aboard!"

The officer was bold in his appearance and had the face for it. He had a square jaw and a cleft chin, a long straight and pointed nose and would be handsome if it were not for the raw and rugged life that he had applied himself so harshly to. Like all men who had clung to the ratlines of a brackish vessel under the brazen sun and salted winds, his former polish had been steadily eroded away.

The ship's bell rang out again as a notice for their guests to depart. The crowd began to file down the gangplank onto shore, turning to wave and shout good-byes - all of them being from some part of England.

In the distance, Captain Grey embraced his fair-skinned and dainty wife, turned and knelt to hold his young son, and then stood to watch them depart. Hands aboard deck shouted different farewells from the bulwarks in French, English, and variations of

Dutch.

Mister Whittier and three other distinguished men of his age who seemed to be the ship's owners, shook hands with the captain, each in turn, and then departed the ship last. Mister Whittier stopped and turned at the top of the gangplank and shouted to all forty hands aboard on deck and those hanging above in the yards and shrouds.

"A short and greasy voyage to you, men!" he cried.

"Huzzah!" the men cheered in unanimity. It was each man's belief that he would return much richer, most of whom who had nothing at all, and a blessing from the owner was received with much welcome.

The old gentleman descended to shore holding onto his hat as the ship's bell rang out again and all men began to take positions. The captain passed beneath the hurricane house to the captain's door and disappeared down the cabin stairs.

Workmen stationed on the dock removed the gangplank to the Fortune. First Mate, James Fletcher, and another man reinstalled the bulwarks that had been removed from the gangway on the starboard side. Two rowboats that contained two men in each were positioned in the water at the ship's bows waiting for the hawser-ropes to be lowered. The Second Mate, Bromley Lock, faced the crew from the bow and called out.

"Four hands to man the windlass, two to pay the warp to the boats!" he shouted.

Several anxious men volunteered for the position and began to work. Two proceeded to feed the warps, the ropes, around the spindle of the windlass and two others fed them through the hawse-holes at the bow. A massive bight was rigged at the end of each line and those ends were lowered to the rowboat crews below. The four men seated in rowboats took hold of the warp and secured one inside each of the boats upon bitts. They took up oars and began to row out from the ship towards the center of the dock as men aboard the Fortune continued to feed them through the holes from above. The First Mate called out again to the men from amidships.

"Stand by to make sail! All greenhands steer clear of trouble! Sway the fore and main upper tops'l yards!" he ordered, looking at the men standing on the main deck. Joseph stood among those at the ropes along the outer edges of the main deck where they began to pull on the lines. The fall of the fore topsail halliards led along the larboard side of the deck, running aft, and that of the main led forward on the starboard. The men began to walk up the length of the deck, heaving on the halliards that had tied off the topsail yards. As the yards rose up, the men ran from one side of the deck to the other to tail onto the fall of the other halliard. This caused the fly blocks to come down within a few feet of the deck.

Harpooneer Three, Nigel Jackson, who was standing along the starboard side among the men hauling on those ropes, shouted to them.

"Bowse the halliards! Hoist away!"

The two upper topsail yardarms across the fore and main masts rose to their proper positions to set the sails. The topsail yards were secured to the masts by a parrel that allowed them to slide up and down.

"All experienced hands get aloft to shake the fore

and main tops'ls!" shouted the First Mate.

The appropriate numbers of men began to climb the ratlines on the shrouds upon the fore and main masts to make their way aloft, ascending both sides. They took their positions across the horses, which were foot-ropes, summing six to eight men across each yard. The sails, furled and attached to the yards at port during preparations were ready to loose.

Further, across the water of the dock, the men in the rowboats arrived at the quayside bollards which were made of whalebone imported by Greenland whalers. They threw the eyes of the warps over them and signaled by flag to the ship.

The men at the bow were prepared and had the windlass threaded with three turns to reel the ship out from the dock. The Second Mate, Bromley Lock, a hefty man in his early sixties who had been at it a long time, took the signal from the bow and turned aft to sight the Third Mate, Redford Whitby.

"Mister Whitby! She is fast to the bollards!" Bromley called.

"Aye, Aye, Mister Lock!" Redford returned. He quickly turned aft and made his way to the wheel from the cabin skylight.

"Mister Whitby," shouted Mister Fletcher, "the wind's direction?!"

Redford looked forward to the larboard side of the quarterdeck to the dog vane, a wind vane made of cork and feathers situated upon a half-pike from the wheel.

"West by North! Three points on the Larboard Quarter! A fair wind, Mister Fletcher!" the Third Mate answered.

The First Mate again bellowed his orders to the men. "Square the braces! Mister Whitby, hard-a-starboard! Cast off! Cast off hawsers from the bitts! Let go the fasts!"

Four crewmen under his command pulled off cables that were hung around two wood posts in the deck that ran out to the mooring posts ashore, causing the ship to be free from the dock. Workers on land began to draw in the cables over the water. Mister Whitby turned the wheel to the right and it moved on the tiller to the starboard side.

"Mister Lock, we are cast off!" the First Mate called.

Bromley Lock turned to the four men at the windlass with a shout, "Handspikes in and heave to!"

Two men who were at the ready with handspikes inserted them into the holes on the barrel of the windlass which was an eight-sided post that lay horizontal. They began to heave down, causing the barrel to rotate and reel the warp in. The pawls produced a clicking as they caught in their holes so that the barrel could not lose its position against the pressure. Two men pulled down on the handspikes as two others coiled the reeled portion of the warps on the deck. The long warps became taut and rose up from the water in front of them. The ship began to turn its bow quickly to larboard and moved away from the shore, pointing to the center of the dock.

"Well, Joseph," John Morgan said quietly, "we're off and away."

"What new and peculiar things I wonder we'll find, John. Let's just keep our thinking aimed to those tropical seas and dream of the solitude and beauty of the islands that live there," he answered with cheer.

"What else have we?" smiled John.

First Mate James Fletcher gave the command.

"Loose sail! Let fall the tops'ls!"

Scotty Watson, an Irishman in his mid-thirties upon the horses of the main upper topsail yard, called out from his position with his native accentuation.

"Unbend the gaskets, men!"

They along the topsail yards untied the knots of cord and the heavy sails spilled down from them with deep thunderous billows. Men across the masts began to call out from the extreme heights, signifying they were finished with the task.

"Gaskets away!" came the calls. "Main tops'l loosed! Fore tops'l loosed!"

James Fletcher hailed hands on deck that manned the cleats. "Veer the tops'l clewlines! Veer the tops'l buntlines!"

Men on both sides of the ship at the cleats and men at the base of the masts at the pins began to overhaul the ropes that led to the blocks at the tops and yards. Each man was anxious to finish and see the great ship push out on the wind for their advantage. The topsails unfurled and were given slack. The sails commenced to unfurl completely as ropes at the foot called buntlines, loosened and ropes at the corners called clewlines, tightened.

The First Mate, knowing the old beast like his own hand, looked aloft and gave a marvelous cry to those eager above.

"Sheet home and hoist away tops'ls!"

It had been some time since he had hailed a crew

with such strength, but it was second nature and comfortable like putting a familiar foot into a remembering wooden shoe.

The fore and main topsails unfurled and immediately moved softly in a cold light wind. The points upon the sails swayed away from the wind's direction as it passed over them.

"Steady out the top bowlines! Brace up sharp! Wind on the Larboard Quarter!" James shouted again to the corresponding crewmen. Those who were entirely new to this kind of situation followed along with the others around them and tried not to be knocked in the head with a beam or wrenched up in catastrophic contortions by a whizzing killer line.

Men, women, and children looked on and waved goodbye from the edges of the dock aware of possible dangers, but complacent in witnessing the crew manipulate the ship's intentions with seeming ease. Some wiped tears from their eyes with handkerchiefs while shouting very heartfelt farewells. The captain's wife was also very tearful among them. There were none who stood there who wanted the men to depart at all and saying goodbye was not written with much pity into the heart of man.

Bromley Lock, seeing the ship being in alignment with the bollards, gave the Third Mate direction.

"Mister Whitby, right the helm!"

"Right the helm, Mister Lock!" Mister Whitby affirmed with a loud shout across the length of the weather deck. He rolled the giant wheel to the left and with the creaks of taut and twisting rope the tiller became centered.

The four men worked the barrel of the windlass

and drew the ship further out into the open water of the dock with great physical exertion. They had not been aboard five minutes after the bell had sounded before they were worked as hard as a coarse man could be expected. The wind then picked up slightly as if deliberately delegated and the sails puffed out and caught it much to their support.

Joseph stood looking over the side at the shore to the faces of those who were waving there among the small intermissions that interrupted throughout his toil. He gazed across the frenzy to the Russell Family Mansion and beyond to the distant city of London as it was beginning to drift away. It was hard for him to look on those images that had made themselves symbols of failure to him. One, being man's personal accomplishment of wealth, power, and happiness and the other, man's universal representation of the same. He held on to the hope that when he saw her again, that monumental and flourishing city disguised as the Ouroboros, he would not be the same. There was not much there for him to love or that loved him, but he always tried desperately to hold on to something and give it a chance. He knew that if it were still standing on his return, he would have something more to offer and a new purpose. Maybe it would be for him and he could forgive that cruel old ancient dragon. Maybe it would be for someone else.

The ship approached the bollards and the warp became unnecessary. Those at the rowboats signaled once more to that colossal traveling representation of world progress with a tiny flag and prepared to cast off the bights from them to see it free.

Bromley Lock ordered the men at the windlass,

"Belay there! Surge ho!" and they ceased turning upon it. The pull upon the bollards deadened and the warps sagged down to the water from the ship's forward momentum. The men at the rowboats finished their task and waved to the Second Mate.

"Mister Fletcher, the warp is cast off!" shouted Mister Lock.

"Mister Whitby, larboard helm!" the First Mate called aft.

"Larboard helm, Mister Fletcher!" he replied. Mister Whitby rolled the wheel to the left, walking with it as it moved to the larboard side of the ship.

The men at the windlass continued to crank the barrel and draw the warp up through the hawse-holes to the moving ship; now only a slightly easier endeavor because of their wet weight. The Fortune began to turn away from the bollards to the right and face the exit of the Greenland Dock to the route that led over the crisscrossing paths of the beloved whale. As it became square, another whaler entered the dock ahead of them. In a gatehouse at the opening into the Thames, a man stood positioned to direct the traffic. After the ship's head passed the oncoming whaler, moving right, the command was given to the helmsmen.

"Midships, Mister Whitby!" the First Mate cried.

"Aye, Midships!" he answered.

The Third Mate centered the wheel again to the right, causing the ship to continue in a straight line. The bow faced the corner of the wet dock, off to the right of the exit to allow the oncoming whaler to pass comfortably. James Fletcher called again to his crew.

"Standby to hoist the mizzen tops'l yard! Man

the sheets! Man the halliards! Man the braces!" he chimed.

All hands on the main deck who were available uncoiled the mizzen topsail yard rigging that was stowed away under the mizzen mast. The topsail yard tie led down from the mizzen masthead to a fly block that created a leverage system with the halliards.

"Hoist long tackle! Hoist away!" First Mate Fletcher called.

The men lined up behind one another and took hold of the mizzen topsail halliards which was not done by walking up and down the deck like the fore and main topsail yard hoisting. Going hand over hand, the men stood firm and pulled the rope to themselves. The mizzen topsail yard rose to its final position. The men tied off the halliards and those at the braces secured their lines.

"Chock, Mister Fletcher!" the Second Mate reported.

Mister Fletcher quickly returned with another order. "Lay aloft and standby to loose the mizzen topsail! Mister Whitby, helm-a-starboard!"

As the yardarm men climbed the shrouds on the mizzen, Mister Whitby's confirmation could be heard below. They secured the topsail yard at its position and climbed out upon the horses to the ends. It was a job done by those who were not afraid of falling to their deaths and upon observation from below would seem that they even invited it. After those daredevils with hearts of stone, every man who had signed up for a journey such as this, had positioned themselves aloft, the ship came alongside the returning whaler. Mister Fletcher stood at the larboard side as the crewmen of the other barque began to cheer hardily and shout. After their huzzahs to the Fortune were quieted, the First Mate called to them in the passing.

"Ho there! What have ye in the hold?!

A man across the way reported, "She's bursting to the hatchways and scuttles and no place left for grog nor grub! Two years nine months out! Taking my Lay to buy the queen's golden chemise!"

All hands of the Fortune aloft and below let out a great billowing laugh that seemed to rattle the boats as whistles soared over the water.

"Luck to ye lads! Oil for ye water and ambergris for ye wine!" shouted the man.

The Fortune's crew gave a strapping cheer of builded excitement and waved to the passing ship whose sails were blackened from her greasy smoke.

Mister Fletcher's smile quickly faded as he resumed his business. "Mister Whitby, larboard helm!"

"Larboard helm, sir!"

The First Mate was poised amidships and looked forward to the nearing gatehouse. The man who faced them upon a high deck began waving a bicolored flag to signify a safe and approved exit. The First Mate made it known to all men.

"A clear passage to the Thames! Shake the mizzen tops'l! Right the helm, Mister Whitby!" he said and all hands jumped to the orders. Eight men positioned aloft unbent the gaskets from the mizzen topsail as the Third Mate took further direction that would draw them only scarcely closer to their hard-earned finish.

"Right the helm, sir!" Mister Whitby answered.

The crew began to work the ropes and the ship steered straight for the gate. James Fletcher paced the weather deck and saw that the vessel was made ready to take on the large curving river to the sea. By the moderate strength of the wind, he determined that he was able to sail her full.

"Man the weather halliards and tops'l sheets! Let go clewlines and buntlines!" he yelled to the available men with his booming voice. Those on deck overhauled the corresponding ropes causing the sail to open from its corners to meet the yardarm below.

The First Mate called again. "Haul taut! Sheet home to weather! Hoist away! Sheet home to lee! Haul out top bowline!"

Men all along the after deck tied off rope ends and pulled others downwards. The ship caught more wind and picked up speed.

Jago, a hefty rough-looking Englishman and the ship's cook, stuck his head out the door of the galley with his arms up against the doorposts. Along the sides of his face were long curly black patches of beard which were thick upon his jaw line, but absent from his chin. He smoked a brown meerschaum pipe with an apron tied around his waist while watching the men work.

"Idle hands man the spanker and jib! Ready flying jib!" Mister Fletcher shouted. "Man the fore topmast stays'l! Make ready to loose sail!"

The men at the rear of the ship headed to the spanker which was a large fore and aft sail hanging out over the back of the ship whose top yard, called the boom, extended aft from the mizzen mast. Those at the forward of the ship headed to the bowsprit and climbed out over the water upon the footropes to loose the gaskets. The surging waters broke apart beneath them against the nose of the rushing bulk and would suck any man down to his death if he were to lose his grip. Three headsails were furled in nets along the jib boom by the canvas men of the dock and lay in wait for their opportunity of testing. Seven men climbed off the bow onto the netting attached to the massive needle that pointed the course and began to untie them. As they went, the Fortune passed out of the Greenland Dock into the influential river that changed the English country forever. Men high and far atop the mizzen boom loosed the gaskets and the First Mate called to them for the next point of action.

"Shake fore and aft sails! On head sails - let go downhauls! Run up halliards! On mizzen boom - haul taut weather topping-lift! Overhaul brails and lee vang! Draw taut clew-outhaul!" he shouted to the fore and aft sail crews.

The men all across the ship jumped to work quickly. Those on the deck hauled on tackle reeved through blocks on deck, raising the headsails that would give the ship its surety of direction. Some men loosed rope and led it over hand, paying it forward to open the spanker. The top corners of the triangular headsails rose up along their stays to a fully opened position.

Mister Fletcher called to the men at the headsails. "Tend the sheets! Belay!"

The bow's crews pulled and tied off proper ropes. The fore and aft sails were made fast and the men made their way back onto the security of the main deck. The ship was at a good distance past the gate at the center of the Thames and the First Mate gave the order to turn to the right and take the river out to the Strait of Dover - their bridge to the unpredictable open sea.

"Mister Whitby, ease to Larboard helm!"

"Ease to Larboard helm!"

The great mass turned slowly to the right. The wind moved across the stern to the starboard side and the ship began to pick up even more in its momentum. The First Mate called again to the current helmsman.

"Mister Whitby, right the helm!

"Right the helm, Mister Fletcher!" he confirmed.

The Third Mate centered the wheel and looked upwards through the hatch in the deck above him at the wind gathering into the topsails. James Fletcher came near his final orders to take the ship to its fullest potential and assign part of the men to their ease.

"Let's make speed, men! Up t'gallant and royal yards! T'gallant and royal yardmen in the tops!" he called.

Men who had been going aloft climbed upon the ratlines and made their way high upon the masts. They traveled all the way up to the tops of all three masts; a task not for those with a fear of staggering heights with little to stand or hold onto. They were all manned at once because the upper sails were smaller and required fewer men to set them. Those who were on deck watched and readied themselves at the proper lines.

Doctor Braddock Stowe, the ship's surgeon, straightened the items on his desk. He looked to the ceiling and the corners of his tiny workspace below decks, sizing up his new home for the next couple of years. His operating room was very small and simple, but he would have to make it perform when the blood-spraying wounds or shattered bone came through the doorway. His face held an expression of one mentally preparing himself for new long-term obligations. The muffled banging sounds of the men's steps as they worked above reverberated through the timbers to his place beneath. He stood, taking inventory of his books and other supplies for the journey that he held with much reverence and cherished for their value. Raising the acute edge of a scalpel to his face, he paused and gave it a blank stare in acclamatory thought.

Above, the First Mate was dealing with his situation that was already at hand. He shouted to the men in the tops with the near satisfaction of seeing the new crew execute his decisions with accurate efficiency.

"Lay out and loose royals!"

The royals, sails positioned at the very tops of the masts, fell away down by the men aloft. "Man royal halliards and sheets, weather royal braces!" was his call again. Men who stood on the tops hauled on ropes fastened to them that raised the topgallant and royal yards. "Let fall! Sheet home!" Men on deck far below then hauled on ropes that opened the royal sails and brought them into fully opened positions. The royal yards across the ship rose to their final places. "Lay aloft and loose t'gallants!" he shouted to men on deck and aloft. "Man t'gallant sheets, weather t'gallant braces!"

The men in the rigging stood upon the topgallant

horses across the ship and loosed the gaskets on the sails. Shouts fell from above that the task was completed; the ropes fixed that would hold those sails in their places at all corners against the direction of the wind.

"Let go t'gallant clewlines, lee braces! Haul taut! Sheet home! Hoist away t'gallants! Steady out the t'gallant bowline!"

The orders to the men on deck were fired away by the First Mate like the fury of Mons Meg, the six ton cannon of Edinburg Castle. Before one task was completed, the men were showered with another command. It was not unlike a siege set into motion by King James the Second himself. Across the ship from bow to stern, men began to veer and haul upon the ropes. They tied them off to pins and cleats along the bulwarks and at the base of the masts. The upper sails became set and the work aloft was nearly finished. The topmen began to climb down and some slid on ropes to the lowest yards. For most of them it was second nature as if their mothers had bore them upon the thin traipse of a topman's beam and weaned eighty feet in the air in a mid-shipman's hitch held in a strained topmast rigging.

Twelve-year-old Samuel Dobb, the ship's boy, chopped potatoes on a low stool inside the galley. He threw them into a tub of water, but tried unsuccessfully to look out past the wide cook in a slim doorway to catch the action.

"Loose the mains'l! Loose the fores'l!" Mister Fletcher cried to all hands.

Men aloft loosed the gaskets on them and called out as the job was finished. Mister Whitby kept his eye on the dog vane and the upper mizzen sails as the First Mate charged him.

"Mister Whitby, the wind's direction?!"

"Holding West by North! She's three points free in a leading wind, Mister Fletcher!" he replied.

"Man the tack and sheet! Let go clewgarnets, buntlines, leechlines! Let fall!" shouted the First Mate, sending the men hopping across the entire deck.

They hauled upon ropes and overhauled on lines to feed the slack needed to bend the last two sails aboard. As the massive canvas captured the wind, the men cheered aloud and whistled to celebrate the beauty of the Fortune in her full splendor. The ship was clean, painted and greased, the sails were new and everything was well and ready for the long journey ahead. Mister Fletcher got a slight smile of gratification upon his usually deliberate face as he made his final orders to sail full.

"Very good, men! Get the tack aboard! Haul aft the sheet! Brace in! Mister Lock, see that the men receive a ration of rum for work well done! Splice the Main Brace!" he cried.

"Aye, Mister Fletcher!" he said under the loud huzzah of all hands aboard. Bromley Lock traveled to the galley and called the preoccupied cook for assistance. The ship's bell rang out and the sound traveled as a signal to those below decks. Mister Fletcher turned aft and went away into the door that led to the captain's cabin. The working men on deck continued to veer and haul upon the ropes that fixed the massive fore and main sails into place.

The Fortune traveled down the Thames and

passed by ancient harbor towns along the way. Joseph kept his eye upon the land, knowing that it would be a rare sight in the months to come; still struggling to understand the position that he had been in for so many years – even with his faith.

Jago and Samuel Dobb descended into the lower deck by the main hatchway to fetch that clear drink that was liquid cheer for the hearts of all men. As they went, Mister Fletcher entered from the doorway by the helm and made his way to the ship's tryworks, making an announcement to the men.

"We set to divide the watches and make boat crews! All hands amidships!"

The men aloft and all others began to make their way to the center of the deck and stood in a large circle around him where he presented a formal opening speech.

"Welcome aboard, men. I am First Mate, James Fletcher. I have served seven prosperous years aboard this here ship under the command of Captain Grey. He be an honest man and will treat everyone with due respect."

Mister Fletcher turned and pointed to the Second Mate who was a fair man in heart, suited properly for leadership duties and had certainly put in his time upon the pitching decks of the sea. He was a man fortunate enough to arrive into his early sixties with white strips of beard growing from his cheeks, but was as strong as an ape and twice as nimble. Being at sea nearly all his life, he was not given the luxury of much leisure nor delightful foods that fattened the princes of greater men and unbeknownst to him at the times it was better for him. He had found the famed fleeting Fountain of Youth, but like all things held so long in spellbound wonderment, it did not come as any expected or wanted. That place of retirement was so close and it was one well deserved if there ever was one to purchase it with great drops of sweat and bitter striving, but it was not apparent to any man that knew him if he recognized it. The habits died hard for some old seamen and many of them did it right there on the decks that carried them.

"This man here is Second Mate, Bromley Lock," said James. "He and I both have served many years together before the mast."

James turned to the wheel with a nod. "He currently at the helm is Third Mate, Redford Whitby. We choose the men of the boats' crews as we see fit."

Mister Whitby, like most men who had risen to officer ranking on a whaleship had seen more blood and gore than the warriors of King David of the Tribe of Judah. All of it had not thwarted him, pressed by either necessity or fervor, he was still there. He was humble and the crews before had always liked and respected him greatly and that warmth kept his fifty-something spirit in recurring elevated positions. Other than that, he was a simple man, there to fulfill his duty in life and finish strong with as many true friends and years of service that he could muster. Of family, he had none that were not lost and knew upon those early years mingling with the generations before him on weathered shoals, he had found them.

"We run three whaleboats off the Fortune," the First Mate continued, "and our boatsteerers are accurate and skilled men - men I have seen in the action and a thrill takes me each time. Harpooneers step forward!"

Three men, in the ages of forty-five to fifty-five, stepped forward from the circle. Mister Fletcher then moved to a big Dutchman who was some four inches above six feet in height and solid as a barrel packed with iron and pointed.

"This is Boatsteerer One, Mister Bastiaan Rasmussen." He approached another: an African. "This is Boatsteerer Two, Abimbola." He then pointed to the last, who was an Englishman. "This is Boatsteerer Three, Nigel Jackson. These men will be first to strike the whale and cause our pockets to be a-lined with silk. Now, for the Watches..."

James Fletcher approached Abimbola who was standing in the fore center. "All men this side of Abimbola on the larboard up to Mister Phillips, the Steward of the Pantry, is to be on Larboard Watch...all other men to be Starboard Watch. I'm officer of the Starboard Watch and Mister Lock'll be of the Larboard."

Jago and the boy returned from below decks with a small cask of rum and a few tin metal cups. The cook put a swig into each as the boy carried them back and forth to each man in the circle, going two by two.

The First Mate pointed his finger to a man wearing a dirty black apron; his hands stained in the lines of his skin with soot and wearing long curly patches of hair on his face.

"The blacksmith is Mister Prescot Stearne. He'll be a-keepin' the irons sharp and straight, the spades and knives all in good working order, the lances ground sharp. I swear upon my life I haven't seen one as skilled as he. Mister William Bazely is the cooper," the First Mate said as he pointed to a light brown-haired man who was short but muscular. "He'll keep the casks knocked up aright, large or small, for whatever we need 'em." Mister Fletcher pointed aft, amidships, to the doctor who stood on the main deck behind the circle of men, listening. "The ship's surgeon is Doctor Braddock Stowe," he continued. "He's there behind ye, men. Anybody got a problem, go see him. It's what he's here for." The First Mate turned and pointed to two others on his right. "The chips are Mister Rawley Chapman and Mister Cornelius Sorensen. They'll be in charge of repairs to the ship and whaleboats. Our fine cook is Jago! I advise you don't say too much about the woman who bore him if you want to keep an expected time at grub each day! We got any greenhands aboard?"

After a laugh from all, three young men among them, Esmond Burne, Alen Reid, and Rupert Phillips, raised their hands.

"Ye men keep your eyes and ears well usable!" Mister Fletcher demanded with severity. "This be dangerous work, but over time it'll be second nature. I want everyone to go down the line for these men whenever possible - show 'em the ropes. And remember, you'er one once yourself."

Everyone nodded to the First Mate and the Fortune drew up to a sharp left bend in the Thames.

The Second Mate called out to the Third. "Make ready to ease to starboard helm, Mister Whitby!"

"Aye, Mister Lock!" he returned.

Mister Fletcher turned and looked at the men

around the circle. "We're gonna put together the boats' crews straightaway. Be in want of twenty-four men to fill positions. Mister Lock, commence to assignin' your crews," James said as he looked over them and came near to the starboard side, approaching the men there.

The Second Mate worked around the larboard side and began questioning the men for possible inclusion to his boat crew. He was particular in his choosing to be sure those in his small company could handle the levels of stress and terror that might at times show itself in those tiny twelve-foot compartments.

The boy approached Joseph with a metal cup of rum, but Joseph, being in no mood and never taking a liking to such indulgences because of the possible consequences, raised his hand and passed on it. He was aware that it would not take the sting away for him no matter how many barrels of it he were to swim in; only creating more on its way down.

James Fletcher approached a fair-skinned man of his late thirties and paused in front of him.

"Your name?" he asked.

"Aengus Murphy, sir."

"An Irishman I see."

"Aye, sir," Aengus replied boldly.

"Your hands and feet, Mister Murphy...are they all accounted for?"

Aengus Murphy took his hands from his pockets and held them out, turning them around for inspection. All his fingers were there. Mister Fletcher scrutinized him up and down, marking muscular development, watching for any abnormalities.

"Your former experience, Mister Murphy?" the First Mate asked.

"Four years on a merchant out of Dublin Port. Three years on a British whaler in '78 assigned to Third Boat, Mister Fletcher," Aengus said straight with confidence. Behind them, orders to the helmsman from the Second Mate carried over.

"Mister Whitby, ease to starboard helm!"

"Ease to starboard helm, sir!"

Mister Fletcher was satisfied and gave the Irishman a nod. "Very good, Mister Murphy. You be on First Boat crew then."

"Aye, sir," he replied as he stepped back against the bulwarks.

Mister Fletcher moved forward and stopped at Joseph.

"Your name?"

"Joseph Michael, sir."

"And you, man, do you have former experience on a whaleboat?"

"Aye, sir. Two years on an English whaler under Captain Tailor in '81."

"You look young and able, Mister Michael. What is your age then?" James asked with some intrigue in his look.

"Thirty-three, sir," Joseph replied.

"How about it? Do ye have all the necessaries to perform the duties required on First Boat?"

"I do, Officer Fletcher."

The First Mate gave Joseph a hard look up and down and then into his eyes to read his face - something that Joseph had been accustomed to in such a line of work.

"Well then, very good. You're raised to my crew, Mister Michael."

"Aye, sir."

Joseph, not having an opinion over the matter one way or another, stepped away and peered out again across the larboard gunwales to the life on land.

Going along behind them, Mister Lock inspected hands and feet of the Second Boat prospects. A man stood before him holding his leg out and turning his heel. Joseph eyed the passing shores and looked beyond the harbor towns as the officers continued to question the men.

Below, Rupert Phillips, the new Steward of the Pantry, made his way down a ladder bearing a tablet of paper. Jago followed and the two men began to go over the items in the hold. Barrels of beef, pork, hardbread, flour, and numerous other supplies were stowed below. Large casks of water were lined in rows in the hold to be used for drinking and ballast until they were emptied and filled with oil at sea.

"On this side, Jago, I've counted forty casks of salt beef, fifty-four casks of salt pork, and sixty-three casks of flour. At counter end, we've stowed the fresh water and through that way there leads to the hardbread supply. If there be any more I can be of service?" Mister Phillips asked.

Jago gave a nod while eyeing over the hold.

"We'll eat favorably...for a while anyways," Rupert said as he stared upon the stows. The two men smiled at one another and Jago raised his eyebrows in hoping.

On the weather deck, Rawley Chapman and

Cornelius Sorensen set about organizing their work area, preparing the carpentry tools that would be in great use throughout the journey for emergency repairs: hammers, nails, wedges, chisels, and clamps. Prescot Stearne prepared his assortment of lances, harpoons, and spades to be sharpened upon the grindstone; his chore to make all abused iron blades razor sharp.

The Second Mate continued to question the men for the Second Boat on the larboard side of the deck. He approached the strange distracted man that Joseph had encountered alone in the forecastle before the ship's parting.

"Your name, sir?" Mister Lock asked him.

"Smith…Alistair…Smith"

"Have you whaleboat understanding, Mister Smith?"

"I do," he responded shortly and then stood still in silence. The officer was pressed to poke him again for a bit more.

"Well, howbeit, sir?"

"At ten years past, I made me way on an Arctic whaler into the north, but it ne'er suit me, so I been land-bound since. It may take some to seize me bearin's, but I've experience, Mister Lock."

"Very well, sir, you're on Second Boat," the Second Mate decided at once, not being too critical of a man's repertoire.

"Aye, sir," Alistair replied half-smiling for whatever reasons and the officer did not care to ask.

James Fletcher called out again to the Third Mate in watching the twisting Thames ahead of them. "Mister Whitby, right the helm!"

"Right the helm, sir!" he answered with a loud shout.

"The Starboard Watch will now report to duty. The Larboard will replace in two hours' time on the ship's bell," the First Mate cried to all hands. "Sound the bell!"

At the chime the captain emerged from his cabin below decks and made his way towards the partially mustered men. Redford Whitby was first to see him enter from the corner of his eye and gave a shout.

"All hands assemble! Captain's on deck!"

The captain was a worn-looking Englishman with a short gray and white beard; a larger man with a round belly, but strong. His voice was always deep and rugged even when he spoke softly and his face, which he usually kept under his hat, was lined with years. He made his way into the center of the crew and delivered a speech.

"Good afternoon, men!" he called in a loud and clear voice that immediately demanded the attention of all hands aboard.

"Good afternoon, Captain!" the crewmen quickly responded together.

"I am your captain, Captain Henry Grey! I've been Captain of this here ship near seven years! This be her third whaling voyage under my command and I've not had one gripe from her yet! She takes five hundred casks in her hold and by God we're gonna fill 'em all! She's fit and able and I'll put on the line she lasts longer than any of you if handled aright. I be a fair man. You want respect then you earn it here as anywheres else. Now, I won't tolerate too much drunkenness for there be work aplenty aboard the

Fortune. All men aboard will hold fast to the Ten Commandments! I especially will have no man takin' the Lord's name in vain on my decks and such a trespass will warrant a fitting punishment! No rowdy brawlings aboard neither! If you want a fight, I'll damned well give you one! All hands keep your running after the devil for when we raise land! He'll be there awaitin' for ye as sure as old age!"

The captain paused a moment and looked around at his crew who stared upon him with bold faces before he resumed with what he had to say.

"We're here to catch whales, try out their oil, and take the bone. The work isn't light when the work is to be done, but when the casks are filled and the decks are scraped I don't mind you to take it on easy...you'd have earned it! Every man carry his load! Every man do what is necessary to keep this ship to anchor and the payoff'll be well worthy! Show proper respect to the officers says I and it'll go well with you! Is that understood, men?!"

"Aye, Captain!!" the crew shouted together.

"We be in the Strait of Dover this time tomorrow, then cross the English Channel three days thereafter. We turn south, over the devil's belt to the South Atlantic, round the Horn into whaling grounds of the South Pacific!" the captain proclaimed. He paused for a moment, looking across them, upon the face of each man.

"Let's fill the hold, men, and soon return home! That'll do!"

A cheer burst forth from all hands and the First Mate quickly asserted his position again with an order.

"Starboard Watch to duty! Mister Alexander, relieve Mister Whitby at the helm!"

Thomas Alexander, an American on the Starboard Watch and relatively young, being in his mid-twenties with shaggy light brown hair with sun streaks of blonde, confirmed the charge.

"Aye, sir!"

The men then began to be at ease and have time to socialize or not. Some members of the Larboard Watch descended into the forecastle to relax and shake off an oncoming headache of temulency from the morning in port and some who were specially made for the life crawled into their bunks for a nap. Some who were never used to the solitude of the sea stayed on deck to see off Britain and to breathe in the clean air that skimmed over the waters away from the city.

Joseph stood overlooking the passing shore along the snaking River Thames. Nearby, an old Frenchman stared across the river with him, but for a moment neither of them said anything from their deep daydreams or acknowledged the close presence of another. Much of it followed until the man extended his hand to shake with Joseph after a deep breath and exhale. He spoke with a heavy French accent and seemed somewhat sullen among so many that had high spirits.

"Bernard Dupont," he said in a soft voice.

"Joseph Michael," he responded, shaking Bernard's hand.

The Frenchman turned beside him and looked again across the currents of the Thames.

"I miss my home, my city...Paris...ze love, ze

women, ze quality of a life. It lays England to a shame. Have you been to my France?"

"I have not," Joseph replied, "although I have learned her language in part." He looked intently upon Bernard.

"It is ze land of beauty and architecture." Bernard paused for a moment and his thoughts went to some faraway place in the lost chronicles of time. Joseph watched the reaction that was played in his eyes as if the man were standing before the gates of some elaborately painted city, executed with great minuteness whose welcome was drawn up by the hand of a master - born for that single purpose. "Have you ever loved?" he said without removing his gaze from the water.

After the time it takes one to relive hard memories from the past and then return amid a solemn expression, Joseph answered him. "Mister Dupont, I have."

"A secret treasure buried within those who have loved her...forever to burn with an eternal light in eternal darkness. My heart remains there." Bernard said with a tormented sigh.

"It sounds remarkable. I hope you shall return, Mister Dupont... à voir une fois de plus votre amour perdu," Joseph said with a short melancholy smile. With his words, Bernard began to smile as well and he turned to Joseph once more.

"I'll never be complete until I return home...to Paris." Bernard then drifted off, speaking softly to himself, but Joseph could hear him. "Et je vais l'attendre jusqu'à mon dernier jour."

Joseph's face reflected his inner feelings of

remembering lost love as he studied Bernard who gazed across the water to Paris, to his home, in his thoughts.

The First Mate approached three men along the larboard bulwarks who were talking together.

"Pardon, men…" he interrupted, "which of you be Royston Davies?"

The man who had climbed aboard with the hidden infectious arm stepped forward and answered.

"Me, sir."

"It is my understanding that you have experience in a cookery?" asked Mister Fletcher.

"Aye, sir. Worked several years ashore in a kitchen service for a breakfast," replied Royston.

"The cook is needin' a good assistant in the galley and, if ye be willin', it'd excuse you from some of the other more strenuous duties aboard. Be ye interested?" the First Mate asked with raised eyebrows.

"I am, sir."

James smiled and extended his hand to shake.

"Very good. See Jago when you can and he'll allot you further instructions."

"Aye, sir," Royston answered with a short nod. He extended his right hand and the men shook on it. Just under his sleeve again, the dark-colored skin infection barely showed. The First Mate turned, put his hands behind his back, and walked away.

Royston, almost subconsciously, pulled his shirt back down over his arm to cover it - an arm that itched and burned and steadily became worse.

Chapter 2
A Blow!

The Officers

The Captain – Captain Henry Grey
First Mate – James Fletcher
Second Mate – Bromley Lock
Third Mate – Redford Whitby
Surgeon – Doctor Braddock Stowe
Harpooneer 1 – Bastiaan Rasmussen
Harpooneer 2 – Abimbola
Harpooneer 3 – Nigel Jackson
Blacksmith – Prescot Stearne
Cooper – William Bazely
Chips – Rawley Chapman, Cornelius Sorensen
The Cook – Jago
The Boy – Samuel Dobb

Starboard Watch	*Larboard Watch*
Diederick Nielson	Vincent Moreau
Cormac O'Kelly	Bernard Dupont
Esmond Burne	Mingo
Gamba	Royston Davies
Thomas Alexander	Colm Doyle
Aengus Murphy	Alen Reid
Badru	Zareb
John Morgan	Rupert Phillips
Charles Digby	Scotty Watson
Kwame	Alistair Smith
Simon Laurent	Waitimu
Augustin Jorgensen	Kallum Morrison
Joseph Michael	Robert Ackley

$\mathfrak{T}$hree days after departure, the Fortune had crossed the English Channel and passed the northwestern corner of France. The day was sunny but cold at sea. All aboard prepared themselves for the whaling tasks ahead and dealt with the downtime with hobbies and fun which was not at all minded by them so far. The men of the Larboard Watch were on duty upon the weather deck - the time being one o'clock PM.

Above the forecastle at the bow, some gathered to watch a skilled music and dance performance. Cormac O'Kelly, a big heavy Irishman, played a fiddle, Alen Reid, a Scotsman who was his opposite in weight and height, strummed a mandolin, Colm Doyle, an Irishman who was burly with hands like hammers and a face full of hair, made a tune with an ocarina, and two strong African men, Badru and Kwame, kept rhythm with small hand drums like congas. The tune was an endemic eclectic mixture and men joined arms and danced to the music as heartily as if they were completely drunk and surrounded by a dozen lassies. Joseph sat smiling upon a box among the others as he observed, much too timid and stiff to compete with such reckless abandon. He took notes at their enthusiasm for a time when he would not have his own options to merely observe and retain his integrity.

Men watched in amusement from aloft, hanging about in the rigging and upon the yards above smoking tobacco pipes; a beloved pastime. Charles Digby, an old Englishman and a master of nautical knots, sat upon the mainsail yard with Esmond Burne. He held two pieces of rope in his hands to teach the young twenty-eight year old man the craft.

"Now, to make a Bowline Knot on the bight of a rope," Mister Digby explained in his rough voice, "you take the bight in one hand and the standing parts in the other. Throw a kink over the bight with the standing parts, the same as the single-knot. Take the bight round the parts and over the large bights, bringing it up again. Then it's finished." Charles spoke almost through the side of his mouth and he squinted one eye at his audience as he spoke. It made the listener pay attention and even caused one to feel that he might want to stand at attention to be more relaxed. The experienced seaman held a complex double-string hoop and handed it over to his student who wanted desperately to not disappoint his teacher. "All right Esmond, now you give it a lick. You get that one and I'll start ye on hitchin's and seizin's," he said.

Prescot Stearne stood sharpening a mincing knife

upon the grindstone as Samuel Dobb turned the wheel with his eyes upon the dancers. His hand fell slower and the wheel nearly stopped as he was distracted.

"Here, Samuel! The wheel!" the blacksmith shouted at him.

The boy jumped and continued to spin the grindstone harder than before; not having put in his time in life to deserve the comforts of leisure that seemed to flaunt itself so much around him.

Kallum Morrison, a Scotsman in his mid-twenties, was on duty at the helm. He kept his eye on the binnacle in front of him that housed the ship's compass. As a smile grew across his face at the music that flowed from the bows, he gazed aloft to the movement of the giant sails.

Jago organized the buckets of coal that lay at his feet at the base of the stove. He scoured over the salt beef stowed in the harness cask to freshen. Atop a table at his right were chopped unwanted fragments of vegetables in a tub. He raised the lid on the pen and inspected the potatoes and other vegetables that he had stored there. Royston Davies, wearing a waist apron, stood behind him against another wall washing kids, the wood food trays, in a bucket.

When the song finished and the laughter and carrying-on receded somewhat, Cormac O'Kelly saluted the African men that beat the drums.

"Badru, Kwame, a fine accompaniment...a noted backing! Very good, fine sirs! You'll be Irishmen yet!" he jested.

The surrounding men gave a laugh. The First Mate entered the main deck from the captain's companion stairs and called to the men from aft.

"We pass northwest France, men! The Channel's cleared! All hands ready for a-whaling!" James cried. Second Mate, Bromley Lock, returned with the order.

"Four men to the fore and main masthead on Larboard Watch! Eyes out for blows! Mister Morrison, hold course South West by West!"

"Aye, Mister Lock, South West by West!" Kallum replied with his hands grasping the large rugged wooden pegs of the ship's wheel.

Mingo, a young African, and Vincent Moreau, a Frenchman in his late thirties with black hair, climbed the rigging of the main mast on the various stretches of ratlines that were analogous with spider's webs. They ascended high as tiny spiders to the crow's nest which was two metal hoops at the top of the mast to stand watch for whales. Two others, Alistair Smith and Scotty Watson, ascended the foremast to the crow's nest that was positioned there for better security of no distant whale passing by unseen. From below, they climbed nearly out of sight and seemed to pass into the clouds for being so incredibly high.

As they went away aloft into what was like a permanent goodbye, Nigel Jackson stood on deck at the shrouds on the foremast with one hand resting in the ratlines. He began to tell the men around him a story in his heavy British accent that shook all of them alive.

"In a run out of New Bedford, Cap'n Reilly first ordered the watch to the crow's nest," he said. "To our amazement, it weren't an hour in 'fore the calls came down. We get out in the water and it's the damned biggest fish I e're seen. I was in the fore boat 'n I was ne'er experienced, so I wanted to get right up

74

on 'im to be sure. The beast rolled and looked at me square eye to eye 'n brisk he did it. I raise me arm to sink the iron into that big eye when he finned under the boat and struck me balance! All men went over and the tubs were sunk! We come up again and the bastard weren't nowheres to be found!"

The men who stood near laughed out at him.

"I still says that American, Mister Alexander, down in the foc's'l, rocked the boat!" Nigel squeezed in. Again, the laughing erupted, but this time with loud whooping noises and hand claps.

"Oh yeah, he was there. You can believe it. I come home and think I've steered clear of 'im. And surprises!" Nigel Jackson cried, "Here he is again, a-waitin' for me!"

The men busted out with laughter again above while Mister Alexander was unawares, lying in a bunk alone in the forecastle. He quietly turned a page in a small book that he was reading in the room's dim natural lighting.

At the back of the ship, the captain sat at his large desk in a much more comfortable setting. His cabin, decorated much more like a home away from home, had a solid bed with headboard, hanging lamps from the ceiling, windows along the stern of the ship, comfortable chairs, and a tall clock that stood against the wall. Counter to another wall, farthest from the door, lied a rack containing five muskets and two flintlock pistols to be used for protection against pirates or any other emergencies. Hanging beside them were three powder horns and three small casks of gunpowder. Violence was not a major part of the whaleship and if a man-o-war were to decide to give the captain trouble, he would have no choice but to comply with surrender. The muskets were there for small emergencies that could be handled at the ends of five of them and nothing more and most likely in place for an occasional game bird if the opportunity arose. He stood over his maps and charted the course to the furthest eastern edge of South America. On one corner of his heavy cherry wood desk sat a small hand-painted image of his wife and son in an oval brass frame. He set aside his parallel ruler and divider and walked to his windows. His mind traveled already to his wife and son and although he was where he was supposed to be, wanted to turn back to see them again. He had left her before, but this time he found it to be much more taxing upon his mind. He wanted the water to spit out the great beasts as fast as he could slay them and imagined the Good Lord bringing them quickly alongside as He did to Simon Peter as an act of goodwill for his burdened spirit. Putting one hand against the old wooden beams of the wall, he stared out across the endless ocean behind and watched it, deep in thought.

Over the next two weeks the weather changed. The men began to dress very light and most went shirtless under a new much warmer climate. The ship crossed the Atlantic Ocean near the equator beneath clear and sun-soaked skies and they were cheered by it like an unusual gift of early summer.

Men of the Starboard Watch trimmed the sails according to the wind's new directions as others coiled whale line into tubs. The rope was laid out on the deck and the end was passed through a snatch block on the mainstay overhead. It then ran down into a tub and was coiled clockwise as it fell. The helper, Augustin Jorgensen, stood and turned the line to the left as he pulled it downwards. Bastiaan Rasmussen, the First Boatsteerer who was also considered an officer and bunked in their quarters, kneeled at the tub and gave the line a Flemish Coil which is and always was turned in the direction of the sun.

Charles Digby and Esmond Burne continued practicing their knot-work aloft in the idleness that sailors loved and hated to turn it into something constructive. Esmond twisted a rope around, handed Charles a knotted lump of nothing and quickly gave up. Charles shook his head as Esmond laughed.

At the helm, Joseph was at turn and looked to the binnacle to maintain the course. He found being at the wheel under the cool shade of the hurricane house, watching the needle through the glass to be soothing. There was much to hate at sea and when he recalled some of the paths that he wore deep in England, there was much to love. The compass told him he might find more South Southwest.

Samuel Dobb hung aloft with another chore, tying stops in the buntlines as men stood around on deck smoking sweet mixtures of black Cavendish in their pipes and telling stories.

The captain made his way to the weather deck to stretch his legs and walked among them looking up towards the crow's nest. He double-checked to be sure the men aloft were keeping a watchful eye and gazed across the water himself with his telescope. He waited anxiously as did the other men to get into action and break up the monotony that was hard to be accustomed to, even with so much experience.

The cooper, preparing for his portion of the labor and with a bit of building anxiety, knocked up a medium-sized cask with a large heavy mallet. Using a wedge, he beat against enormous steel hoops that circled bowed planks, forming an elongated barrel so tightly seated together and even that they were waterproof. He patiently waited for the oil to fill them.

Over time, the musicians continued to conjure their melodies upon the forecastle and it flowed unbroken as the waters from the mountaintops. Men danced and spun across the deck while others clapped their hands; all doing what they may to be busied. If there were any of the devil's mermaids beneath them for a hundred miles, they themselves would have been bewitched by the warbling of so many men and their instruments.

Late at night, some days after, the crewmen that bunked in the forecastle were resting in their beds. A single lantern hung from a hook in the ceiling and swayed with the gentle motion of the ship. Rupert Phillips, who was young, intelligent, and a native of northern England, leaned forward on his elbow to speak to his companions from his top bunk.

"Three weeks out and no sign of a whale…it always like this?" he said somewhat disenchanted now that he saw it with his own eyes.

The old gray-bearded Englishman, Rawley Chapman, who was like a sort of father figure to all the men because of his age, answered from experience with sensibility to Rupert's concern. "Aye, sometimes months before a sightin'. I expect the cap'n'll post a reward soon to get us jumpin'," he said. "No worries. Take the time you got now to be rested for it. It'll be wished for sooner 'an you suppose."

The men chattered amongst themselves again upon the subject when Thomas Alexander proceeded to tell them a story. The noise died down quickly and the men gave attention. From his top bunk, Alistair Smith watched Charles Digby roll a gold pocket watch around in his hand below. It was a unique and beautiful thing; not something one would expect to find in the possession of such an unrefined tar such as him, but it was not uncommon in the gritty sea chests of sailors. The finest gold, gems, jewels, and hand-made creations of whalebone and exotic woods were not always found on land.

Thomas leaned on his side from his corner top bunk as he began to speak.

"The tale of two lovers: Hero and Leander," he said. "Hero lived on one side of the Hellespont and Leander the other - Hellespont, the Strait connecting the Aegean Sea with the Sea of Marmara. Leander was young and he lived in Abydus. Hero was a priestess of Aphrodite in the city of Sestos. Hero could not marry because she was a priestess, but ne'retheless Leander would swim across the Hellespont at night to be with her, guided by a flaming torch she held high on a pinnacle of a tower. One night, in a terrible storm, Hero's light was blown out and Leander lost his way. In the darkness, he became exhausted and perished. When the light of day returned, Hero saw his body washed ashore. She became overcome with sadness and cast herself from the tower to her death on the ground below, joining her lover forever."

The men remained quiet for a moment in burdensome thought in the dimly lit room.

"There was a woman who loved me much the same as that once," Colm Doyle said, breaking the heavy silence of the forecastle.

After a short pause, the men gazed at one another with a smirk and then, unable to hold it any longer, laughed aloud.

"Your mother!" Robert Ackley injected. Everyone, including Joseph, laughed again, but much hardier.

Alistair Smith stared into the single flickering flame of the swinging lantern, lost in some vision or fantasy with no expression; only hearing the deep hollow sounds of the ship as if they were speaking to him.

At eight o'clock the next morning the skies were clear. The captain entered the weather deck where all men were gathered and stood amidships at the main mast, shouting clear in the hearing of his crew.

"It's time men! I'm lookin' fer a man that'll bring me a whale! I be a-ready to get my hands dirty! I'm ready fer the decks to be greased with silver and the bed at night e'er sweeter and softer with an oil in the hold!" The captain walked to the foot of the main mast and gave another shout. "First man that sights me a whale takes a reward! Mister Bazely, your hammer!"

The cooper passed the captain his shipwright's hammer and the captain climbed atop the fife-rails, the framework around the main mast which stood about three feet high and anchored a portion of the running rigging. He took from his pocket a leather pouch and shook some coins within.

"Two quid men!" Captain Grey exclaimed. The eyes of all crewmen widened at the sound of it. He produced a nail and hammered the pouch of British silver to the mast and the clink of it that jingled the coins inside reverberated in the minds of every man who stood there. "...to the man that spies the blows of the first whale!" he bellowed.

"Huzzah!" the men aboard cried and followed it with shouts and whistles as their thoughts quickly spun in circles around the hundreds of different things they could finally do with the money. Some thought of meats, some of sweets, some of a golden tooth to fill the hole, some of immoral women and their lusts, and others, an enormous bottle of the strongest rum that men could achieve.

"Godspeed to you all!" said the captain. As the men clapped their hands, Henry got down and Jago hailed the Third Mate on deck from the galley.

"Mister Whitby, grub is right!"

Redford Whitby turned to the crew and relayed the call.

"All hands to grub!"

The men began to line up on the larboard side with much to talk about and dream about, down the length of the ship and pass by the galley. Jago stood inside slopping the food onto kids as Royston Davies, who wore his shirt and apron at all times, stood in the doorway to distribute to each man his ration. Joseph approached in line among them as they drew near to the curve at the galley.

"I wonder what the cook has spoilt to day?" John Morgan said as he turned around in line in front of Joseph.

"Probably what he's spoilt every day," Joseph replied with a smile. "Come, now. It's not all bad as of yet. We're only spanking, John. What'll it be when a year's gone and the barrels in the hold have been scraped dry? I don't want to think about Jago's face in those days."

John mirrored Joseph's look with a snort that was of both laughter and direful gloom and continued forward in line, hungry and anxious. Aengus Murphy took his plate from Royston at his turn.

"What say you, Jack Nasty-Face, has the cook been enlisted to butcher our palates?!" Aengus said, squinting at him with a suspicious eye. Royston kept his head down and glanced quickly through the corner of his eye to Jago without an answer. Aengus leaned to the side and peered into the galley door at the cook who remained indisposed at his work with care.

"What's this Jago?! Yesterday's stockings rolled

in batter?! You wouldn't choke your dog with this would you?" All the men in line let out a laugh as Jago turned around, pointing his wooden spoon with a retort.

"You'll be chewin' your own stockings for fare if there be another word, Mister Murphy!"

The men laughed again as Aengus prepared a response.

"You mean for a change, sir?!"

The men howled with rowdy shrieks and the decks above and below echoed with it.

Jago shook his head knowing how futile his attempts would be to get in the last word with the Irishman and returned to the pots to dip out the men's breakfast - a brown lumpy liquid and a piece of hardbread. Each man eagerly passed a crate of limes and took one; not only for health, but sanity. Joseph and John Morgan made their way to the bulwarks at the forecastle with their ration and sat on the sole with their backs to the wall to eat.

"I thank you, Lord, for this sustenance," Joseph prayed softly. "Bless that which I am to receive, in Your service. Amen."

John Morgan took notice and paused to look at him. "I would hardly refer to it as sustenance, Joseph!" he said.

"All the more reason to pray, John!" Joseph said in a half-preaching half-joking tone. Both smiled from ear to ear and John, having been rebuked, laughed out.

"I tell you," John stated, "there was this young African lad in the Gulf of Guinea that kept tugging on me – a dirty and mangy mongrel of a child. He was a servant in the slave port. After I gave him a doll made of twisted oakum I couldn't shake 'im loose. He followed me like a dog would if I let meat fall from my pockets. He kept this chattering in his language and waving me on to follow him and so after a day of it, I finally resigned. I went with him a ways from the seaside into the stinking paths of some remote huts and he brought me in one. They had a fire going and over it a great roasted pig turned on a spit. I stood amazed and beside this was a table laid upon the floor with bowls of fruits and rice, berries, beans and savory broth. There were colors of oranges and browns, greens and yellows. I nearly fell to my knees and wept!"

Joseph laughed while chewing his food.

"I had not eaten so well in my life and there it was...under the guise of a threadbare leaning shelter stuck in with mud and straw."

"I shall always keep twisted dolls of oakum in my pockets for when I spot a dirty waif," Joseph proclaimed with laughter. "For it could be a cherub, God's messenger, a holy being come to save me!"

"Now you're learning somethin'!" John cried with wide eyes, but with a determined face.

The captain and the officers, being the First and Second Mate, the doctor, and the three harpooneers, sat at a table inside the officer's mess within sight of the officer's bunks. They ate a much finer breakfast of sweet breads with butter. The room was clean, tidy, and more spacious than what the rest of the crew endured in the forecastle. A rim along the table kept the cups and plates steady during the movement of the ship as they were advantageous enough to be sitting at one while they ate.

"Mister Jackson, it is my understanding that you were once married to a woman of the Cayman Islands," Mister Fletcher said with all men looking to the Third Harpooneer.

"She were some lovely thing to look upon, she were," Nigel said with his mouth full and his eyes to his plate. "She would dance bare upon the sands of those tropical shores, her dark hair and glossed skin to reflect the moon's light...and feed me she would, by her own slender hand, avocado and papaya with coconut milk. Why, no man had beheld such beauty afore in all history of earth and time. Just to speak of her turns an old salt as I into an skilled poet."

The men rested their arms onto the table and slowed themselves from eating, being amazed at his reply.

"I had her there to myself for a month...on white sands to adore and to love...as a Siren Queen Enchantress with only one to admire her," he said.

Nigel broke off, finished with his story, and continued to chew alone as all other officers looked upon him, completely frozen. A pause the size of five Indian elephants sat on top of the others and the men at the table looked at one another, desperately wanting to press him for more.

"Well now, what became of it, man?!" James shouted in dismay, almost angered at his silence and hanging onto the edge of the table in captivation.

"I departed," Nigel responded plainly, looking up to James.

"You departed?!" James asked with legitimate

confusion.

"Aye."

"For what cause?!"

"…For the seven other wives I'd left three-hundred-twenty furlongs away a-waitin' for me." Nigel said with a smirk.

The men at the table burst forth in laughter, even the captain, and none of them dared ask him of his married life again.

"I did once fall for a lass," Captain Grey said amidst the clamor, "whom I did meet upon the shores of Basseterre in the West Indies on a lull for fresh water ballast in my youth."

The men immediately became still in wonder to hear him.

"But it was not predestined to be," the captain proceeded, "for she could not marry a man who were a stranger to her people. My heart was torn from me that time spent upon that isle and was hard to mend - the zealous lad shifted…lost. But alas, years of time to wane when a hollow shell of a man only remained and duty was an only aim, one would catch my eye and win my heart again when least expected. Upon the very streets of my schooldays in England she was found, healed the wounds of a tiresome past, and become my faithful wife."

The men, cheered by the captain's story, smiled at him in good sentiment.

"Very good, sir," the First Mate said to him softly with a nod. The men at the captain's table gazed upon him as he took up his food again to eat and they followed.

$\mathfrak{T}$he ship sailed across the ocean on starboard tack on another sunny day. It was the three o'clock hour with light winds. The weather had turned very warm and the men did appreciate it at open sea. First Mate James Fletcher stood on deck and marked the hour.

"Sound the bell! Starboard Watch to duty!"

The bell obeyed him and the men aloft at the mastheads and others began to swing down through the rigging to change places.

Joseph got upon the ratlines of the main mast on the starboard side and climbed aloft to the crow's nest. Joining him on the main masthead was Gamba, a young and mostly quiet African man and an easy one to spend so much time with alone. The First Mate called out to all of the crew.

"Any volunteer for Steward of the Hold?! Need a man to mind the placement of casks below when the oil be a-flow! Any volunteer for the duty?!"

Alistair Smith stepped forward.

"Aye, Mister Fletcher! I volunteer."

"Mister Smith, be ye able to organize the stowage in the hold and keep her to rights?"

"Aye, sir!"

"Very well, Mister Smith...It be upon you."

Aloft, Joseph and Gamba passed two men coming down from the masthead. Joseph climbed into the steel hoop on one side and Gamba the other. On the fore masthead in front of them, Diederick Neilson and Simon Laurent took their places on lookout. The day was beautiful and the view, quite stunning. Joseph clung tightly to the steel ring, the only thing keeping him from a fall to certain death, and looked down over the many layers of puffed canvas, like stacked clouds, with a smile. He stood at a dizzying height of a hundred feet from the weather deck and there was no other sound but the wind blowing into his ears.

"A feeling of freedom like none other. Would you agree, Gamba?"

"Aye, Joseph."

"Quite a transition from the streets of London."

There was a short silence between them.

"Other than returning home, this would be the greatest part of a whaling voyage, I say," Joseph remarked as his face seemed to be in an expression of one daydreaming.

"My name, Gamba, means reflection. My people in Bouake believe dat de spirit of a man returns to de waters of de earth, where he's from during life and death. Dat life, as de man lives, is a reflection of his ancestors before him. He sees dem when he sees himself in dat reflection. Dis is what I think about when I look to de sea. What about you, Joseph? How did your father call you?"

"My father was a hard man," Joseph replied. "He kept to his work and was not seen often. Then, he became ill. Doctors consumed his savings in his efforts to be healed, but to no avail. When he lay there he said to me, 'Joseph, I was wrong. Forgive me for not being there...for you.' I was young. He died of his sickness and I were left with no inheritance. I took up work to care for my mother as I do this day. He gave me my name, I expect, after Joseph the Patriarch of Israel; a man sold into slavery, into Egypt, a foreign country, and then overcame his circumstances by becoming second only to Pharaoh; a man who took hardships and, with the help of his God, the God of Israel, made them into blessings. My father gave me one thing: a name that would teach me to overcome the disadvantages that would try to hinder me."

Gamba stared at Joseph as his words sank in deeply.

"A lesson for all men, my friend," Gamba said.

Joseph nodded with a small smile as they both beheld and enjoyed the beauty of the glimmering sun upon the waters of the sea.

𝔘pon the main deck, days later in a clear evening as the sun was setting, Alistair Smith sat alone upon the goosepen step that lied beneath the tryworks. He whittled a piece of wood with a small knife and the shavings fell into a pan at his feet. He was solemn and quiet and took no notice of the sound of music, clapping, and laughter that drifted towards him from the bow of the ship.

There, Colm Doyle played a fast and fancy song on his two-handed ocarina along with the beat of a single drum introduced by Waitimu, a thin African man in his mid-forties who had the beginnings of silver hair. The Larboard Watch was at ease and they passed the time as they could. A small crowd gathered around the performers as some danced, some sat on the deck, and some hung in the foresail yard above.

Alistair Smith continuously looked upwards to the main mast while he whittled and fixed his eye upon the captain's purse; the bag of silver coins.

Mister Doyle's song closed and immediately Alen Reid rang in with a Scottish shanty. As he did, others joined him in the chorus.

"Right Ho! Ann Clair so fair a Maiden!
None e'er so like yer comely Grace!
I went to thee in woe's a-laden!
Thy tears to heal from off thy face!
Right Ho! Right Ho! My damsel Fair!
Make Haste! Make Haste! In Auburn Hair!
And in the mists of Castle Island!
Thou cam'st to me in Shetland Lace!

Now griefs of ill, worn on by years!
And lines that crease my guise at night!
The burdens laid upon an fellow!
All disappear in thy sweet light!
Right Ho! Right Ho! My damsel Fair!
Make Haste! Make Haste! In Auburn Hair!
And in the mists of Castle Island!
Thou cam'st to me in Shetland Lace!"

The men cheered and clapped for themselves.

"Shipshape, Mister Reid!" Scotty Watson added over the plaudits in his own approval. As the men sang along the ship's bows, the blacksmith held a double-pronged harpoon in his hand. The boy stood beside him, watching.

"Aye, Mister Dobb, sharp and straight," Mister Stearne said to him. "Not a whale's hide under the sea that'll keep out a two-flued iron of my craftin'. It holds fast and not a thing can shake free its grab! In it goes quick, but not will it be hauled out, not without ripping apart the flesh and breakin' the bone. Unlucky, that beast or creature under the sun that is pierced through with the fire of one of these!"

Samuel Dobb's eyes grew wide as his imagination ran. The blacksmith turned the razor-sharp point around in his hand - a man who was master of the artistry.

On the morning of a sunlit sky, two days following, the sails brimming with the faithful winds, the ship sailed large with a quartering wind on starboard tack. The weather clew of the mainsail was hauled up to allow wind into the foresail and the spanker was furled. The morning was quiet and fair.

The captain took a sighting on his sextant at the bow, measuring the position of the sun to the horizon to exact the ship's location. Augustin Jorgensen sat on the sole of the weather deck doing needlework on a piece of sailcloth - a Woolwork picture. He embroidered a scene of a ship anchored near a harbor to constructively pass his time. His colors were limited to browns and greens, the supplies of a sail mending kit. Joseph sat quietly beside him admiring his work.

Suddenly, and finally, a shrill cry came from the masthead. All men jumped to their feet and those below clambered up from the forecastle. Alistair

Smith stood to his feet, amidships, and looked up into the rigging as another cry echoed down to them.

"A Blooooooooooowwwwwwww!!!!!"

Robert Ackley, the man who called from the masthead, stood on starboard side with his finger pointed ahead.

"She blooooooooowwwwsss!!!! She blooooowwwwsss!!!" he blared again. He added swirling pitches in his hail, like some call of a Loon, applying his own distinctive carol to his moment of glory. The captain jumped and ran to a place on deck to look to the crow's nest from the bows.

"Where away?!!" he called to him from below.

"Right whale on the weather beam! Two miles, Captain!" Mister Ackley replied from the towering height above.

The captain quickly dashed to the starboard beam, amidships, brought his spyglass to his eye, and searched the distance. A great V-shaped spray of water shot high above the surface of the sea as the whale lunged forward, swimming slowly and unwittingly into the danger of the lance.

"A fish! A fish!" crewmen on deck began to shout as they pointed.

"Make ready to wend four points to starboard!" the captain ordered.

"Man the mains'l and spanker gear!" the First Mate cried to those of the Starboard Watch. Men across the ship took positions to trim the sails. As the mainsail and spanker gear was manned, James Fletcher gave the orders that a whaleman loves to hear. "Boat crews ready the boats! Put in your tubs! Put in your irons!"

The whaleboat crews uncovered the three whaleboats that hung on davits along the larboard side of the ship and placed the large heavy tubs of coiled rope into them. Each boat carried two tubs: one of two hundred twenty-five fathoms of line and the other of seventy-five fathoms; the second smaller one for the occasion that the whale dives deep. Men took up bundles of harpoons and lances and put them aboard the boats. One man climbed into each of the three whaleboats and readied himself to fend it off from the side of the ship as it was lowered to the sea. They were handed a water-cask, compass, lantern, and a cask of hardbread to stow aboard in the event of an emergency.

The captain clung to the bulwarks with spyglass raised, waiting for the right moment to give the order. The First Mate took a position near First Boat at the stern. The Second Mate was ready at Second Boat, amidships, and the Third Mate and his crew at the bow.

The whale raised his enormous flukes into the air and dove down, disappearing below the surface. The captain saw the right moment to launch.

"Lower away! Lower away!" he cried.

In just seconds, a man in each of the three whaleboats unhooked the tackle and let go the runner line. The boats quickly dropped into the water and as they did, men began to scramble down the side of the ship or slide down the falls into them. Joseph was among the men of the First Boat and climbed down alongside Mister Fletcher. All men of the boat crews took their positions and the tackle was loosed. The ship passed on away from them as they stepped small masts upright and began to sail in the direction of the whale.

The whaleboats were each thirty feet long and six feet wide and could carry six men. The officers rode at the sterns and the harpooneers at the bows. As the sails traveled up the masts catching the wind, they began to move. The officers took hold of a long oar at the rear to steer the boats. The men ran line from the largest tub aft across the oars, around the loggerhead, which was a small post at the stern and back over the oars to the bow. The harpooneer got hold of it and tied the line to his harpoon. They kept quiet and made no shouts, being careful not to startle the whale when he broke the surface.

All three boats went under sail and pressed further from the ship. As they went, they spread apart and prepared for the creature's emergence. Bastiaan Rasmussen, Abimbola, and Nigel Jackson were ready in the bows with harpoons lying at their hips.

After several minutes of great nervous tension, the whale surfaced ahead of them, closest to First Boat. The others turned to that direction and made an angle to come up on him from the rear and side. After pulling down the sails, the men quickly took hold of the oars and began to row. Bastiaan Rasmussen stood and put his thigh into a padded notch in the edge of the forward box. He drew close to the unsuspecting whale with his heavy harpoon raised over his shoulder. The men were wide-eyed and anxious as they watched him.

"Give it to 'im!" the First Mate cried, breaking the silence.

Bastiaan launched his spear with great skill and

strength and plunged it deep into the whale's body.

"A size-fish!" Mister Fletcher shouted.

Alongside him, but at an even greater and very impressive distance, Abimbola darted his iron into the whale from the Second Boat to secure him.

"A fall! A fall!!" the men cheered.

The harpooneers pulled against the lines to set the flues and they held fast. All hands backed the boats away from the great beast with their oars and prepared themselves for his wrath. The harpooneers threw out a few fathoms of slack line and changed ends with the First and Second Mates, who handled the deadly lances. The men tossed lines across to one another and connected all three boats end to end.

The whale immediately rolled, beating the sea with his giant tail in his surprise and wrath. He barreled off at great speed, causing the First Boat to spin around and be pulled behind which put Officer Fletcher at the forefront. Joseph, who was before rowing backwards, then faced the whale as all men were dragged along at fifteen knots through the spray of the waves. Whoops, shouts, and nervous laughter rang out as the whale took them on a ride over the surface of the water; the boats connected in a single file line. The rope was passed over the loggerhead and the men used it like a reel on a fishing pole to haul themselves in or out from the wrathful beast.

Aboard the Fortune, the captain shouted to the helmsman on the main deck just moments later.

"Mister Moreau, Helm-a-larboard!"

"Helm-a-larboard, Captain!" he confirmed.

Vincent Moreau turned the wheel left and the tiller moved with it. The captain made his way forward and the ship's head turned to the right as they procured a maneuver to cut the boats off at an angle.

"Haul aboard! Haul out main tack and sheet! Spanker outhaul! Clear away the brails!" the captain bellowed over the noises of the sea.

The mainsail was opened by the crewmen aboard as well as the spanker. The main tack was got down and the main sheet aft. A man aloft overhauled the buntlines. The ship came rapidly to the wind as all hands aboard took part in the steering of the ship.

"Brace up headyards!" Captain Grey ordered. "Overhaul weather lifts! Haul aft jib sheet! Mister Moreau, right the helm!"

"Right the helm, Captain!" Vincent replied.

The men scrambled to the orders and the ship turned quickly for the boats that were pushing farther away from them on the sea.

After thirty minutes in the pursuit, the whale slowed from blood-loss and exertion. The men pulled on the line and brought themselves closer alongside him, keeping clear of his dangerous massive flukes which had been known to destroy whaleboats in times past.

The First Mate took hold of the six-foot iron lance with a razor-sharp point and stood as the whale moved slowly in front of him. The boat came alongside the whale's body and James plunged the lance straight into his side, piercing his lungs. He pulled the lance out and stabbed him again, repeatedly, causing blood to gush from the whale's side and turn the sea red.

Alistair Smith stared on from the Second Boat, wide-eyed, gritting his teeth with an excited snarl in his lip.

The whale sprayed great clots of blood straight into the air from his spiracle and the men shouted for it. Some of them, including Mister Fletcher, were spattered with mist and droplets and it dripped from their faces.

"She spouts red! She spouts red!" Redford Whitby cried in victory, soaking in the excitement.

The dying whale went into a flurry and swam in a large circle as the sea turned completely red with blood. In a moment, the circle diminished and the whale thrashed his tail onto the water one final time, rolling over on his side with one fin raised into the air.

"Fin out!" the Second Mate yelled.

All cheered and whistled. James Fletcher turned and called them.

"Let's get in a towline, men!"

Mister Lock drew his boat near to the dead whale and made a cut in its head. He passed a line through the hole and fastened it to his boat. The men joined the boats together again with ropes, spaced out at a distance of thirty feet, and began the hard row to the ship.

Captain Henry Grey kept the Fortune moving in from the side towards the boats and gave the order sequence to stop and wait for them.

"Prepare to slow ship! Spill the fore and mains'ls! Furl the t'gallants and royals! Get fore tops'l aback! Heave her to, men!" he commanded.

The men aboard the Fortune took to executing the orders of heaving to the ship as the wind blew over the starboard beam.

"Helmsman! Hang the rudder!" the captain shouted when the great vessel slowed to a stop. The helmsman allowed the rudder's pintles to fall into their corresponding braces and men below decks secured it into position with wood-locks.

The boats, in a long line leading to the whale, were rowed steady and hard. The officers gave a shout to keep up the grit.

"Heave cheerily! That's it! Put in your backs for the day's charity, men! And we'll fill the hold with oil aplenty!" Second Mate, Bromley Lock called, forcing vigor upon the panting men of his boat.

Charles Digby, who rowed in stride in front of Joseph, started a song to stave off the strain of the chore.

"I went a-whalin' on a bark from Solin,
And cast my lot with the men on her,
But when the Isles of Wight came callin',
I stole off there with my heart astir!"

The men of First Boat joined in, including the officer.

"Beauty hey! Beauty thine!
The Isles of Wight have I made mine!
I left a lady on the mainland!
To trade her for the island wine!"

Aboard ship, the captain gave his commands to secure the whale. "Get down spike-tackle and cant-falls!"

The boat crews drew in after some time at the oar

and fixed the whale along the starboard side of her with the tail at the bows.

A set of walkways, called the flensing stage, was lowered out over the ocean from the weather deck. It extended ten feet from the ship and upon this, men were able to cut up the whale while it was in the water with long-handled spades. A railing along the walk kept them balanced and from falling off.

The wind blew over the beam and crewmen left to the maneuvering of the ship got her hove to which partially raised the whale up from the sea. The gangway was removed in order to bring the huge pieces of whale blubber aboard by the purchase. Preparing the blubber hooks for work, the men raised the cutting blocks and tackle aloft. The whale's flukes were wrapped around with an iron chain leading to the windlass through the hawsehole at the bow and then secured to the fluke bitt. The captain and the First and Second Mates traveled out upon the stage over the ocean with cutting spades in hand; the satisfaction of slicing up the whale given to the men in command.

The crew prepared the tryworks to be fired by dumping water into the goosepen at its base to keep the deck cool. The main hatch was then removed to open the lower deck and hold. The first order of business for the officers was to cut off the head - a difficult task that demanded experience.

"Put it on its side now!" the captain shouted to the crewmen who heaved upon the tackle.

The whale rolled over by the tug of chains with its eye out of the water. Captain Grey and the officers made an incision around the socket of the jaw by thrusting their cutting spades into the blubber. They extended a cut around the eye in a semicircular curve to a point, forward of the fin. Blood permeated the water around the ship and sloshed against the hull in red waves. Redford Whitby, who was standing on the main deck at the gangway, called to men positioned at the ropes.

"Lower cutting tackle!"

Abimbola climbed down the outside of the ship on rope and chains and stood upon the carcass as the cutting tackle was lowered to him. He took hold of the giant hook, inserted it into the blanket piece of blubber, and climbed back, clinging to the main chain-wales of the shrouds.

"Heave away windlass!" Redford cried to the men at the bows.

The loosened blubber peeled off, readily, as the officers cut it clear at each side. The blanket was raised and the whale rolled slowly over until the jaw faced away from the ship when the heaving was stopped. The Third Mate ordered them again with a cry.

"Lower away second tackle!"

The windlass crew overhauled on a line that sent another hook down to the whale that was suspended from the cap of the lower mainmast. Again, Abimbola descended onto the whale and attached a chain strap over the jaw. He then took hold of the second hook, attached it to the strap, and climbed out. The officers upon the stage cut around the other socket and severed the throat, thrusting the spades deep until they reached the backbone.

"The jaw be free!" James Fletcher shouted.

"Hoist out!"

The jaw of the upper part of the head was loosened and then wrenched out. It was hoisted aboard as the blanket piece remained suspended by the opposite tackle. Joseph was among the men who took hold of the large jaw, draped with baleen, as it came aboard on the chain. The some four hundred slabs of whalebone were up to twelve feet long at some points, weighing five hundred fifty pounds alone.

"Heave in on the blanket piece!" the captain ordered.

As the blubber hook rose, peeling away the massive piece of blubber, the men laid the great jaw onto the deck. Joseph and several others cut the bone slabs from it with sharp blades and set them upon a board laid across two casks to be scrubbed and cleaned with brushes. It was all a dirty business and took a particular type of person to work a whale processing barque at sea.

"My favorite part, Joseph," John said with a big smile while slapping his hand against them. "What I dream of when I lie down at night…picking the young prawn from a whale's mouth."

"Just keep it thrown overboard or Jago will try to salvage it for breakfast," Joseph said softly, but all the men around him heard it and laughed. "Just keep that brush firmly in your hand, John, or some admiral will put a musket in it." Everyone laughed again and they buckled down harder and scrubbed away as if what Joseph had said could happen immediately.

John laughed. "Joseph ought to be a ship captain with the way he can motivate a man to work," he said to the others.

"Nay!" Joseph stated with stiffness. "It would be excessively tempting to pirate these seas and force others to serve me as my slaves as an iron scourge…to get rich on the bloody backs of poverty-stricken subjugated men."

"That sounds like us!" cried Mister Doyle.

Everyone laughed again as Joseph cracked a subtle smile.

"There it is, fellows! You've heard it for yourselves!" exclaimed John. "A born leader!"

The blocks of the blubber tackle rose and met at the lower masthead slings. "Block and block!" the Third Mate called, signifying the giant pulleys had moved as far as possible. The other tackle was lowered and hooked onto the blubber at the gangway. Redford Whitby used a boarding knife to poke a large hole in the blanket for the second tackle. Taking the heavy blubber hook that had raised the jaw, he inserted it into the hole he had made, slicing off the seven-foot wide blubber strip just above the second hook.

"Lower into the hold!" he cried. "Hoist away second tackle!"

The hoisting and lowering crews lowered the long strip of blubber into the blubber room below the deck through the main hatch. Two men stood on each side of the hatchway and led the large slippery bloody mass down.

Several who were waiting beneath, received the large blubber strip as it descended and settled. The men pulled it from the hook and sent the iron back up. They quickly started on the thick blubber, cutting it into to strips called 'horse pieces', three to four feet long and eight inches wide. During this, the captain and the two officers above hacked a spiral in the whale from head to tail as it slowly turned around in the blood-soaked water. The Third Mate and the men aboard continued to raise one giant hook and insert another, peeling the whale like an orange. As the captain stabbed away with his spade, the Second Mate called out to the other men that were near.

"Ha! Look!"

Five shark fins poked through the red surface in a frenzy of blood. They attacked the whale carcass and bit chunks out of it.

"I got a meal for ye, mates!" Bromley said to the unwanted dinner guests in a mocking threat. With his spade, he stabbed two sharks in their heads as they came up under him at the stage. The surrounding men cheered and whistled as the sharks turned on one another to devour those who were bleeding. Men on deck, including Joseph, bounded to the bulwarks for the show. "This is what happens to thieves around here!" Bromley said with an angry laugh. The men whistled and cheered to see their most hated species kill one another in madness. If they would have had a moment longer, bets would have been in place.

"Get a fire in the tryworks!" Redford Whitby called from the gangway after the men had had their sport.

The horse pieces were brought up from the blubber room by hoisting in wood tubs as fires were started under the two huge kettles of the tryworks furnace. Men brought the tubs to a mincing station on the main deck near the tryworks and placed them upon a long plank laid across two casks that were waist high. Large tubs were filled with these pieces and the small ones were returned to the blubber room to be refilled. Two men, one on each end of the plank, minced the pieces into 'bibles' with large two-handled knives. They were so called because they appeared to be such with heavy thick blubber pages that could be turned upon a spine. They stood over them with a sturdy grip on each side and pressed in with their body weight repeatedly to force the shapes and slices. From there, the books were tossed into another large cask near the tryworks to be boiled down.

Below their feet, Alistair Smith went over the casks in the hold to determine which ones would be filled with oil. Some that had been stored with drinking water at the beginning of the voyage were now empty. He rolled these to the center of the hold and prepared them to be sent up to the weather deck. He stopped and stared at an area that was filled high with casks laid on their sides to the ceiling. A thought formed in his mind and the place seemed to grow eyes in the black crevices and look at him.

At the bow of the ship above, Joseph and his eager team stripped the jaw of the baleen and scrubbed it clean with brushes and buckets of water. There were unsightly globs of dead crustaceans and masses of plankton that had collected between them like tartar on the gums of a giant and now was the time for the men at the bow to earn their meager pay. The clean slabs were then stood straight up against the rigging and bundled together by count for the corsets of the ladies of London and long whips of the horse drivers that carried them.

"I ever tell you of the time I was invited by the Lord Mayor of London to attend his daughter's birthday ball?" said Charles Digby to the greasy men around him. Everyone stopped and let out a hearty laugh, but Charles was straight and cool and looked at them with an eye of surprise at their unified response.

"Now, I believe I've heard it all, mates!" Rawley Chapman resounded in mockery. "Did I ever tell you 'bout the time King George asked me to accompany is lovely wife to Belgium for an opera while he was busy attending to other more pressing matters?!!" he shouted with a winy sophisticated articulation.

The men laughed with full force as they kept one eye on the both of them, pulling and sloshing away at the mutilated flesh.

Charles appeared to be offended and quickly answered his antagonizer.

"Why, it is true! I cannot lie! I had nothing to wear at the time you can be sure and straight away got to the hatter and the tailor and the bootmaker…"

"And the perfumer!" injected Nigel with a shout from the quarterdeck with his arms sunk to the elbows in intestines. Everyone burst with more chuckles and chortles.

"Aye, I'll take it from here, Mister Jackson!" he continued among cheers. "There I was all prim and proper. Smart and trim was I there with top hat and tails. I got me one of those gentleman's canes with a red glass ruby cut in all manner of ways like a sparkling diamond; like the king's sceptre. Sharp as a lance and ready to kiss the hands of as many ladies as would walk through a door…and impress every single one would I and send 'em home in the evenin' to lay next to their husbands a-dreamin' of that fine mysterious gentleman who had held 'em so gently, turned 'em so carefully, led 'em in Waltzing so extravagantly. As each one would touch my white glove, it was as if the entire room would pause to see her loveliness in our handsome parade. After was all said and done on our final bow, the Lord Mayor himself, his wife, and his orchestra nodded and applauded our exquisite display. Three days after when I got to the bottom of the letter I seen it was addressed to a Charles Madison Elbert, a chap three streets down and inside a more fashionable neighborhood. The currier had got it all wrong. In my excitement and thrill, I hadn't worked my way fully to the bottom of it to discover I was no less a different Charles."

The men stopped working to bend over with laughter at him. The officers were not exempt and never missed anything Charles had to say when he spoke of himself.

At the tryworks, Badru took a long double-pronged fork, stuck it into the cask of book pieces and piled the kettles with them. The blubber sizzled in the hot pots like bacon in a pan. The result was a valuable commodity and there would be nothing to compare to it. America's Benjamin Franklin himself said there was nothing finer or more suited to oil the delicate and intricate workings of a man's watch and so many years after, still held most true. The deck became extremely greasy with coagulate, covered in blood, oil, and gurry. The men were soaked in it up to their knees and it seemed to be absorbed into their skin that way, another mandate of a whaleman - it being impossible to avoid.

"The tongue is aboard!" Redford Whitby reported to the men operating the tackle. The whale's giant tongue was hooked through the center after it had been severed, raised up onto the deck, and pushed over to the mincing station for immediate slicing. "Make ready to bring the lip!"

Men hauled again upon the windlass and the whale's lower lip rose up from the sea, hooked through a chain like the jaw. It was also a valuable portion of the carcass and would yield much oil. Two men guided this large and odd shaped piece to the hatchway and lowered it down to be carved up. As everyone across the ship continued to work, orders could be heard from the main deck to bring in the flensing stage and to replace the gangway. The rest of the whale was left to the teeth of the growing number of sharks and the slow digesting creatures that moved over the dark floor of the ocean below. Anything of any worth at all was harvested from the great beast whether it was organs, flesh, or bone and by the time it was through, would be separated into hundreds of pieces.

Down in the hold, a chain harness was lowered from the hatchway and Alistair Smith came climbing out from the dozens of casks that lined the walls and crawlspaces. To him, it looked like a monstrous hard-clawed hand that would reach into the dark pit where he hid to feel about to find him and kill him. The vision left him quickly and he stepped out into the exposing light in remembrance, somewhat in a lingering imaginary but amusing fear and secured the chains to the first large cask and signaled for it to be hoisted away.

From the main deck, thick black smoke rose up from the boiling pots and a new and familiar stench pervaded the noses of the men as it rose to the very heights of the sky. Joseph stopped working and took a deep and laborious inhale with squinted eyes. It was not like bacon or cattle or savory meats when cooked in the fires and it seemed for once the crew would suddenly invite Jago to fry up whatever he wanted for their suppers to fend it off. The smell lined their nostrils now like heavy cream and was not going to depart anytime soon at all; not even if a man were to jump into the sea and snort the saltwater in and out of his lungs like a fish.

"Aaaah! That familiar fragrance arisin' from the pots!" the captain cried with a great smile. "Makes a lubber choke, but a whaleman healthy!"

The men laughed at him as the tolerance for the stink that had to be acquired over time with the looming prospect of money mingled within, set them apart from other human beings. Esmond Burne cleaned the slabs of the jaw near Joseph and could not resist making a subtle comment as the olfactory wave hit them.

"I be a lubber, then," he said.

Joseph and the surrounding men laughed at Esmond, a greenhand who was not accustomed to the very unique and memorable foul odors.

"What do you mean, Esmond? Jago's meat's had no different a smell for us yet!" inserted Aengus Murphy, the cook's leading supporter.

The men laughed again.

"And I've not had it yet, neither!" Esmond cracked.

The men broke up repeatedly, never being weary of a slander upon the inedible material they had to call food.

The processing of the whale went into exhaustive effort across the entire ship for hours and into the night. Large casks were hoisted through the main hatch and lined along the bulwarks. Men went along and lashed them to the side of the ship to keep them secure. The cooper beat them with his mallets and pried them open, making them ready to be filled with oil. One man forked the book pieces into the pots as another dipped the cooked ones out with a strainer, casting them into the fire - ultimately fueling the flames with only tried blubber and saving the coals. Another carefully dipped out the boiling hot oil with a large ladle and poured it into a copper tank that sat alongside the tryworks to cool. They worked the system quickly and effectively to finish, to get clean, and to rest. One whale would keep them busy for nearly an entire day, from sunup to sundown, and they were eager to see the reward in silver that would await them at the end of the winding Thames.

The captain walked along the deck and was pleased at the bustling of the men. He felt that it would be a good voyage and prosperous. His mind wondered to the things he would do with his wife and sons on his furlough and then his thoughts began to change. Maybe he would situate himself on land afterwards and give the sea to only his past. It suddenly sounded right and in his heart he made the ruling right there in his step. He knew that she would be overwhelmed with joy at his decision and later, when he found the time, would express it to her in a letter. He made his way aft past the wheel and into the door to his cabin, closing it behind him with an entirely new feeling of satisfaction that he had not had before.

The sun shone strong and clear upon the waters at nine o'clock the next morning. The ship was at full sail, moving along the ocean in a good wind. The sails took on the appearance of a working whaler and were stained black by the harsh smoke of the tryworks. All was astir as the crew further cleaned the deck of remaining blood and grime from the day before. The Right whale had been processed and cleared away completely, a job that had taken the entire day into the night.

"Mister Watson, more ash here, sir!" Third Mate Whitby called.

"Aye, Mister Whitby!"

Scotty, being on ash detail, took ashes from the tryworks that were stored in a large tub and sprinkled them on the deck near the bow with a shovel. The crewmen scraped it into the sludge on the sole with long-handled brushes while others scrubbed the kettles until they shone like giant silver punch bowls. The men were as black as the busy chimney sweeps of London who had no boy to send up the pipes instead.

Alistair Smith approached the cooper who worked repairing a large cask, hammering on a steel ring against an anvil to beat it into a rounder shape.

"Mister Bazely, I'll be in want of several ryers to fill the odd corners of the hold."

"Aye, Smith. Reckon how many?" William asked.

"Four, I says."

Alistair glanced around the ship from where he stood. He looked at some of the other men as they scraped the grease from the deck and then returned his gaze to the tradesman. "For now."

The cooper gave a nod as Alistair turned and walked towards the blubber room ladder to disappear into the hold. In the midst of the cleaning, the captain entered the deck for the first time of the day to speak and the Second Mate called all hands.

"Captain's on deck!"

The men stood to their feet that were not and everyone became silent.

"A fine job, men!" the captain shouted in his clear voice. "I am pleased to see that it went ill for no man in yesterday's catch and the execution of it was perfection by my standard! Well done, gentleman! Now, to make good on the reward I swore to ye!"

Everyone's eyes lit up, anticipating the moment even though the money's path led to only one man. The captain climbed onto the belaying-pin frame at the foot of the main mast with a step on a nearby crate and pried off his moneybag with a hammer.

"Mister Robert Ackley!" the captain shouted. "You sighted first whale and dirtied these here decks! The reward be yours!"

The captain, still standing atop the frame, threw the purse to Robert who caught it with a beaming smile.

"Aye, the decks be a-foul and to get her clean'll be work indeed!" said the captain. "But be of good cheer! Jago! Rum for all hands!"

The men rejoiced with a cheer as they stood around in their grimy black clothes. During the commotion and clamorous shouting, Alistair Smith remained still and expressionless with his eyes fixed upon Robert Ackley who was patted on the back by all men around him.

On a dark and cloudy night, three days afterwards, the forecastle was lit by one lantern that swung from a hook in the ceiling. All men lied in their bunks as it was late. Thomas Alexander neared the ending of one of his usual nightly stories and everyone gave him their ear.

"...And so Poseidon struck a stone with his mighty Trident in the contest with Athena for the patronage of Athens and there he created the first horse," Thomas said as he was finishing. "But the gods determined that his invention was of less benefit to mankind than of Athena's creation, the olive tree, and gave her the victory."

The listeners weighed the decision of the gods carefully and no one spoke. After a moment of pause, Aengus remarked from his meditation. "Well now, I have to disagree with the gods of Athens," he said in a soft low voice from the shadows of his bunk below. "The horse has been a much more beneficial creature to us now." For a moment more the men awaited his conclusion as he paused. "It's in every plate that Jago feeds us!"

Everyone let out a laugh at Aengus' constant barrage of Jago's food drollery and did not for one minute have any surprise. When the commotion receded after the two cents collectively were thrown into the hat with much more comical defamation, Alistair then began to speak.

"'ave any of you here ever heard the story of the Night Watchman?" he said with a tricky smile. The men became quiet and those that could, turned and looked at him. No one answered.

"Then I will spin you a twist," Alistair said with a mysterious and plain face. "This... Night Watchman...walks the streets of the night, a commissioned guard of London. Behold, one night as he passes through the cobblestone alleyways in his turn, a lighted window catches one eye. So, he draws near and there inside, in her room, is a lady: the Spring Beauty, Miss Evendale. He is taken by her at once and is transfixed at her. Each night he comes again, standing in the alleyways or upon the rooftops to watch her and to long for her. The Night Watchman, being in her trance, sends to her presents - gifts of perfume and flowers, always a secret admirer. As it happens, he discovers a fiancée - her new lover. The Watchman catches him unawares and sends to her his head, wrapped in a box...and with it, a note which states that her admirer's dedication to her is unmoved and that he'd do anything for her. She becomes afraid and packs her things into a traveler and leaves London all alone."

Alistair looked around to the other men who had their eyes fixed upon him in the lantern's light.

"Why alone, you say?" added Alistair. "She had no others, not family nor master…and along her way, on the outer edges of the city, she changes carriages. The new driver, her secret admirer, takes her far into the country, far from anyone. And in his distress, beats her, and walls her up in a tomb with stone and mortar."

Silence was upon them all. The younger men, including Mingo and Samuel Dobb, were hanging on the edge of their bunks, staring with mouths open. Alistair started a slight smile as he lay back against his pillow.

"So ends the tale of the Spring Beauty, Miss Evendale, and the perpetually elusive Night Watchman," he said slowly and near under his breath.

Not another word was spoken among them. Each man had a different reason and each man had the same. Joseph kept Alistair in his stare across the room from his bottom bunk in apprehensive wonder as the wind blew over the forecastle door above - the wooden ship creaking in its pitches.

Chapter 3
The Writing on the Wall

$\mathfrak{M}$en were aloft on all three masts inspecting the sails and rigging as the sun shone full and brightly over them. The day was favorable and the Fortune made her course South West by South. Charles Digby straddled the fore topsail yard with his feet resting on the horses while training Esmond Burne to tie a new knot setting. Joseph was fortunate enough to be hanging nearby in the rigging overhead to watch them.

"Now, Esmond, to day you shall be practiced on a knot of special magnificence," Charles said in his bold voice, "the Running Bowline Knot. 'ave ye heard of it?"

Esmond only laughed. Charles noticed Joseph listening in from above.

"What about you, Joseph?" said Charles.

"I know of it, but I admit, Mister Digby, I'll be

your student to day as well," he replied.

"Very good, then. There'll be a class to day," Charles returned, looking down to a long segment of rope in his hands. "To conjure up this knot, you take the end of a rope 'round the standing part and through the bight. Make the Single Bowline Knot which you know upon the part here and you're finished. You're on deck, Mister Burne."

Not far from them, aloft on the main topgallant yard, Kallum Morrison and Alistair Smith went over the clews of the topgallant sail to be sure the ship was in proper form and in good health. Alistair was positioned on the leeward side at the lee clew and stepped as one intoxicated. His eyes were red from it. Kallum fixed a new middle-seizing in the rope that had been worn down at the foot of the sail by the strains of the wind. He finished the splice, climbed across the footropes to where Alistair hung onto the rigging with his back turned, and tapped him on the arm with a marlinspike. Alistair turned and looked at him and took the long pointed iron tool into his hand.

"Let's get a new eye seizin' in the lee clew 'fore this one gives out," Kallum said, pivoting and climbing off in the weather direction in the rigging. Alistair did not answer, but stared motionless at the marlinspike in his hand as if in a trance. At that moment, calls and whistles arose from the ship's bow in a fuss, but Alistair was not stirred.

"Hey! Watch 'em now! Take 'em!" men shouted on the fore deck. "There's meat on the bows for the cook!"

Dolphins swam in a pod at the bows, racing alongside and ahead of the ship. The Fortune, being in warmer latitudes began to see them regularly. The men gathered at the head of the ship along the bulwarks and made a ruckus as Nigel Jackson quickly climbed out on the martingale stays, under the jib-boom, with harpoon in hand.

"Take one for me! I'll be next! There's sport on the martingales! Put one right in the blow hole!" the men shouted from the bows behind him.

"A relief from the cook's terrible spoon!" cried Aengus Murphy. "No horse in the kids to day! Watch men! Only dolphin to be spoiled!"

Nigel wrapped himself in the ropes near the 'dolphin-striker', barefoot and bare-chested, and let go his harpoon straight down over the water. The iron sank directly into the blowhole of a dolphin and men began to cheer wildly as others quickly made their way to the bows in the rigging above for a rare moment to be entertained with something new.

"Eh, Jago!" Aengus cried as he turned aft towards the galley, "Come see what we're having tonight!"

As the men at the bows had their sport, Alistair wobbled slightly, staring off into nowhere. He clutched the rigging with a languid grip as calls from the Second Mate came up from below. He wanted to walk upon the blue waters to another place and the shimmering ripples that stretched to the horizon in front of him below looked like a curious staircase that would take him upwards but only straight forward. He smiled at the illusion with amusement and extended his left foot as if he thought it would be humorous to step off the ropes straight onto it to see what would happen.

Alistair took no heed to the order and allowed a

line to un-reeve from a block and tear a portion of the main topgallant sail away in the wind. The Second Mate caught the event and quickly sent Samuel up to him.

"Mister Lock wants to see you in the officer's mess, sir," said the boy. Alistair grinned and turned away, going down to the weather deck.

He entered the room where the Second Mate stood alone, waiting with an angry demeanor. He stared into Alistair's eyes, breathing heavily, realizing the cause for the offense.

"You report to duty once more unable to see a hole through the grating," said Mister Lock, "and I'll have stripes put on your back...is that clear enough, Mister Smith?!"

Alistair sneered with a defiant half-smile and kept his eyes frozen upon his officer without a word.

"Dismissed 'til followin' Watch!" Bromley said in outrage, giving him one long stare before turning his back.

Alistair's expression slid down into a threatening glare as he blinked his eyes slowly in his drunken condition. He stepped forward to lay virulent hands on him while no one was around.

Bromley turned and took a step back against the table, wide-eyed and completely startled.

"Mister Lock, sir, what'll be the orders for the mast-head watches?" said Samuel, entering the room unaware of events that were about to transpire.

Alistair stepped back, interrupted by the boy, and walked out, around the turn to the stairs for the main deck.

At the same moment not far away, the captain sat at his large desk in his cabin below with maps and charts strewn across it. He took hold of a large book, his whaling log, inked a stamp and pressed it against the page. An image of a black baleen whale was revealed in the fresh ink as he pulled away. He took up a feather pen, dipped into the well, and marked in his book the take of the whale: 41 barrels - oil, 529 pounds - bone.

Over time, the ship traveled across the ocean and the equator along the northeast edges of South America on varying tacks. The weather remained in the captain's favor over the next five weeks of their long voyage. During this time, the crew took to the whaleboats on multiple occasions and harpooned into a pod of one hundred Blackfish, making a prosperous day where the men were immersed in the hard work of trying it out.

To their delight, the captain and his crew took another Right whale along the coasts of Salvador which had them believe was a temporary hotbed. There, Joseph heaved on the line that drew First Boat near the dying and bloody creature. The Third Mate continually lunged forward with his lance alongside Mister Fletcher as the men behind them shouted in the victory of death. The tryworks bellowed obtruding black smoke for some time, smearing the sails above in soot like a mischievous whitewasher and its oil was bailed from the silver kettles with a thousand hauls. Their tracks were marked above them in the sky like the record of a melting mollusk made of pitch. If there were anyone around for two hundred miles in any direction, they could find them easily by their pollution of corrupt smell. In many ways their grime could work against them or for them. There were some who roamed the seas like jackals that would not be deterred at such defilement to find out what they held aboard.

The cooper knocked up small skinny casks with a wide blade and mallet, fitting the ship's countless small spaces tightly with oil.

Alistair Smith continued working in the belly of the ship guiding the casks as they descended to him on a chain to rest alongside many others. He kept an eye out while performing his tasks to see if anyone could observe him.

Work pushed late into the evenings as the sun made its rotations; the water ballast in the hold traded for oil, week after week. The captain made a habit of pressing whale stamps into the ship's log and it bled to a second page alongside several others. His book was topped with writing and numbers stating dates, times, and locations of the kills, but there was never too much.

The bows plowed forward through waves in all manner of weather as the figurehead of the woman was silently marking time.

After another two weeks had passed, the Fortune advanced into the southern latitudes where the weather had gradually returned to being colder.

The captain sat at his table with all other officers in the officer's mess among the light of candles in the night. As expected, the men were dressed to warm themselves and their cups were nearly emptied of the fruit of the vine that also assisted in the conquest. It was a permanent ritual that every one of them anticipated for the duration, executed in the hours before retiring. The Fortune was sound in that it had no draft to chill the bones of sleeping men and they loved her for it. When the scuttles and hatches were closed they were sealed to airtight and only a man's movement or breath would flicker a candle's flame. It was a comfort that warmed their hearts as well, not giving too much or any thought at all to the condition of those passing the nights in the bows. There, it was a stinking business altogether; the bulk of the crew lined in tight rows closely and in layers like the barrels of the hold. When the wind was cold their air supply would be stifled by the latches, breathing in one another's smells. It was welcomed by most all when one would light the tobacco of a pipe to choke out the lingering subtle nagging of odors. It was a way of life and those odors were rarely recognized by them, but there were times after so many weeks at sea in the colder latitudes where the idea of a bath in a cold bucket was universally refused that it could not be ignored.

"I remember, Doctor," Second Mate, Lock, said to Braddock Stowe who sat across from him, "on a night in mid-September not many-a-year past, the captain mastered the helm in a foul sea. We'd been out for some two and a half weeks in the shoals of Serekunda of the Gambia in trade for goods. We were aught to be broken apart under the gales that were and near to empty the hold to right her, but Captain Grey fought that storm like a Sperm under the lance throughout the night. Aye, and saved the Fortune did he as one man."

The doctor's eyebrows rose on his forehead along with a few of the other officers' as he flashed his look to the captain who sat with his gaze down onto the table, smoking his pipe.

"If Her Majesty of England were to look on at such a triumph," Mister Lock continued, "he'd be Admiral of the Royal Navy, I says! Hard-a-weather be him and few there be as hardy a seaman!"

The doctor looked on quite amused and smiled as the others tapped their hands onto the edges of the table in a gentlemen's commendation. Captain Grey took in a deep breath with a large smile and leaned forward in his seat.

"It's been very well, gentlemen!" he said from under his thick white beard. "Tonight... we have wine! A drink to the Fortune!" All men raised their glasses.

"Aye, to the Fortune, Captain," answered Mister Lock.

"To the Fortune!" the other officers chimed together. In cheer, the men raised the glasses to their lips and drank.

At two o'clock that morning, the captain lay in his bed asleep. A faint moon penetrated the windows at the stern against the back of his bed and illuminated him in blue mists. A distant whale call far out at sea roused him to wake like the haunting lament of one crying out from the dead. He quickly sat up by it and the song drifted slowly through the windows again as an aimless smoke on a lifeless wind, bringing him back from some better dream. In his thought, he saw his wife's face as she wept for him and it was deeply troubling. It was merely her broken heart of his absence he was sure, but returned solid to his bed knowing the tide would turn soon enough. He wiped his hand over his face as he stood to his feet and looked out across the dull sparkle of a nearly invisible light.

Above him at the ship's wheel, Joseph stood alone upon the silent deck watching the night sky in dreams of his own, gazing upon those bodies as men and poets oft do when he is reminded of his fleeting breadth. That moon was faithfully behind him as he went ever on and when it went again into the future horizons Joseph considered it a foretelling of destiny. It was quiet sound wisdom portrayed in physical display as childlike men slept and he pondered it.

"I will follow," he said softly to himself to it with a short smile.

Only few sails were loosed as was the custom and the hour, subdued. The captain exited his cabin and met the helmsman at the hurricane house by his door.

"Oh, good evening, Captain!" Joseph said, startled by his presence, being hailed back from outside the confines of time towards the real flickering light of the binnacle where his feet stood upon seasoned timbers of old.

"Good evening, Mister Michael," Henry replied

with a short nod. He walked forward and put his hand on the binnacle which lit his face by the lantern inside as his mind went to the disturbed visions of his sleep. He looked up over the canvas into the night sky as he spoke a thought to the only other that shared his consciousness.

"Do you have any family, Mister Michael?"

"I do, sir," he answered with a newly warmed face."

"Can you tell me of them?"

"My father was a farmer from Thorpe Tilney and met my mother as a young man. They had only two children in all their years of marriage - I have a younger sister who stayed home in England. They were good people and my mother taught me much the same as I came along. I remember my childhood with much fondness and I owe it to them for all manner of wisdom that I have later gained – something that must be sought and when found, hearkened to. My father and mother loved one another in that truest form and when it is there, the children know it. It seemed to be a simpler time and less weighty. They did well and their example was one that I wish all men would gain. It is a priceless gift and I regret that so many are not in a position to receive it," he said with a melancholy smile.

Captain Grey looked on with sincerity, pleased to hear memoirs that lifted the spirits.

"Do you ever miss them?" he asked.

"Over time, my sister was wed and we had to go our separate ways. My mother is now the only survivor of my parents. I have not lent as much as four days in four years, sir, to their concern and now as I stand here, staring into the night sky, I am sorry. My mother had much prudence and one thing she was sure to instill into me was a peace with God, a respect for life, and a thin silvery thread of hope. As I have made my way across land and sea from north to south in sand and ice, in fire and in water," he said with a confident twinkle in his eye, "I've found that I've required it."

Captain Grey's face lit up with a smile as he appreciated what he saw in Joseph's countenance. He nodded softly to him in some alleviation from his words.

"Your story is much the same as mine, Mister Michael...and one day, I too will go back and not again take for granted those simple treasures, these that are most important that The Lord has given us."

"And I as well."

Joseph smiled in concurrence with his captain, a man who was human like the rest of them in balanced purpose to finish the race as honorable and as pleasing as could be.

The men for a single moment were created equal under the earth's satellite as two molded segments of iron made in God's image, designed to sharpen one another. In the mutual realization of it there was a temporary suspension of difference before any more was spoken.

"I'll take the watch, Mister Michael. Get some rest."

"Aye, Captain," Joseph answered softly, being extremely glad. "A good night, sir."

With a courteous nod, the simple whaleman left his post and traveled away into the darkness, down into his forecastle bed.

Captain Grey put his hand on the wheel and stared down into the binnacle. The course held South Southwest by the compass. The great circle was tied off by rope to hold it into position without assistance. He removed a pipe from his coat and placed it into his mouth. He pulled a tinderbox from another pocket and took from it a piece of char cloth to light his tobacco. At the binnacle, he raised the glass of the lantern and inserted the cloth into the flame. He brought the fire to his face to burn his pipe when a burst of heat lightning whipped across the sky above. It instantly grabbed his eye and pulled his gaze upwards.

A flickering fire, the Ampizant, like a dim yellow star, immediately appeared on the main masthead and began to move. Henry quickly puffed out the burning char cloth and threw it down in fright. He ran amidships under the main mast and stared up to a glowing fireball that moved downwards towards him. With wide eyes of dread, he took the pipe from his mouth and stood frozen. The fireball crackled and fizzed as it passed down through the rigging and forced him to quickly look away to the side in fear. It crackled much louder and against his better judgment, could not resist returning to it again no matter what the cost. The traveling sphere quickly descended as if it sought him and connected itself in an electrical arc, touching the gunwales at the captain's side. Before he could manage a blink or a twitch of muscle, the charge lit upon him for a split-second, causing his entire face to burn with electric light.

Captain Grey immediately cried out in fear, but

not enough to wake any man and fell backwards against the bulwarks with a jolt; his head propped against it at his shoulders. He breathed hard in panic, rubbing his face frantically, trying to wipe off the mysterious glow that had already accomplished its purpose and vanished. He lay there trembling and stared straight ahead in a daze, knowing and fearing what it meant.

𝕴n the galley on the following day, Royston Davies stood at a table alone, rolling greasy chunks of fish into a ball of dough. He stopped in irritation and rubbed the back of his neck. As he pulled down his neckerchief, a new black sore hidden beneath was apparent on his flesh. He rubbed it slowly in habit with his bare hand as Jago entered the doorway in front of him, smoking a dark brown crooked cigar. The particular cook paused to study his assistant's progress and Royston smiled at him with a nod.

"You get 'em Greyling heads chopped up in 'ere?" Jago said.

"Aye, Jago," Royston confirmed. The cook turned his back and the two men continued to prepare the ship's meal.

The bell clanged to signal the change of duties in a light rain. A cold wind had picked up under the overcast sky and the crew was dressed accordingly. The Larboard Watch advanced to duty and the Starboard Watch yielded. The Second Mate prepared his company for tacking ship. The topsails were single-reefed and the topgallants were set over. She was close-hauled at six points off the wind on larboard tack and the helmsman, an African man named Zareb, called out to the Second Mate.

"Mister Lock, wind South by West!"

"Larboard Watch prepare to go about on starboard tack!" cried Mister Lock. "She's six points off the wind! Helmsman, keep her a good full for stays!"

"Aye, Mister Lock!" he answered.

"Ready about! Stations for stays!" shouted the officer to those unfortunate to be at duty under the wet sky.

The Larboard Watch got into their positions to turn the ship through the wind and see that everything was clear.

"Ready! Ease down the helm!" shouted Mister Lock.

"Ease down, sir!" Zareb answered and turned the wheel slowly a-lee spoke by spoke. The Second Mate shouted again.

"Ease off jib sheets! Spanker boom amidships!"

The corresponding men in those positions took action at the lines to move the sails. "Helm's a-lee!"

At this signal, the crew let go the fore sheet and head sheets, making the bow able to swing through the headwind. Joseph and the men of his watch retreated to the forecastle from the oncoming rain with a great sense of relief.

"Rise tacks and sheets! Haul lee spanker topping lift! Let go the weather one!" the Second Mate called.

The crew ran up the clewgarnets so that the clews of the course would clear the nettings when the yards were swung. The lee tack and weather sheets were shortened and the lee spanker topping lift was hauled taut. The ship turned into the wind and the fore sails were aback against the mast.

Joseph got down the ladder and began to make himself comfortable and dry. Men crawled into their bunks after they had stripped themselves and others rested upon sea chests never minding the clammy garments. John Morgan sat beside Joseph upon a chest and spoke his thoughts as he wiped the cold water from his face.

"We need a good rain to wash the stink from these decks...and from the men," John said half-smiling. "If only it could rain in here."

"Aye," Joseph replied, "but would it change anything?"

John looked at him with a laugh. "I suppose it would not...reminds me of the farm, that stench...where I was raised," John said, staring up at the rugged beams of the ceiling overhead. "I figure it weren't all bad now that it's been put so far into the past. I just needed to clap eyes on the better part of the world to fill the bill."

"The same for me," said Joseph, "but I could have stayed there my entire life and tended to it with much joy, but trouble pressed me on...into a new life - a life in the city and a life at sea."

John turned and looked at Joseph to study his face which had turned distinctly sober.

"What will you do, Joseph, when you sail home to England?"

"I will return to my former life, my friend...to my home in the country. I were happier there. Whether the reward from this voyage be much or little when I see the old city again, I shall make my way there ne'ertheless...changed and grateful."

"That would make you happy?"

"With the way that it weighs upon my thoughts, I can think of nothing else."

"Would you take a woman with you, Joseph?" John said most sincere.

"I would like that, John," he answered with a sad face.

"I never had luck at all with them, hence the isolation at sea. But I can say that it was probably always my fault. I never could hold a regular position of work...always looking for something more exciting. There are no hours spent like those doing something you despise or that make you feel that you are slipping away in life into a dreadful obscurity. Here, I can think. My mind is clear - that load is lifted. To have a woman is to have a great burden. To keep her you would have to fight and it would not be very long at all before you would be in some war bearing arms. To have her and to keep her you would have to leave her and it doesn't make much sense. There is some that I've seen that I admire within my heart...as if we had a loving past. I hold on to this if ever such was needed because it would turn out the same in the end anyway. We all go on to see God alone," said John.

"I suppose for myself, the load has never been cast off since I had to leave the old place behind. It's been hard pressing, the memories of the former days...before the exceeding advancement of man. I wonder what it was like for the forebears. I wonder if it's all more difficult now."

"I believe you ponder it too much, Joseph. You need to live your life and love it as it has been given. You need to see what good is in it now."

"I would like to."

"You could let it go."

Joseph looked at him with a small smile and a short nod. John was right, but he did not understand what it really meant.

"Aren't those the very things you've declared to me in times past?"

"They are, but it seems that it is your turn to day to impart it to me," Joseph said with a humble but happy expression and a snort.

"The future is looking you in the face each day," said John, "and there's gonna be a bit more of it for *you*." John got a long grin on his face and put his hand on Joseph's shoulder. "Tell her I said hullo when you meet her."

Joseph's spirit was lifted and somehow he knew John was right again. He entertained the thought for a moment with small gladness and a building hope that his friend had spoken life into a dead dream - and it heard him.

"Well, what about you, John?"

"I expect I'll remain at sea forever," he stated with genuine cheerfulness, but not really knowing where it all would ultimately take him or for how long. "It's a glorious thing, this life - only tied to an ship under open sky of starry nights…that freedom in a world of war. What more can a man want?"

Joseph smiled. "When you put it in those terms, John, it would almost persuade someone into believing they've fooled the world out here."

"But we have," John said with a gleam in his eye.

Joseph laughed at him and for a very brief moment he agreed. He nodded but before he could say anything more, whether of denial or acceptance, a piercing cry came through the hatch above from the masthead.

"Blooooooooooooooooooooooooooowwwww!!"

The men in the forecastle jumped to their feet and clambered up the ladder to the deck in the light rain. The Larboard Watch was still going through the motions of tacking ship and all men took hold of something fixed nearby and looked to the crow's nest.

"A blooooooooooooooooooowww!! She blooooooooowwsss!" came down the desperate cry.

The captain sprang onto deck from below wearing a wool raincoat and hat as the Second Mate returned an answer to the call.

"Where away?!!"

"A Sperm! Three points a-fore larboard beam!" a shout returned from the complex enigmas of rope-work that amassed itself throughout the sails overhead and obstructed all views from any angle.

"All hands keep ship about to starboard tack!" cried Mister Lock. "Mains'l haul! Brace up sharp!"

The yards on the main and crossjack were swung around together and then braced up sharp on the new tack by the quick working sailors. The captain hurried to the larboard side, his spyglass to his eye, and found the Sperm whale among the gray misty crests in the distance.

"Let go and haul!" Mister Lock cried as the rain beat down onto his face.

The headbraces were manned and the yards swung around to the opposite tack. Men hauled on the fore and top bowlines as the old lee-braces were let go. The ship made a successful turn and sailed close-hauled to the wind on starboard tack.

Just seconds behind, Doctor Braddock Stowe burst onto the deck to gaze upon the sighted whale. He looked to the sky and upon the water that ran to the weather deck from every mass and became increasingly apprehensive for what could come of it.

From his spyglass, the captain eyed a single blow from one Sperm whale shoot high from the surface. "Mister Lock," he cried, "it is a lone bull! Boat crews make ready to lower!"

Without wasting a moment, the men stole their positions along the larboard side as always and uncovered the boats. First Mate, James Fletcher turned with a great shout.

"Get ye tubs aboard! Put 'em in!"

Two men assigned to each boat took positions at the falls by the davits and prepared to lower them away. One man from each crew jumped the gunwales of the Fortune into the boats to fend them off from the ship and they had it organized so well they could have executed it in their sleep. When settled, the emergency supplies were quickly loaded.

Kallum Morrison, who was part of the Third Boat crew, noticed Robert Ackley was not at his station to get aboard.

"Mister Whitby," he shouted, "Mister Ackley isn't at duty!"

The Third Mate looked immediately up and around, unable to locate him in haste and called aft.

"Mister Ackley! To your station, man!"

The giant creature brought up its huge tail and dove below, disappearing into the choppy surface of the sea. The captain climbed up into the rigging and held onto the shrouds of the larboard side with the stress of it and pointed his finger to the whale.

"Capture that stronghold of ambergris! Lower away boats! Lower away!"

The vessels dropped into the water and men scrambled down the lines after them, clinging to the sides of the ship as it plunged forward. Redford Whitby took one last moment on deck to call for a replacement.

"Mister Neilson! Balance Robert's place in the boat 'till we turn 'im up!"

"Aye, sir!" Diederick answered and left his point at the ropes and climbed down with the Third Mate into the restless Third Boat at the bows. The men unhooked when they reached the crashing water and cast off from the ship. Alistair Smith took a position in the center of the Second Boat and started to row out against the wind with the others in adrenalin-fueled heightened strain. Joseph was in coordinating practice on First Boat and kept his eye upon the face of James Fletcher who stood at the stern in front of him awaiting direction. All three boats moved away from the ship into the waves of the vast deep, but soon after, the turbulent ocean set itself to hinder them.

"I've lost sight of 'im in the swells. Waif the masthead!" James cried to the other boats.

Redford took hold of a red flag and stood waving at the ship. The man at the masthead who scraped the underbelly of the cloud cover, signaled with a flag to them in response and they interpreted his direction.

"He's away on larboard bow!" Mister Whitby shouted. "Steer him, men!"

Abimbola was busy running the whale line across the boat around the loggerhead as they rowed and got his iron ready to throw. He held it in a notch that he had worn in the knuckle of his right hand and as they pressed further, he rubbed it repeatedly deeper with pressure. When it flew away on its launch, it would be quick and it would be sure.

Third Mate Lock spoke softly but forcefully to his crew, looking toward the whale's position with trembling. "Heave men! Pull in close! Take the swells in your stride! That's it! Bring her to!"

Alistair Smith pulled his oar in time with the others and the repetitive and rhythmic motions put him into a hypnotic trance. On each row there were beats on a native's drum. The wooden stick thrust into a taut skin and was propelled away with a deep hollow pulse. Each one echoed over the surface of the waters and he tried desperately to keep in time with it. It was what he wanted. It was how to stay in balance. He kept his eyes fixed upon Mister Lock, glaring at him with the eyes of the devil. He heard nothing that was spoken and nothing that was called, but there was a voice. Mister Lock was unaware of the consequential evil that had gotten into the boat with him, but unwisely kept his eye set on the lesser beast: the massive seventy-foot Sperm whale and its jets of vapor that shot straight into the air.

Joseph rowed hard with all of his strength and the First Boat remained the furthest from the whale of the three. James Fletcher pushed them to row harder as the rain continued to fall. All three boats progressed a great distance from the ship and the giant surfaced again not far from them. With stealth and silence, they came upon the ideal position to strike him; he being enormous like another ship himself. The Second and Third Boats lingered a moment longer for James to near before any action was dared taken. Nigel Jackson remained seated, anxiously rubbing his hands up and down on his legs to remain nimble for his moment of accountability.

The tension was oppressive and there was a point of authentic fear among them. Men of all three boats looked at one another in it even as they rowed ahead. James Fletcher stood trembling with his eyes as wide as tea saucers, readying himself for the cry. Nigel Jackson got to his feet in the Third Boat, pressed his leg into the notch, and raised the harpoon and rope over his shoulder like a madman.

"Strike!!" James cried, almost frantically. "Up to the hitches!"

In an instant, Nigel Jackson threw the harpoon with all his might and sank it deep into the monster's back. Immediately, he stooped down to his feet, took hold of a second, and sent it the same way, plunging into the meat of the whale with a spray of blood.

"A Fall! A Fall!" The First Mate screamed almost maniacally.

"Stern all! Steer clear!" Redford shouted to them with his heart threatening to rip itself from his chest.

In dread of him, they quickly rowed away and tied the boats together in only a matter of seconds.

The great Sperm was immediately enraged as

expected and thrashed around on the surface, wallowing and rolling in tangled lines to free himself. He flipped his huge tail upwards, causing a giant wave and waterfall and dove deep. The behemoth spiraled down as he went and the cables that held him as a ferocious marionette on many strings jerked hard behind him into agonizing straight lines.

The men clung to the sides of their tipping boats in terror as the First Mate shouted over the deafening roar of tidal waves upon water.

"He sounds!"

The boats spun around as the whale pulled them quickly forward and the officers took a front seat to the ensuing ride. The whale line of the Third Boat began to whistle and shriek upon the loggerhead as it passed through the chock in the bow. The harpooneer threw buckets of water over it as it burned with smoke and tried to catch fire. Others pitched seawater into the tubs of line to attempt to spare their strength and vehemence.

"Get a turn 'round the loggerhead 'fore he takes it all!" Redford shouted to Nigel from the front of the boat.

Nigel tossed another loop of line around the pin to slow the whale as much as possible without killing them all. The bow sank down to the water and nearly went under when the boatsteerer let off and raised them up again. It spun and unrolled from the tub at an amazing rate, almost too quickly to measure its speed and would have whipped into a deadly knot if it were not for the careful spin it had been primed with. The largest tub, holding two hundred twenty-five fathoms of line at the after part of the boat, quickly ran out and the second line from the smaller tub, amidships, kicked in, dragging the boats behind. Redford Whitby gave the signal to the Second Mate.

"The reserve line is on!" he nervously yelled.

"Make fast the main line to Third Boat's reserve!" Bromley cried to his crew.

As the boats flew along and crashed through the smaller swells of the sea, the main line from the Second Boat was thrown to the Third Boat and tied to their reserve. As the men accomplished this, the reserve tub ran empty straightaway from the Third Boat.

"Reserve line is out!" the Third Mate shouted with amazement. The main line from the Second Boat began to run out just as fast as anyone had ever witnessed and was determined to catch the boat on fire, even in the rain.

"Get two turns on the loggerhead!" Bromley cried as he turned to Abimbola from the chock. The harpooneer got his hands into the rope that lay deep in the tub and threw two loops over the post. As he did, the spinning line abruptly stopped.

"He's broken off!" Abimbola cried.

The men went silent. Each one clung to his boat as the rain poured down and soaked them through. The rain spattered against the surface of all things in great drops and no other sound dared resonate. After a moment of rising with the swells end to end, James Fletcher gave caution.

"He'll breach! Careful, men!"

"Get the boats apart!" Bromley shouted in an effort to save as many lives as possible if there was trouble. "Peak your oars!"

The line was unhitched between the boats and they quickly drifted a short distance apart in the uneasy water. The men of all boats raised the paddles of their oars straight into the air in an effort to save them. They waited silently, rising and falling upon the raving of the deep, anxiously searching over the dark surface with wide eyes. There was nothing to appease the tension, nothing to assure death had no intentions for them; only an insensitive wind. Bromley Lock breathed heavy as his eyes searched the distant water and no matter how many times he had seen such a thing, no man is ever ready when his life is cut short. He clung to the sides of the boat that came to a point where he sat and hoped he would again master the animal that could kill them all in a swan song that the nightmares of men are made of. Everyone in his boat desperately searched for a sign of the whale and knew that now they were in his realm and at his mercy - defenseless against his awesome power. The three boats quietly drifted a hundred feet apart on the water.

Then, in an instant, the rain stopped. A dead silence rolled over and only the heavy breathing of the men broke it. Bromley's twitching face revealed his nervous spirit. Joseph held on and in wisdom, whispered softly to himself.

"There shall no evil befall thee, neither shall any plague come nigh thy dwelling."

The whale came directly beneath the Third Boat at a very great depth. He swam straight upwards towards the surface from the utter darkness, directly beneath its keel with unrestrained and unquenchable power. Traveling at an extremely great speed, he came near the boat in only a few seconds from the eternal depths. The boat was dark against the light of the surface and the whale, in his rage, aimed straight for it with malevolence. As he came within forty feet, he opened his enormous twenty-five foot long jaw, lined with forty-five sharp teeth, each weighing over two pounds; the jagged chasm of doom.

The great Sperm breached directly upon the Third Boat as if shot from the mouth of a volcano. The tiny wooden structure was clamped in his bite and was raised straight into the air in uncontrolled vengeance. The men cried out in terror as they went up into his mouth. Nigel Jackson fell away from the side, fifteen feet to the water and splashed hard into an immediate disorientation. The other men were thrown out seconds afterwards at twenty-five feet, back to the ocean far below. Diederick Nielson, seated at the center of the boat, fell forward into the corner of the whale's mouth and his leg became caught between the teeth at his knee. Simon Laurent was seated behind him near the center and plummeted down over him as the whale continued straight towards the sky. Simon's head fell into the whale's mouth and his neck became wedged at the opposite corner of his jaw in a harrowing pinch.

The beast propelled completely out of the water, all seventy feet of his greatness, straight up into the air, gushing blood in profuse spurts in all directions; a rain to those men as that of the end times. He bit down onto the boat with terrible force. Diederick cried out as his leg was crushed in half at the knee and concurrently, Simon was instantly beheaded. The whaleboat shattered into matchsticks as if from an explosion and Simon's body along with Diederick plunged back into the swallowing ocean with him.

The whale landed flat, using his entire mass against the surface of the water to thwart and injure them, just inches from the Second Boat. It rose into the air on a colossal twenty-foot wave that threw all men overboard. Bastiaan Rasmussen was just at a right position in his boat and stuck his harpoon into the monster's side as he crashed down.

Alistair Smith hit the water alongside Bromley Lock. Their fall was tremendous and both men sank deep beneath the turbulent white waves of salt. Bromley rolled around, looked up, and saw the light of the surface under Alistair's legs. Alistair moved his head around, got his bearings, and found Bromley swimming up from the darkness beneath him. As Bromley rose to Alistair's level, Alistair quickly grabbed him around the throat and began to squeeze. Bromley's eyes widened in shock as they began a violent struggle. Bromley attempted to get to the surface for air, but Alistair clung to him tightly and kept him down. He tried to pull on Alistair's face and head, but to no avail. A long knife appeared from Bromley's pant leg and stabbed upwards with a wild powerful thrust.

Alistair saw it flash in the light from the surface above and swerved to the side. He got his hand on Bromley's forearm, twisting it around into a position that nearly broke it. Bromley's hand writhed in pain under the maneuver and he dropped the blade. It sank away from them quickly to the bottom of the sea as the overturned whaleboat drifted above their heads. Bromley struggled upwards, but Alistair's head was much higher.

Holding Bromley by the hair, Alistair pushed him down to his waist. The motion caused him to be forced upwards and his head broke the surface inside the capsized boat. He gasped for air under the darkened cover while keeping his grip down and hard against the Second Mate. He sucked in a quick breath to sustain him and pushed down again as Bromley pulled him under, struggling bitterly for his life. Alistair turned him around, wrestled him under the neck from behind with his right arm, and squeezed. Bromley began to lose strength without oxygen and reached back in severity. He got his left arm around Alistair's head and strove to force pressure on him with any means. He pushed against the water, desperately trying to get his head to the surface. His thoughts went immediately to his mother and father. They were still alive although they were in very old age. He did not want to die there and leave them forever wondering what went wrong or never knowing the truth. He was angry, but it quickly faded as he feared the very worst.

Alistair got his left arm under Bromley's left arm across his chest with an unstoppable madness and constricted him with immense strength. The remaining air that Bromley had saved in his lungs was forced out through his teeth against his will. His eyes widened, knowing what was happening as Alistair loosened his grip with a jerk and caused him to inhale a great gasp of water. Alistair gritted his teeth, his face twisted in lunacy, as Bromley violently convulsed to his death. Alistair laughed within himself in a frightful shudder as the dead man's arms drifted out, motionless to his sides. He wished there were others down there with him that he could kill, he wished he could breathe the water like a fish and continue with what he purposed to execute. He did not want to stop and relished the struggle that would threaten his own existence. He immediately released the arm around Bromley's chest, kept his other very tightly around his neck with rapid twists, enough to break it if unintentionally careless, and swam upwards to the edge of the overturned whaleboat. He pushed his face into the air and gasped for breath, barely managing to keep himself alive throughout the fight, but forgetting that he needed it like all men. He looked around and saw the others clinging to the broken pieces of the Third Boat in turmoil as some attempted to swim towards him.

"Help! Help here! It's Mister Lock! He's injured!" Alistair cried desperately while panting. "I've got 'im here!"

Three men came to Alistair, got hold of the Second Mate's body, and tried to raise him from the water. They flipped the boat over and quickly pulled each other into it. Bromley Lock was hauled in by the shoulders and they laid him on his back upon the floor of the boat. Alistair knelt by him as the men gathered around and looked on in despair. Diederick cried out in pain from a distance, treading water with nothing to cling to.

"Hold now! We're coming, man!" was the reply. They paddled to him and pulled him from the water to reveal that his leg was gone. He drenched the boat with his shooting blood.

"God's mercy!" Nigel shouted. "Hurry, to the

ship!"

The men rowed hard with only two oars left undamaged and recovered. The giant whale bled out as they went and was exhausted. James Fletcher stabbed him to death with his lance and the blood covered them as he rolled over and raised his giant fin into the air from the water.

Aboard ship, the crew hoisted the Second Boat from the water and brought Diederick and Bromley aboard. The doctor stood eagerly awaiting them with much fear. Badru was also among the injured with a severely broken arm.

"My arm, sir," he said softly to the surgeon without much excitement.

"Get Mister Nielson and Badru below!" Doctor Stowe shouted to the surrounding able men. "Mister Stearne, get me irons red in a fire!"

Redford Whitby darted across the deck as soon as his feet touched the sole with the disheartening report.

"Captain! Captain!" he cried frantically. At the main mast, Henry met him with a look of great fear.

"It's Mister Lock, sir!"

The captain immediately drew near and knelt by Bromley, whose skin was pale white. The doctor pressed on Bromley's chest and water poured from the sides of his mouth. He reached forward and felt for his pulse. After a moment of observation he looked to the captain who knelt beside him with a distressed overcast face.

"He's dead, sir," the doctor said in disappointment. "He's drowned."

Henry was silent and his eyes turned downwards into a stare of disbelief. "Captain, if I may?" Doctor

Stowe requested in the moment of confusion. The captain slowly nodded his head with a stare as if in a daze and the doctor rushed off below decks. After a moment to regain his thoughts of authority, Captain Grey looked to the Third Mate with the orders.

"Get a boat out to Mister Fletcher and assist the tow," he said firmly.

"Aye, Captain," Mister Whitby answered solemnly with a sigh of grief, pausing to say one more discouraging thing. "Um…Simon Laurent, sir, he's been killed as well." He turned with his head down and dashed off to the spare boats on the skids, over the cooper's station, relaying the command.

As the captain knelt beside Bromley, Alistair stood near, looking upon the face of the dead man. He wiped his mouth with his forearm and held a disgusted look as he turned away.

Captain Grey ran his fingers up under his hat and slid them down over his face in anguish as the rain continued to beat down upon them.

Chapter 4
Voices in the Ceiling

Inside the Surgery, Badru sat watching several men hold Diederick onto a table as he struggled with the pain. His blood covered everything - those around him and the floor. Doctor Braddock Stowe produced a small jar from a locked drawer.

"Keep pressure on the leg!" he commanded as he hurried in and around the men who assisted him. "Diederick, this is opium. It will dull your pain."

He poured the liquid into Diederick's mouth and the blacksmith nervously entered the room with two red-hot harpoons from his fires. Doctor Stowe placed a wood stick wrapped in leather between Diederick's teeth and turned to the African man who stood nearby.

"Zareb, keep this in his mouth!"

Following the order, he moved behind Diederick's head, gripped the stick tightly at each end, and pressed down.

"Mister Nielson," said Braddock, "I am going to cauterize the wound to stop your bleeding. If I do not, you will die, sir." He turned to the blacksmith who waited at the door with beads of sweat pouring down his forehead. "Mister Stearne, please."

He handed over the harpoon that issued black smoke from its burning tip.

"Hold him! Tightly!" Braddock shouted.

He pressed the red-hot point into Diederick's severed leg quickly and the blood and tissue sizzled like the sliced whale in the tryworks. Diederick bit down into the leather with the full force of his bite and screamed in agony as the men struggled to hold his violent writhing upon the table.

In an hour's time, the tow was painstakingly executed and the main deck buzzed with men who cut in on the massive Sperm's carcass. The fires were stoked and burning hot and the captain stood upon the flensing stage with three other men, including the remaining officers. Their mood was heavy and laden with dread. It had taken the entire crew with influence and all remained solemn as they worked; their thoughts fixed upon the dead and injured. Notwithstanding, the captain and the surviving Mates were pressed to continue with the requirement at hand and hacked away with their spades and cut the large section of the head above the mouth loose in the grease and grime.

The Sperm was a sizeable catch and the process of its harvesting was formidable. It would take much of the next twelve hours of time given to them and its yield would be well worth the labor, but that price paid put on the charge to render such a creature into barrels was only what was needed to see it.

"Haul on the Junk!" Henry shouted to the

handlers upon the chain. "Bring it aboard!"

The most prized piece, the hollow cavity in the whale's head which was filled with Spermaceti oil, was lifted and torn off by a large chain that was looped around and brought over deck. The waxy cream oil was everywhere, including on the men, sloshing around upon the deck in pools against the bulwarks and barrels in the movement of the Fortune.

Joseph worked in exhaustive stride below in the blubber room, slicing it into manageable pieces and throwing it into tubs. They were filled to overflowing and felt as if they were topped in lead by weight. All who were aboard heard Diederick's moans through a wall at the other end of the ship, but those below were more unfortunate to perceive all of the chilling nuances. Joseph paused, looking aft in the direction with shaken nerves over the entire spectacle, and took a deep breath while continuing to cut. Within his heart, he prayed for the terror of the poor man whose life was forever altered.

In the surgery room, Doctor Stowe took hold of Badru's left arm and quickly set the bone back into place with an instant thrust. Badru cried out with only swigs of rum to relieve his pain. The doctor placed two wood splints on each side of his arm and bound them tightly with cloth.

"I have done all that was necessary, Badru," he stated with compassion. "Now the rest is up to you."

Men on deck bailed the oil from the tryworks into the copper cooling tank. Others at the mincing station sliced the horse pieces into books. The deck was slippery and the men skidded around on it as they moved. At one portion of the fore deck, five men slipped around on top of an enormous heap of intestines, slicing out any ambergris. They ran their hands inside an endless gash and squeezed everything they felt through their fingers.

Prescot Stearne returned to his anvil and pulled a twisted mangled harpoon from the fire. He held it up in front of him - the damage done by the whale was clear. Laying the thing down, he hammered away with great force and straightened it.

As the day pressed on, the whale's head was severed and secured to the side of the ship, pointing nose down to dip out the most prized portion of the floating flammable form. James Fletcher cut a hole in the center of it near the exposed ragged neck bone and made an order.

"Ready to bail the Case!" he cried. "Lower Case bucket!"

Four men attended the task and a bucket was lowered down with a pole attached above it. One directed the bucket, two operated the guy-lines to force it into the Case by means of the pole, and the fourth to hoist and lower. The bucket was forced into the opening and the oil spilled into it quickly around all edges of the rim. The hoisting man pulled and brought it out. The man on the bucket unhooked it from the line and poured it straight into a barrel that was lashed to the bulwarks.

"Ah, Spermaceti oil," James said softly to himself in an astonished remorse. "None other like it in all the world." He paused for a moment with a sigh. "We've lost two men for you to day."

"Has any man met Robert Ackley in a

roundabouts?!" the Third Mate called from the tryworks.

All hands on the main deck searched their surroundings and high aloft.

"Nay, Mister Whitby!" came the answers from fore and aft.

"Not been seen 'afore the Sperm made 'is debut," Redford said with curiosity. "What about to day, then? Any clap eyes on 'im atall?"

"I suppose I've not seen him aboard since the sun's been raised," answered Mister Doyle.

The men immediately pried their memories and everyone came up amazed. James Fletcher joined Mister Whitby in the hunt and a call flowed down into the blubber room through the main hatch to them there.

"Is Robert Ackley among you, men?" Redford shouted.

"Nay, sir!"

James spotted the boy as he fueled the fires of the tryworks.

"Mister Dobb, get aloft," he said, "and find Mister Ackley." The boy nodded, got his feet upon the shrouds, and began to climb with determination.

"I need a few men to give search!" cried James. "Some who are less soaked in gurry. Robert Ackley is not accounted for!"

Abimbola, Nigel Jackson, and Rawley Chapman left what they were doing and descended through the main hatchway into the hold. Alistair Smith rolled barrels around with a large two-wheeled cart down in the obscure.

"Is Robert about?" Nigel asked the steward in

passing as he searched over the nooks and crannies of the large space, the belly of the ship.

Alistair looked up at them and shook his head. The men walked around, inspecting between barrels and all the spaces of the rows and columns. The area was a great expanse of storage and filled with many rooms. Alistair stood watching without moving. It was as if they were trespassing on his personal property. His face was constant cold and he had no concern for their agenda. They passed over the area lightly and then climbed the ladders out, finding nothing. Alistair rubbed his mouth and jaw to his neck in a neurotic and irritated manner and then continued with his work.

The search party and the officers met together at the forecastle and Samuel Dobb returned from aloft above them, descending upon the fore shrouds.

"Anything, Mister Dobb?" Mister Fletcher asked with nervous concern evident on his face. The boy shook his head. The men of the search party turned away quickly and descended into the forecastle, but found no one there.

"Which of these be his?" said James, pointing to the sea chests that lined the floor.

"This one," Mister Chapman replied, signifying the one nearest the ladder.

The officers unfastened the great rugged box and found it filled with Mister Ackley's belongings.

"There's nothing missing?" Redford stated in amazement.

"What of the captain's money?" said James in a stern and foreboding voice.

The men were astonished and looked to one

another as if startled by a strange sound. Peering into the chest in an ominous silence, they saw that it was certainly not there among the man's items. As all were still, afraid to make any assumptions, James turned and climbed out with a deeply seated nagging thought.

On the other side of the ship, the captain sat at his table staring down at his books in sadness as the First Mate knocked and then immediately entered his room.

"Sir," he said in distress, "it's Robert Ackley. He's...disappeared."

The captain looked up from the table to James, his feelings of both fear and worry written into his eyes. He inhaled deeply and sighed with a look that expressed inner perturbation, but said nothing.

Late that night, the flickering beam of the lantern brightened the forecastle. The men were uneasy as they lay in their bunks, meditating on the day's ill-fated events. After nearly thirty minutes of silence wherein no soul spoke, Esmond Burne broke it.

"How does it happen?" he said, restlessly, "that a man vanishes into the air on a barque at sea?!...into nothingness?"

Only the creaking of the beams made any sound at that moment in the room and when the pause was finished, John Morgan answered with his thought.

"A merchant of Spain I layed onto for passage to the East overtook a storm and lost two men to the sea...an' all transpired nearly unseen."

"Time will certainly tell the matter. We have plenty of it here," Thomas Alexander said in a sober

157

tone, looking side to side to his companions from his bed. Everyone held their peace for a moment longer; each face still in the lamplight.

"No man speak of it again another word I says…things there be nay an answer to," Charles Digby said low in his frustration in his own maimed and individual style of speaking. "An' if an answer were, an one we'd might wish to un-know and forget! Sufficient unto the day is the evil thereof…cursed be it and nevermore shall one like it return."

Joseph and the others were quiet, tired and worn from the resistance of both good and bad. He had his thoughts, his meditations upon his God, and there is where he maintained hope for times that were hard. If he was in an unexpected struggle and there was the possibility of some threat, he rested in the words that came from the One who could save him. Staring up to the ceiling above, each man wondered what strange thing had occurred and reflected upon the deaths of those among them.

On a sunny but colder afternoon the following day, the chips finished a coffin for Bromley Lock. Rawley Chapman and Cornelius Sorensen put the final nail in the lid tight as all hands aboard were busy cleaning the decks, covered in soot and grime. The captain showed and all men gathered as they were at the sound of three bells in reverence.

"We assemble here under the mast," the captain said in a sorrowful spirit, "to lay to rest two of our fellow crewmen - the officer: Second Mate, Mister Bromley Lock and whaleman: Mister Simon Laurent. They put in their lives on the Fortune, to take the behemoth, to bring his oil to life on land; a noble living for a noble purpose. These thrived on the hunt, although it were dangerous to them and to all. Farewell. We'll remember you, our whalemen brothers." Captain Grey paused for a moment. "Go now unto the sea and be at peace: officers, leaders, whalemen and devoted friends. We mourn a great loss. May God have mercy upon your souls."

The bell rang out again and four men slid the single coffin overboard, the only body they had retrieved.

Joseph looked upon the captain's grief with a heavy heart as he watched the box drift away upon the water with the man inside and slowly sink out of sight. To himself he spoke.

"Our lives are but a thin vapor on the wind."

He took in a deep breath and slowly let it out with a strong desire to know his purpose.

𝕿he temperatures had dropped by the next morning. The men dressed in jackets as the weather became chilled in the southernmost latitudes. The cooled casks of whale oil were let down into the belly of the ship by Alistair's direction and by all accounts he was a diligent and notable Steward of the Hold. He loosened the chains from the final cask to descend and signaled to the crew through the main hatch above.

"Ready in the hold!"

"That'll be the last of 'em!" a voice returned from the square opening of light.

Alistair hitched the large barrel onto the cart to move it into storage when the Steward of the Pantry descended the hold-ladder not far from him.

"Mister Smith," Rupert Phillips said, greeting him with a nod.

Alistair did likewise as he continued to work. Rupert examined the hold closely with his tablet and made note of the content.

"So you've taken in nine casks to day?" Rupert asked.

"Aye," Alistair responded with a cold look.

Rupert walked around them, some large, some small and crawled in and out between the bulkheads. A thin cask about five feet long, placed on its side against the hull, caught his eye and he called to the manager of them.

"Mister Smith, here, this ryer...I don't recognize it, its makings!" he shouted from inside the partition wall.

A shadow passed over Alistair's face and he turned to meet Rupert at the item of question.

"What's it doing against these?" Rupert asked.

"It be the ambergris, Mister Phillips, not yet stowed."

Rupert got a puzzled look.

"I have no record of it here," he said. "Are you certain of it?"

"Aye," replied Alistair with a reassuring smile.

"After this here, I'll have it put to sleep proper."

"Well, to be sure, let's have a look inside to be in good reckoning."

Alistair's eyes deviously flashed over the room. No one, he was sure, was in the hold but the two of them. The men stood enclosed in an area between bulkheads and casks and were well hidden from view. Alistair reached into a hole in his pant leg and slipped out an iron marlinspike, gripping it tightly in his hand. As Rupert's back was turned, Alistair gritted his teeth and rushed onto him in an instant. He swung across Rupert's head and instantly cracked his skull. His victim went totally limp as a rag doll and dropped to the floor. The killer quickly exited the room and ran to the open area of the hold under the main hatchway where he tilted the last cask of oil back on its cart. The great weight was dragged along slowly with his strength and rolled into the place where Rupert lay. Taking a mallet and iron wedge that hung from a column to the ceiling, Alistair smacked open the big cask of Spermaceti oil with a hard swing. He peeled away the lid and began to work as it seemed more quickly than before. He dropped the lid to the floor and took hold of Rupert by the wrist. He lifted him up over his shoulder and submerged his feet into the milky white oil. Alistair quickly plunged him completely in, forcing Rupert's head beneath the surface. The displaced oil rose up over the edges of the cask and ran down the sides of it.

At that moment, two men managed a ladder and entered the hold on the opposite side of the ship. Alistair turned away in alarm and his glassed eyes were split wide as he pierced the dark.

Rupert, who was not dead, lifted his head from beneath the thick white oil and gasped for air with a gurgling moan of pain. The sounds of his torment ruptured the cold silent cover that the shadows granted and threatened to give its designer away. His eyes were held closed beneath the weight of the viscous oil that ran down his face and over his mouth as his body contorted itself in slow involuntary writhing to retain survival.

Instantly, Alistair took up the iron marlinspike that lay atop another cask beside him and stabbed straight down into Rupert's neck with its pointed end. Rupert's head went under the oil again with convulsions and disappeared as Alistair stabbed down multiple times into the oil, slinging it into the air. The center of the white oil turned red with blood as Alistair quickly replaced the lid and hammered it down into place. With wild crazed eyes, he glared down upon the sealed cask and breathed heavily as the euphoric sensation of executing an unseen quick kill pulsated through his body.

Later that evening, before sunset, the decks were quiet and the men seemed lifeless, being in no mood to play music or sing. Most of them kept to themselves or held short and quiet conversations. Joseph sat along the bulwarks near Augustin Jorgensen, again watching him work. This time he carved an image of the Fortune killing a Sperm whale at sea on a Sperm whale tooth with a sharp square iron nail. They were dressed warmer for the coming chill of night.

"I first make de shape and design with light scratches to plot out what I want," Augustin said, speaking softly to Joseph. "Then, I make de lines a bit deeper and go over them again many times before de work is completed."

"Turn out to be a fine piece of Scrimshaw, I'm sure," Joseph responded softly with a low-spirited smile. "Your gifts in the arts are refined and always reveal themselves to be quite impressive to the eye."

"I wonder what my talent is for...its reason," Augustin said very seriously while working. "If only I could make a life wit my art."

"In ways you are," Joseph responded. "Look at you now. You're earning a living and you've been able to indulge in something that you love all the while. I've seen many people in the world so pressed that even the thought of taking some time in their lives for their passions is infeasible or impossible. I see a blessing anywhere in life when a man or woman...or child is able to have a way of escape; something that brings them joy."

Augustin paused and looked upon Joseph.

"What is it you do to pass de time?" he asked.

Joseph smiled softly. "I have a very good imagination, Augustin," he answered. "I sometimes go to different places in my thoughts and I ponder the expanse of much."

Augustin's eyes grew wide and a big smile appeared on his face, showing his stained and dirty teeth.

"I like dat, Joseph. Imagination... Ha! Ha! Ha!" he laughed without restraint. He continued to engrave the whale tooth while rolling the idea over again in his mind. "Imagination... heh heh," he chuckled again.

Joseph smiled to himself in some sorrow for those dreams that he wondered would ever come to pass as the ship's bell sounded and brought him back again to real life.

"Starboard Watch to duty!" the First Mate commanded.

Joseph stood and joined Vincent Moreau on the ratlines of the main mast, ascending towards his turn at the towering heights of the crow's nest. No other men hung about in the rigging as the weather did not permit any enjoyment. Joseph gazed upwards to those lines that seemed to stretch into infinity, straight upwards to a vanishing point that poked a hole in the plain gray featureless void; Jacob's Manila ladder into heaven. He put his shoe into a square of knotted rope and began the climb into nothing.

As nightfall descended, he remained standing, quietly leaning against the steel hoop around him. Vincent Moreau was behind, but both were silent, being lulled by the complete silence that was everywhere around them like another closer companion. The distant bell rang and Redford Whitby's cry drifted up to them from far below on the wind.

"Retire the mastheads! All to deck!"

The four men who had been stationed at the crow's nests made their way down, but Joseph lagged behind, going slowly, entranced by the daydreams that took him in those times. At the main topgallant yard, he traveled down the rigging and moved into position under a sail to see the moon for the first time of the evening; that enigmatic inspiration for so many artists and composers. He stopped and leaned against the ratlines, hanging there with his arms wrapped in the web, watching the watcher and his endless stars. He was alone for the first time as long as he could remember as every other man had left him. His thought went as far as eternity to the very furthest reaches of the outer fabric of the universe.

"The heavens declare the glory of God and the firmament showeth His handiwork," he spoke softly. He paused for another moment in meditation and then continued the long descent to his bed below.

The forecastle was silent as the ship creaked and groaned under its weight. Alistair lay calmly in his top bunk whittling a sliver of whalebone with a small knife. He looked up from his carving and watched Charles Digby roll his gold watch over his fingers again.

Joseph lay in his bed, uneasy, slowly looking over the faces of the others in the lantern light. Another bed normally occupied was empty, but no one gave it any thought for men were free to go as they pleased and some lingered on deck for the night air in many evenings, no matter the weather.

"Thomas," Samuel Dobb said, breaking the long silence, but not most of their contemplations, "could you tell another bit of story, please?"

"Eh, not tonight, lad. Only the thought of sleep occupies the space betwixt me ears," Thomas replied without moving and his eyes closed. "Maybe on the night to come."

Alistair looked up from what he was doing and gave the boy a calculating stare.

"I got a story for you, boy," he said in a dry voice.

Samuel peered at Alistair from his bottom bunk over the room with a small amount of apprehension and no less curiosity.

"There was a boy...like you," Alistair began, "who worked in his father's smithy day and night. He had no mother, but his father paid him no mind, only to get more work out 'o him...made him into a slave. When the boy would tire and become faint with the heat of the fires an' become slack, his father would beat 'im an' lock 'im in an iron storage box for a night without supper. He lay there in the darkness...in that cold darkness and thoughts began to take shape and twist and turn about in his mind. After a time, the boy learned a way to trick the lock from inside and escape the strangling fingers of its biting cold 'n cruel nights. As it happened, the boy was especially weary in a day bereaved of food - he slept too long and did not return to his father's box by morning. The father, rising early, caught him lying without on a bed of straw near a coal fire for warmth. Again, the man lay hold of him and suffered his son no pity in the lashes that were put to. So it was, after the day of business was had, the father went to settle the coals for the night and the boy met him there and pushed him into the furnace and burned him alive."

Alistair stared at Samuel with an angry face and the boy was afraid.

"Why don't you shut your mouth?" Bernard Dupont said to Alistair, leaning forward in his bed.

"I'm sick of your stories."

Alistair smiled at Bernard and lay back in his bed, continuing to cut against the whalebone in his dirty hands. Joseph gazed upon Alistair from his lower bunk and remembered his words.

On the morrow, the air was chilled and the men wore coats in the morning hours. The crew ate their breakfast across the deck and below in the forecastle. John Morgan sat against the bulwarks near Mingo, a young and always sober-natured African, as he dug around in his food.

"Hard fish and hardbread...'n I thought Old Horse was what would finish me," John said in a dreary tone of despair. He looked up at the sea from the edge of the bulwarks and imagined a long bridge to land where there were luxury foods on tables with no one around. "What I'd give for a leg of lamb...roasted over a fire...the juices dripping and sizzling on the coals. What about you, Mingo? Would you trade your hardbread to day?"

"Yes," Mingo answered seriously.

"For what?" John asked.

"Okapi."

"Okapi? What is that?"

Mingo, not looking away from his food while eating quickly, responded, "It like a zebra."

John's expression fell dull and he went back to his plate again.

"A zebra...a striped horse. Uuugh, you too," John whispered softly to himself in disgust and

167

disappointment while stirring his food and shaking his head.

On the other side of the ship, Jago approached Mister Fletcher from the galley.

"Sir, 'ave you seen the Steward of the Pantry?" he said, taking a cigar from his mouth and wiping his dirty hands on his soiled apron.

"I have not, Jago," Mister Fletcher replied.

"He's not turned up this mornin', sir," he reported.

"Mister Phillips! Give us a call!" the First Mate shouted across the decks. "Mark your whereabouts, man!"

There came no answer aboard. James Fletcher turned and called in another direction.

"Rupert Phillips! Where be ye, man?!" Again, there was nothing. "Any man clap eyes on the Steward to day?!" Mister Fletcher shouted as a bit of worry grew in his mind.

"Nay, sir!" the men responded on deck. "No, Mister Fletcher!"

"Sir! Mister Fletcher! I've not seen Mister Digby to day, either!" the boy answered from the bows.

"All hands turn out ship for Mister Phillips and Mister Digby!" the officer ordered. "At the whip!"

"Officer Fletcher! Here!" Badru cried while standing near the wheel at the hurricane house on the larboard side. He peered over the gunwales and pointed with his good arm. "De Larboard Boat is away!"

The First Mate dashed to Badru's place and stared down upon the hull completely stunned. The Larboard Boat was gone and the ropes hung from the davits and dragged the water.

"All hands turn out ship!" Mister Fletcher shouted with his eyes fixed upon the sea behind them. He turned and looked upwards with his hand steadying upon the backstays.

"Sight ye any whaleboat at sea on the mast heads?!" he cried to them up high.

"Nay, sir!" they returned.

The crew jumped and began to go aloft and below. Joseph and the others became alarmed. James Fletcher stood wide-eyed, looking over the crew as they went about searching. Men descended the ladders into the blubber cutting station and looked it over, but saw none.

Doctor Stowe tended Diederick Neilson's amputated leg dressings in his operating station as a search party entered the room.

"Pardon, Doctor," Mister Sorensen said, "has Mister Phillips been sighted to day?"

"No, he has not. Not by me. What is the issue?"

"He's missing, Doctor…as well as Charles Digby," they responded in haste. As they turned and went out, the doctor followed behind, dumbfounded.

Alistair and ten others searched the hold, calling out to the missing men. He made sure that he stood behind and watched each of them with evil in his eyes. They combed over the hold, high and low, but found nothing.

Above in the forecastle, there were five others who investigated. They opened the sea chests of those missing to see what they would find.

"Their things are gone," Alen Ried said. "They've deserted!"

The search parties coalesced on the weather deck to inform the First Mate.

"No sign of them anywhere, sir," one group reported.

"Their belongings are gone as well, sir," followed from another.

James immediately turned and descended the captain's companion stairs as the men began to line the bulwarks of the ship on both sides, searching the water for a sign of the missing whaleboat. In a short moment, the captain and the First Mate reemerged onto deck and Henry brought the spyglass to his eye.

"I am in persuasion to believe the men have deserted in the night, Captain," Mister Fletcher said privately in a whisper. The captain lowered his spyglass, turned, and gave James an angry but troubled look as he shouted to all hands aboard.

"There's nothing more we can do for these men!" he proclaimed. "They have deserted! God's mercy be upon their plight! All hands resume duty! We go forward!"

James Fletcher and Redford Whitby both stood on each side of the captain, looking into his eyes. Captain Grey turned to James, speaking softly to him alone.

"Nothing we haven't seen before, Mister Fletcher." He walked away and paused next to Colm Doyle who stood at the helm. "Keep course Southwest by South, Mister Doyle," he ordered quietly.

"Aye, Captain," he affirmed. "Southwest by South."

Henry entered his companion stairs door and

returned to his quiet cabin below with an even more severe weight that pressed upon his shoulders. The work load was now even greater upon the remainder of the crew, not to mention the frustrations of the unknown. The First Mate initiated the order.

"You 'eard the captain! Back to work!" he shouted with a hard voice that could crack the hull alone. The crew hustled back into positions as the ship sailed on into an even colder latitude. Alistair Smith began tying off running rigging, alongside other men, watching the officers with an unnoticed malevolent stare.

"Idlers of Starboard Watch take a spare from the skids and replace Larboard Boat!" the First Mate ordered.

"Aye, aye, sir!" came their answers and the chips set about to replace the replacement.

𝕿he Fortune made her way over colder waters, south of the Tropic of Capricorn. The bows broke through as the ship traveled ever on for the Horn of South America. Men were kept on lookout at the mastheads in rain or shine, in the warm or cold and Fortuna, the goddess of the figurehead, continued with her plans.

𝕬t six o'clock in the evening, some days later, Jago worked alone in the galley making preparations for the officer's meals. He went over the store and as he opened a special pen where the captain's butter and sugar was stored, found it empty.

"What the devil?" he said to himself, confused and angry.

Below, the captain sat at his charts with his sextant lying on the table's corner. He drew a line between two points and looked over the sextant's corresponding mathematical chart. He marked the ship's position near Carmen de Patagones and began the log with his feather pen when there was a knock on his door.

"You may enter."

Jago stepped into the cabin.

"Sir, someone's been in the galley. The officer's store of butter and sugar is gone," he said calmly.

"What do you mean, Jago?"

"There's a thief about, Captain," he stated with a hard brow. The captain appeared sorely grieved and looked down. He drew a slow deep breath and spoke.

"Keep a lock on the door when necessary. Call Mister Fletcher to my quarters at once."

"Aye, Captain."

Jago exited the room and Henry was left in thought, holding his pen.

At that moment in the hold, Alistair Smith climbed around the casks by lantern light in the darkness of the after part of the ship. While he raised a large water cask by chains on a lever, he heard deadened voices through the ceiling. He stopped his work, looked up to the long wood beams, and listened. He climbed on top of the casks which were lying on their sides upon each other and got his head to the corner at the ceiling. Through the creaking of the ship and the floor above him, he heard the words that were being spoken.

"Keep your eyes and ears open, Mister Fletcher," said the captain, "for there is thievery upon the ship!"

"What kind of evil has befallen us?!" James responded. "Sir, it is the men's position, and mine, that neither Mister Digby nor Mister Phillips fit the character of a deserter...and with the circumstances..."

"How could we possibly argue the purpose or motivation of another man's rationale?" answered Henry. "Am I in any position to make such judgments?! It is my singular purpose to be captain of a whaling vessel, not to determine the why and wherefore of the hearts of men!"

"Assuredly, Captain, there's more to the happenings on this ship than what is believed!"

"I have no reason to believe anything other than plain evidence, sir, that these men have deserted!" Captain Grey exhorted, maintaining his position. James Fletcher calmed himself and looked his commanding officer in the eyes.

"Henry, we have known one another for a long time," he expressed more nervously in a whisper and the subtle look in his eyes changed to something plainly unsettled, "and I say to ye now, there is some deplorable thing afoot on this ship!"

The captain kept his gaze fixed upon Mister Fletcher in a pause with a measure of unease and carefulness without flinching as he turned up his decision.

"Agreed," he responded. "We shall turn out ship at sunrise. On the morrow, sir, you shall have your answers. If there be a thief or some other fiend aboard this barque, Mister Fletcher, then I will be damned sure to get to the bottom of it! And, if I find treachery among us, by God there will be hell to pay!"

Under the floor below, Alistair's face was still as he went into the dark schemes of his mind. While fixed in an insidious stare of poisonous estimation, he pulled a shiny gold pocket watch from his coat and rolled it over in his wicked hand.

Chapter 5
To The Death

During the second watch that night, the men were asleep. The quiet ship rocked side to side as it traveled sluggishly over the oceans and Alistair's eyes popped open. He slowly leaned forward in his top bunk and peered over the room as the dull moonlight penetrated the open forecastle hatch doors above. He stared long and hard at the eyes of every other man around him in that dull light and there was no one like him. He hung his feet over the side and crawled down to the floor without making a sound. Creeping forward with strategically placed steps, he slipped past the sleeping men to the ladder and climbed out. Royston Davies rolled over in his sleep, scratching his chest, and Joseph twitched, but did not wake.

Alistair immediately lay flat upon the main deck and crawled forward in the moonlight to the back side of the tryworks. He peered around the brick and saw Thomas Alexander fatefully at the wheel. The light in the binnacle revealed Thomas' face with faint benefit and he stood, looking up at the stars. Only the ship's fore and main topsails were unfurled, being triple-reefed because of a goodly wind in the night. Alistair got out on the fore mast shrouds and climbed aloft into the rigging, undetected in the darkness and disregard.

He climbed silently up the fore mast to the fore top and then moved aft, up the fore topmast stay to the main topgallant yard. He stopped for a moment, hiding behind the main mast, and watched Thomas, far below, come out from under the hurricane house roof and then return. Alistair moved again in the same manner, first climbing down to the main top and then going hand over hand across the main topmast stay to the mizzen topgallant yard; an acrobat's performance of the insane and not for the faint of heart. Thomas was directly below him under the deck that ran over the galley, the wheel, and the captain's companion stairs entrance.

At that moment, in the officers sleeping quarters below, the Mates, the cook, and the harpooneers were fast asleep - lit by a small flickering lamplight that hung from the ceiling. The doctor lay on his back and a moan traveled through the wall across from him and slowly caused him to wake. A muffled voice came softly again and Doctor Stowe rose from his bed. He lit a candle from the lamp and entered his station where Diederick Neilson lay sleeping in a canvas hammock. He raised his candle to investigate and found that Diederick moaned from the pain in his sleep. The dressing on his leg was dry and there was no more that he could do. He turned and went out.

Yawning and half-asleep, he sat on his bed near the other men and blew out his light.

Aloft, Alistair began a quiet descent down the mizzen mast through the rigging. He made his way just a few feet above the hurricane house roof deck in the dark just as effortlessly as a spider on her own intricate web.

Thomas stood at the wheel and blew on his hands to keep them warm and to keep awake. He wrapped his arms tightly around his chest to ward off the cold that seeped into his gray wool coat. There came a creak on the roof above his head and he looked up at it. There was another and it grabbed his attention firmly with concern. He stepped out from under it with his back against the skylight and looked as high as the Spanker boom, but saw nothing. He spun around and looked up the mizzen mast. There was nothing out of the ordinary. He turned his back and returned to the wheel to inspect the corners of the roof where it met its supports.

Alistair came up behind him from atop the Larboard Boat, pulled the marlinspike from his pant leg, and struck Thomas across the back of the head. Thomas was dead before he knew what hit him and fell forward onto the pegged handles of the wheel - tied off in position from one side according to the opposite push of the wind. He slumped onto the pegs, held there half-standing under his arms. Alistair slid the marlinspike back into his customized hidden pocket and quickly opened the door to the captain's stairs and went in.

Doctor Stowe rubbed his head, unable to return to sleep and stood, wrapping himself in his coat. He rose in his unbalanced position of half-asleep and took to the companion stairway to get some fresh air on deck.

The devious shadow slowly crept down the twisting passage of the stairway in the failing light and at the turn, met Braddock Stowe face to face in the darkness. The doctor's eyes immediately burst wide and terror rushed over him to his core.

"You!" he whispered in horror.

Immediately, Braddock turned to his side to run and let out a cry, but Alistair got him by the throat. He was strangled and struggled to get free from the stairway. He took hold of Alistair's forearms, but could not pry him off. Alistair pinned Braddock's head against the wall with such strength that his feet did not touch the ground. Doctor Stowe raised both legs into the air to kick against the walls, but before he got the chance, Alistair crushed his windpipe and killed him instantly.

Sliding the doctor's body down the wall onto the steps, Alistair let go and wiped his dripping face with his sleeve, staring at him with wide eyes.

In the captain's cabin, Henry was fast asleep and did not move in his bed. His breathing was the only other sound upon the surging of the waters behind the ship and his dreams were troubled. His face clenched in expressions of distress and within, he tried to find a way out.

Alistair stood up from the floor at his side and

bent over to breathe down upon the captain's face in a warning. His eyes were wild and his countenance was twisted with an odd appearance in the moonlight of the cabin windows. He gritted his teeth and breathed heavily with soft growls and deep grunts. A killing rage overpowered him as Henry Grey's eyes opened in helpless ignorance. The hellish shape stood tall with crooked fingers and drooling teeth to take him.

In an instant, faster than Henry thought possible, Alistair got his hands around his throat with tremendous power. Alistair squeezed and the captain's eyes popped open wider with a severely injuring choke. Captain Grey opened his mouth to give a cry for help, but nothing could pass through the lunatic's grip. Henry forced Alistair back with his weight against his own throat and managed to get his legs over his bedside, writhing and convulsing with everything to free himself. Alistair furiously tried to keep him down to kill him there, but the captain pushed hard against him and managed a foothold to stand. Henry drew back a fist and struck Alistair in the side of the head and attempted to rip out his eye, but missed. Alistair was forced back further and the captain pressed him against the wall farthest from the gun rack. Henry came down with his right elbow onto Alistair's left arm and forced it to bend. He pushed forward with his neck, closer to Alistair, and landed a blow to his face across the cheekbone and eye. With this, Alistair lost his authority for a second, allowing the captain to twist free of his grip, but with much eternal sacrifice. Immediately, Henry went for the door, but Alistair was only a step behind.

The captain tried to call out, but his throat was irrevocably damaged and nothing more than a soft raspy sound expelled from his mouth. He thought of his wife and young son. She needed him and he did not want to leave her alone. His spirit began to grieve within as if the time had come to say goodbye and he ripped open the door by the handle and shot through its frame. Not having distance or allowance for failure to turn to the officers' room for fear of being trapped alone, he dashed up the stairs, leaping over the doctor's body to the main deck – The reaper no more than inches behind him.

As Henry threw open the door and got onto the main deck, Alistair latched onto his legs and threw him down to his face. Alistair held the advantage in his hand. He pulled the marlinspike from his side and raised his arm into the air to stab Henry in the heart. While the captain gagged for more air through his crushed larynx, he took hold of Alistair's arm at the wrist. Alistair straddled him and got his knees into Henry's shoulders, struggling with the man's strength. Alistair leaned forward and pressed the marlinspike down with his chest and upper body weight. The marlinspike drove slowly and zealously and its pointed tip nearly penetrated the captain's chest. Henry threw Alistair off of him to the left side onto the deck. Alistair's head and hand smacked against the base corner of the binnacle and the marlinspike rolled over the slats of the sole into the darkness.

The captain stood in his bedclothes and dashed for the bow of the ship, not knowing if anyone else was alive. He got to the main mast on his way to the forecastle or bell and Alistair jumped on his back and knocked him forward again to his face on the deck. The lunatic captured him in a headlock and squeezed Henry's throat again with his forearm to kill him as they rolled over against the bulwarks on their backs.

Captain Grey maneuvered his feet against a large heavy cask and launched himself upwards from it, hitting Alistair in the mouth with the top of his head. Alistair's bottom lip split open and burst with blood as the captain came down into his ribs with a driving blow from his elbow. Alistair's hold loosened once more for only a short second and Henry forced himself from his clutches.

Captain Grey immediately rolled and as he maneuvered away to arm's length, Alistair knocked him in the side of his head with his fist and cut the skin above one eye. Henry drove down with his forearm and pounded Alistair's head into the lower bulwarks as he got to his feet.

Alistair immediately got one hand around Henry's throat and Henry got one hand around Alistair's throat as both men lunged at one other and stood upright. The free hand of both men latched onto the wrist of the other's choking hand and they were a deadly mirror image of themselves in form.

At the hurricane house, Thomas Alexander's body slid over to one side as the ship rolled on a wave. The body fell to the deck and turned the wheel the opposite direction of the tie-off rope as the wind receded. The wheel immediately spun quickly out of control and the rudder turned hard to one side in the water. The tiller slid the body along the ground, up against the wall and the entire ship violently lurched over to the starboard side as the wind continued pushing upon the sails. Nearly all of the sleeping men were thrown from their bunks to the floor in the forecastle and all of the officers, whose beds opened to the larboard side, were thrown against the wall.

On the main deck, Alistair and the captain fell back against the after side of the main mast in the ship's roll. Alistair pinned Henry's head back against it, pressing the captain's face upwards with his palm under his jaw. Alistair let go of the captain's wrist and took hold of a rope end of a knot that hung at their faces. He pulled on it and the knot easily released a block attached to a large iron blubber hook. In a split-second, Alistair forced the hook into the captain's mouth as they struggled and yanked down on the halliard rope that raised it with a hard and violent thrust. The blubber hook instantly pierced the roof of Henry's mouth, crunched up into his skull, and lifted him twenty feet into the air as Alistair heaved down on the rope that ran through a series of leverage blocks.

Men of the crew, including the officers, witnessed the captain's death from the doorways and hatchways as they surfaced onto deck.

"Captain!!!" Rawley Chapman screamed from the forecastle as he was first from the hatch.

Immediately, the harpooneers and the two officers darted in from the after part of the ship. The men of the forecastle raced out onto deck as they struggled to understand what had happened. Alistair, having the captain's body near the main topsail yard, saw the crew coming behind him. He flipped the rope end around a belaying pin at the foot of the main mast at his waist in hopes that Henry's body would not immediately be noticed at its height and backed up to run with immense fear.

James Fletcher, gaining on him from aft, looked up and saw the captain's body swinging above them. He gave a shout of rage and dove forward, towards Alistair, who jumped to the gunwales and began to climb the ratlines. James caught him by the ankle and jerked him down onto the deck with ruthless brutality. At that moment, all men on deck began to shout and those who were able to get to Alistair grabbed him and beat him mercilessly with their fists. Screams of anger and of horror came from every part of the ship. Joseph was among several others who immediately set to getting Captain Grey down from the rigging in hopes that he was still alive.

"Quickly! Pay it out! Pay it out!!" Bernard ordered at the front of the line of men working to free the body. Joseph hauled on the lines with several others as two men carefully caught Henry as he was let down to the deck.

"Doctor!!" Cornelius Sorensen frantically cried for the captain's sake. "Doctor Stowe!"

"The captain is dead!" Bernard cried out in despair. "He's dead!!"

Their shouts rang out in the chaos of Alistair's capture. He fought to escape and attempted to run through his tormentors to no avail. James Fletcher, Jago, and every man of the crew that could press his way into a spot, kicked and punched him without any restraint. Alistair received a serious beating to every inch of his entire body as he laid face down on the sole, covering his head. The men shouted from all around to encourage more brutality from those who were able to get a piece of him.

"Kill him! Kill the bastard!"

"Tear off his arms!"

"Break his skull!"

Several took hold of the ship's wheel and turned the rudder to its former position, righting the ship and giving them a level floor to inflict greater damage. Rawley Chapman, Abimbola, Scotty Watson, and Alen Reid made an effort to get the riot under control by force. Breaking into the circle of the fighting, they began to shout while holding others back with their arms.

"Easy now!" Mister Watson shouted. "Easy now! Hold it, men! Let's have order!! Settle yourselves, now!!"

"Ho! Ho!" Abimbola bellowed out in his deep and penetrating voice.

"Mister Alexander is dead!" they cried from the helm.

"Wait, men! Use restraint! Let us regain control! Easy as you go!" Mister Chapman shouted as he pulled against them with muscle.

James Fletcher saw those who were attempting to restore order and took thought for the situation.

"Where be the doctor?!!" Cornelius called out in the noise.

"He's dead!" answered Mister Whitby. "He's dead on the captain's stairs!"

The men's wrath was refreshed and they began to shout again much louder in the ship's volatile atmosphere. The First Mate quickly made a decision against his own desires and called attention to the crew.

"Hold it! Hold it now! Rawley is right!" he shouted. "Let's keep our heads now!" At that, they backed off and gave their officer a moment to speak his mind with continued cries of rebellion in their rage.

"We've got our killer, Mister Fletcher! And now he's kilt the captain and the doctor!" another yelled.

"He ought'ta burn in Hell for it, Mister Fletcher! And we ought'ta send 'im there without a wait!!"

"I say we keelhaul the bastard!"

"Aye!!" they shouted in agreement.

"He's probably kilt the others as well...Mister Digby, Mister Phillips...Mister Ackley!" Nigel Jackson screamed in fury. "I'll kill 'im myself and his blood will be on 'is own head!"

"Run him under the garboard-strake!!" yelled Kallum Morrison as he kept his foot on Alistair's bleeding and bruised neck.

"Aye!!" many of them answered.

"Wait! Wait, now I says!" James Fletcher cried. "I know the captain's brother! ...and I know *that* man would want to get his hands on this murderin' devil! I've thought over it...and for the captain and his family's sake, I'm gonna deliver 'im!"

"I says keelhaul 'im, Mister Fletcher!!" Cormac O'Kelly screamed. "This worthless dung doesn't deserve the food to sustain 'im to get there!"

"Aye! And cut him to pieces!" they shouted as the idea was fit for the punishment.

"Aye!!"

The men were totally enraged and wanted Alistair's blood too badly to let him live for any reason at all.

"Without the captain, there is no voyage!" Redford Whitby cried.

"I know you men are angry, as am I - more 'an anyone! You better believe it!" the First Mate exclaimed. "There's nothing more I would want now than to kill this bastard myself! But think on the captain's family! They deserve their own revenge! For his wife! For his son!" he said as he looked into each man's face, beginning to calm them. They searched their souls and each man began to remember Henry's loved ones with compassion. "Turn back, I says! We got more 'an enough oil to make it profitable as we are…enough for each man to make his pay and to salvage this voyage and move on! Mister Whitby is right! Without the captain, there is no whaling voyage! There's naught to do but to return to England, and there, if the captain's brother sees fit, by God, he'll stand before the magistrate! If not, then let him kill this cursed scrap of meat himself! Now I mean when I mean that no man shall lay a hand on 'im! That'll be left to the avengers of England!"

James Fletcher turned to them again. "Does not Henry Grey's kindred deserve to see this dog hanged with their own eyes…or to choose to do what they will?!...would you men not agree with me of this their right?!!"

"Aye, sir!" the crew cried together in reluctant concurrence.

"But…until then…" James Fletcher paused as he looked down onto Alistair who was swollen and bleeding from his head and face and then to his men.

"Bring him to the gangway!"

They shouted and cheered in their anger and the sound was a great terrifying roar. They took Alistair by the arms, jerked him up, and dragged him face down to a grating set up against the mast. They ripped off his shirt and tied his arms around it with his back exposed. Forming a semi-circle around the mast, the men watched James Fletcher take down a leather whip from a nail.

"Mister Rasmussen!" the First Mate shouted, "Would you do us honors?!"

Bastiaan Rasmussen was a tall and robust man and a perfect butcher. He stepped forward while undoing his buttons with one hand and threw his coat and shirt to the deck with a wicked stare at his mark. He was covered in large defined muscles and they dripped with sweat. He flexed his chest with a look that could kill and replied softly with a deep coarse voice.

"My pleasure."

The men shouted violence as Bastiaan took the braided leather into his hand and dropped the heavy ragged tip to the sole. He inhaled one large breath to set him, drew back his arm, and cracked one across Alistair's back like a bolt of lightning. Alistair screamed out in agony as Bastiaan planted the whip into the flesh of his back to the bone, repeatedly. Samuel Dobb hid behind the tryworks in fright at the agonizing screams of the damned. The men became silent and watched in bloodthirsty satisfaction as Alistair finally sank down, limp with his executioner's fatigue, and lost consciousness in a pool of blood.

"Enough! Give some to the captain's brother!" James cried. "Mister Jackson! A pail of seawater for the meat!"

Nigel dropped the case bucket over the side of the ship and brought it up by rope. He threw it on Alistair's back and he immediately revived, screaming in excruciating pain.

He turned to the men. "There! You've had it! He answers to Henry's wife and brother now, understood?!! Mister Stearne, Mister Bazely, fix me a cage and put this dead bird in it."

"Aye, Mister Fletcher!"

"Chips! Knock up caskets for the doctor and Mister Alexander. I know you men will do them honorable," he said in sorrow.

"Aye, Officer Fletcher!" Mister Chapman answered with heaviness. He came near to James and both men's faces reflected their grief.

"And a fine coffin for our captain, sir," James said as Rawley looked down, frustrated, and nodded. "We go for to take 'im home."

Chapter 6
The Devil in Chains

The Fortune pressed on through the gloom and the ocean on a new northerly course. By sunset on the following evening, all sails were set and full in the wind to make speed. Upon the main deck, the men stood around in depression – the doldrums being upon them there so far south. No one spoke and nothing other than the wind made a sound over the ship. Augustin Jorgensen rubbed ink into the grooves of his whale tooth design as Joseph looked on in anticipation for the endeavor that had taken the man so long to achieve. He buffed it hard with a cloth and held it to his eye to admire the unprecedented engraving of the Fortune.

"This is an unparalleled piece of exceptional work, Augustin," said Joseph, breaking a long silence. Augustin kept his eye fixed upon it and did not answer. Only a slight melancholy smile grew on his face and after a pause, spoke softly to Joseph while keeping it in his gaze.

"If only she had her captain...," he responded sadly.

Joseph turned his face down in regret for the artist's grief. He understood that the small masterpiece was forever maimed in the mind of its master and that its intentions that were in place at its inception were now conclusively changed. It was an unfortunate thing and another smaller but no less important loss for the tiny world of man.

Augustin marveled at the work of his hands for a moment longer and then extended it to his friend.

"I want you to have it, Joseph. It will always remind you of her and of me wherever you go. I am sorry that not all of your memories will be happy ones."

Joseph's heart was pierced and it was a gift that he would appreciate all the days of his life. He accepted it with his usual melancholy smile and a nod.

"Then I will also give you a gift."

Joseph stood and descended into the forecastle hatch. The other men who sat on deck around him continued to whittle whalebone and twist pieces of rope to pass the day and wondered what they would get into for their living when England was again on the horizon. Some planned to reenlist upon the next British whaleship and even consider the trials of the Greenland courses to make ends meet or to simply pass the days in any way possible. It was something of a challenge to procure a more satisfactory position on a merchant, seeing that those crews were forced less into extended voyages at sea without respite, but on the other hand, dealt with impending threats of enslavement or death by pirates for their merchandises.

Joseph stepped off the forecastle ladder and approached his sea chest. He knelt down, opened it, and pulled out the wooden case that he had brought aboard and set it to the floor. After a deep breath, he loosened the latches and brought forth an old simple Baroque guitar. The thing was rugged and battered. Many years of use and travel had worn off its color and shine and it did not appear for a moment that it would create any desirable sound. He took it into his hands with care and climbed out upon the ladder to face the men.

They gave heed as Joseph moved across the deck to a low place to sit in their hearing. Everyone gathered to him, sitting against the bulwarks on the sole and climbing aloft over his head to listen. He placed the guitar on his lap and Augustin leaned forward in wonder. All men, including James Fletcher, stood quietly watching at the bow of the ship. Joseph placed his fingers upon the gut strings and began a song.

(author's note: download Joseph's song, 'Homeland', on iTunes or Amazon mp3 – written and performed by Wyatt Michael – search: 'Homeland-Wyatt Michael')

Falling, spiraling down through the cosmos,
Searching for souls who will wish on,
Burning with millions of years then,
Crash through the doorways of death,
We long for your life again,
Sometimes their ghosts will follow me.

Long days
Suffering sons who 've had hard ways,
Off in the war of their country,
Lost on a field of dissention,
The blood sometimes calls us to cry,
We long for your life again,
Sometimes their ghosts will follow me.
Stars will fall away,
Men will pass away,
But my homeland will not fade...

As Joseph hummed the final chorus, it was both haunting and beautiful to all ears. He plucked the final note and its harmonic tones rang out upon the silent men. All reflected on their lives and remembered their original dreams with their heads bowed as the sun passed its way into dusk's shining sea. Joseph's eyes met Augustin's who returned with a nod of admiration and a subtle smile of appreciative amazement. Joseph rubbed his forehead with hope for the triumph of his fellow man and was then reminded of the speed of a twinkling of an eye as he looked across the bow to the setting sun.

𝕴n the hold, on the dark and windy night that followed, Alistair Smith lay face down inside a crude iron cage that was strapped to a tabletop, constructed of bent cask rings and twisted harpoon rods. His hands and feet were in iron shackles behind him, held up by chains that led to the top ribs of the cage. His back was bloody and slashed from the whipping post and was bound in the hold alone. The doctor that could have been to aid him was dead at his own hands. Beside his face was a dish full of water and he lapped it up like a dog. After he drank, he screamed out threats to everyone that could hear him.

"Let me out of here!! Let me go, you dirty bastards!!" He choked and gagged as he shouted out profanities as best he could with the jagged ribs of the cage below him digging into his chest. Only the sounds of the creaking ship and splashing waves gave any heed to his voice in the spaces around him. It seemed to him that even the barrels that were stacked in rows had ill will towards him and he cursed their disregard within his stone heart. In his madness and fury, he imagined all the crewmen folded into unnatural shapes within them without air and without light. It was an exciting idea and as soon as he was out, would set to immediately implement its completion.

The Starboard Watch was on duty in the rain above him. The sea turned and the ship began to rock, but Mister Fletcher had already prepared for it. The royals and topgallants had been furled including all sails on the mizzen mast. The flying jib and the jib sails likewise, but the fore topmast staysail was loosed. All men of the Larboard Watch were below deck making an attempt to keep their threads dry.

"The wind and sea have turned a-foul! Kwame!!" Mister Fletcher cried to the helmsman, "Hold course North Northeast!!"

"North Northeast, Mister Fletcher!" came the reply that rolled over the creaking beams and creaking rigging.

The rain began to come down harder upon them. The ship then pitched more heavily. No one became alarmed as it was not a major storm, but the sea ran rough.

"Mister Dobb!" James shouted, "Get below and fetch the raincoats! Shorten Sail! Stand by to take in mainsail! Man clewgarnets! Buntlines! Leechlines!"

The Starboard Watch took their places on deck to haul on the rigging.

"Haul taut! Up mainsail!" James ordered. The men hauled on the ropes and the mainsail shrank upwards to the yard above it. The boy dashed across the deck and distributed coats to anyone who wanted one.

"Lay aloft! Furl mainsail! Take in weather first!"

The topmen, of whom Joseph was party to, made their way aloft to take in the mainsail on the main mast as the ship continued to roll hard.

Jago and Royston Davies were preparing the ship's evening meal regardless of the weather and the working conditions. Royston was not well, his face appeared slightly red and he was sweating when his actions and surroundings did not merit it. Jago, who was focused on the work at hand, took no notice of him as his back was turned. Royston chopped potatoes into small pieces on a cutting board, turned to a large iron pot of stew that was boiling in the middle of the floor, and dumped them in. Jago stood on one side of it with a large ladle and stirred the contents that boiled over coals. Royston nearly lost his balance in the galley and grabbed hold of the prep counter as the ship pitched.

"Better get 'em onions in the pot quick 'fore the sea grows worse," Jago said without looking up, chewing on the butt of a wet cigar.

Royston turned and began to chop an old dried and spotted onion, wiping the sweat from his forehead with his sleeve. He brushed his shaggy hair to one side and in his hairline, encroaching upon his face, was the black spots of some disease. He blinked his eyes hard to keep his focus and his sleeve rose up. His arm was nearly all blackened with sores. His hands were wrapped in cloths that were tied around his palms to hide his skin. Jago paid it no mind, thinking they were for handling the kettles. He coughed into a handkerchief and laid it on the counter by the food.

Aloft, Joseph lay out on the main yard over the ocean. His feet were on the horses and he grasped tightly to the sail, furling it to the gaskets alongside several others. He watched the water splash against the ship below his feet and a look of seasickness came over his face. He hesitated at the task for a moment and clung tightly to the yard. He did not understand it, but was certain he was simply ill from the rocking motion.

"Stand by to take in fore topsail! Man clewlines!

Buntlines! Haul taut!" Mister Fletcher commanded those upon deck. The rope men executed the orders and the fore topsail began to furl up to the yard that it hung from.

Joseph finished his portion of the mainsail and turned to descend while the First Mate shouted from below.

"Let go top bowline! Let go halliards! Clew down!" he called to the men who had just furled the mainsail. "Lay aloft and furl the fore topsail!" The topmen got up the fore mast shrouds.

In the galley, Jago finished the ship's meal preparations and turned to Royston at the counters.

"Stir it once whiles I notify the officers," he said quickly. Jago immediately slid the galley door open and exited the room, closing it behind him.

Royston turned and stood at the side of the large iron kettle, took hold of the ladle, and stared down into the soup. His eyes were red and swollen as sweat dripped from every part of his face. His vision was blurred so he brought the ladle, filled with stew, close to his face to see it. He stared into the spoon and perceived maggots and fat grub worms wriggling around in the broth, crawling over and under the potatoes and onions. Royston instantly vomited into the pot so quickly that it shot from his mouth and he dropped the ladle back into the soup. He turned and fell forward against the door and slid it open in a frightened fever. He staggered out of the galley and fell back against the wall behind the helmsman who was busy fighting the sea and did not notice him. Royston pushed open a storage closet door at the stern under the hurricane house and fell inside. In fear, he kicked the closet door shut as he lay on the floor among the things stored. He began to convulse and writhe as the ship creaked and rolled on the sea. He made a violent choking sound as he exhaled his last breath. His shoulders fell back against a crate and his head hung over it, upside down, and he died with a look of painful horror upon his face.

Jago ran to Mister Fletcher at the bows on the weather deck in the rain.

"Grub is ready, sir!" he said. James faced the forecastle hatch and shouted to the Larboard Watch who was at ease below.

"Grub is a-ready! To the galley!" he called.

Jago turned back to the galley and found the door partially open. He entered and looked, but did not see Royston anywhere. He lifted the ladle in haste, gave the pot one more heavy stir, and dished spoonfuls of stew into five metal bowls aligned on the countertop. Taking three of them into his hands, he pushed the galley door open with his foot.

"Mister Dobb! Lend a hand, boy!" Jago shouted from the doorway.

Samuel rushed in and got the three bowls of stew into his arms. Jago picked up the remainder and headed down the companion stairs with the boy following.

In the officer's mess, the Third Mate and all three harpooneers sat at the table, talking together and drinking rum, albeit their mood was quite serious. Jago and the boy entered to serve them while the ship pitched slightly to-and-fro. The men received their bowls and paid the ship's movement no mind.

"Many thanks, Jago," Redford said amid

sentence. The men continued to speak as they took up their spoons and ate.

Jago and his assistant exited the companion stairs door and the men were lined up to the galley in the rain waiting for them, holding kids they had passed around. The First Mate made a final call to eat.

"All hands to grub!"

Jago entered the galley door to begin filling the bowls as they passed by him. They in turn then retreated to the forecastle in the rain. Joseph stood in line, hanging on to the standing rigging with deep worry that was also painted on his face. His condition escalated with every bump and sway of the floor beneath his feet. He approached the galley door in the succession and Jago scooped out a bowlful for him. The sight of it was disheartening and threatened the complacency of his shaken stomach. Joseph nodded and got to the forecastle hatchway, hanging onto everything in his path as he went. He descended the ladder and found a place upon a sea chest among the other men who had already begun to eat without hesitation. Other crewmen followed in behind him shaking off the rain and dripping wet.

"Ah! I thought the grub would never come!" Colm Doyle said happily with the food in his mouth.

"I'm starvin'!" Scotty Watson added.

"I never thought I'd say it," Aengus Murphy said with a smirk, "but I could use this stew to warm me. The rain has seeped far into my bones!"

"Aye!" John Morgan said as he chewed.

Joseph took hold of his spoon and dug into the softened potatoes and onions. He lifted them to his mouth, but stopped. The ship rocked again to one side and he laid down his bowl and got to the ladder.

"Are you going to finish this?" Kallum asked as Joseph made his way slowly to the hatchway doors.

"Not tonight. It's yours," he answered in a wavering voice. Kallum eagerly snatched the bowl as Joseph climbed out and set it beside him.

"You'd better spread it around, mate. I'll have it too!" Scotty warned. "You wouldn't leave a fellow Scotsman off in the cold?!"

"Nay, I would not, sir," Kallum responded, "but the rest of these filthy dogs won't see a spoonful," he scoffed with fun and sincerity.

Above, Joseph clung to the standing rigging and shrouds on the main deck and made his way amidships in the rain. His face turned pale green as the barque continued to bounce up and down. He clutched the shrouds and gunwales with both arms and wanted to die. Gamba passed by carrying his bowl from the galley and stopped near him on the way to the shelter of the forecastle.

"Hey now, Joseph!" he shouted. "Be ye well, man?!"

Joseph shook his head.

"It's the furious seas," he responded in a weak voice.

"Seasickness?!"

"Aye," said Joseph. "Ne'er were accustomed to it! Go! Get below! I'll manage!"

"I'm sorry, Joseph."

Gamba patted him on the shoulder and hurried from the wind and rain, disappearing down into the forecastle hatch.

At the stern, Kwame labored at the wheel, holding

the ship's course and Mister Fletcher made his way to him.

"Kwame, Mister Jorgensen will relieve you for grub in ten minutes!"

"Tank you, sir!" he said, wanting desperately to be away from the onslaught for a moment. James turned, took hold of the companion stair door, and called to the galley.

"Jago, I'll take mine when you're at the ready!" The cook gave a nod as James entered the doorway and shut it tightly behind him.

In the hold, on their way to the forecastle, Prescot Stearne, William Bazely, and Rawley Chapman approached Alistair's cold iron cage with their bowls of hot stew. Each man stared down at him in contempt and disgust. As they came, Alistair began to shout.

"Let me out! Let me out of here, you maggots! Loose me or I'll kill every one of you in your sleep! Loose me! I warn you!"

"It's time for grub, you dead dog," Rawley said, gritting his teeth. "For us, that is."

"Give me some of it!" Alistair screamed in a panic and rage. "Give me some of that stew!"

Rawley turned to the others. "What think ye, men?" he said, "be there enough stew to throw to the dogs?"

"Not for this damned lunatic," William answered, staring at Alistair who flailed about and twisted wildly in his chains with growls and screams.

"Give me it! Give me the stew! I starve in here!!...I starve!" Alistair screamed.

Prescot Stearne dipped a bucket into a cask of

seawater that sat against a broad hold pillar and threw it on Alistair through the bars.

"Eat that!"

"You're all dead!" Alistair screamed in fury. "I'm gonna gut you like pigs! I'll peel the flesh from your faces while you live!!!!!"

Rawley came close to the cage and spat on Alistair as he passed by to leave the hold. The blacksmith and cooper did the same, taking their stew with them as they went.

"You're all dead men!! You're dead when I'm loosed!!" Alistair screamed in madness, trying to free himself, thrashing violently inside his cage and causing self-inflicted wounds on his wrists and chest.

Above, on the weather deck, Joseph was soaking wet and clinging to the bulwarks. He dry heaved several times with awful wrenching, but there was nothing in his stomach to expel. He rubbed his face with his wet sleeve in utter misery as the rain poured over him. He gasped for his breath and moaned as the ship plunged forward in a turbulent sea.

Chapter 7
The Storage Closet Room

Joseph woke with a jump the next morning as if from a bad dream. The white light of an overcast day penetrated the forecastle hatchway at the corner of the room. He rubbed his face, still feeling seasick from the night before and sat upright in his bottom bunk. The ship's bell sounded and Third Mate, Redford Whitby, called down the hatch.

"Larboard Watch to duty! On deck! On deck!"

The men were painfully roused awake and several of them appeared to be ill.

"I'm not at all right, fellows," Bernard Dupont said, slightly groaning from his bed. "I'd be obliged if one of ye'd ask Mister Whitby to excuse me for First Watch."

Colm Doyle, who also lay still in his bunk, appeared to be in the same condition. "Aye, here as well," he put in with a very rough voice. "Please alert Mister Whitby I'm not myself to day."

If there were any other men feeling ill they did not

reveal it and all hands dressed as warm as possible and climbed away from the forecastle to the main deck. Joseph went with them to have a look at the weather, but Bernard and Colm rolled over in their bunks, coughing.

Joseph beheld a sky that was white and gray. The day was colder than usual and windy much to every man's dismay. The Third Mate was dressed very warm and also appeared to be slightly ill to Joseph.

"Colm Doyle, Vincent Moreau, Waitimu, Mingo! To the mastheads!" Redford cried.

"Mister Whitby, Mister Doyle and Mister Dupont are both not aright to day and've asked to be dismissed from First Watch," Alen Reid reported to his officer.

"Very well," Mister Whitby answered while coughing. "Mister Reid, you take Mister Doyle's place at the masthead."

"Aye, sir."

While the appointed men slowly went aloft, the Third Mate started the orders.

"Larboard Watch prepare to make sail! Topmen, lay aloft to shake royals and t'gallants! Every sail to fly!"

"Aye, sir!" the men answered across the decks. Joseph stood at the bow of the ship and looked across the water to the horizon. According to the calculations of the men as they stood at the moment, he was to make enough to take his mother away from the old city. He took solace in those thoughts and his dreams went wild when the downtime was up. He was happy that he was returning home earlier than expected and the past eight months had proved again so many things. He was no whaleman – at least not for life. The old city would be returned to bitterly cold again by the time he got back, but he did not care. It would be a cold that he would even embrace to stand on its stinking streets, its solid ground again. He was thankful for the blessings that came as well as the ones that came in disguise.

Just as the sails were being loosed, Jago labored with chopping bits of limes, squeezing them into a pot of water in the galley. Samuel sat propped on a stool by the door and appeared very tired, ready to fall asleep at any moment.

"Where's Mister Davies?" he asked the cook sluggishly.

"I expect Mister Whitby's got 'im off somewheres," Jago answered, not giving it any more thought.

"Oh," Samuel answered as his eyes drooped and his head nodded forward off his hand. Jago coughed while he continued to work, not feeling completely himself. The boy shook his head to keep awake and leaned against the wall, slowly rubbing his eyes.

Below, James Fletcher sat at the officer's table alone, staring at a plate of flour biscuits with a large side of jam. He sat without moving and was undoubtedly ill. He put his hand to a biscuit that lay at the closest edge, but pushed the plate away from him. He took a deep breath and coughed intensely on his exhale.

Later that day, the First and Third Mate met at the captain's desk and both men were fevered with what appeared to be flu-like symptoms, but with itching skin.

"What is happening, James?!" Mister Whitby said in fear. "Most the men aboard are ill! ...Oh, if the doctor were here! Oh, if the doctor were here to explain! Look at us! Even my eyes torment me! What shall we do?!!"

James kept his head down in despair and then built up his own confidence with an urging.

"It is only an passing ailment!" he replied with an occasional rasp in his voice. "Nothin' we haven't survived afore as lads! Do not rouse any fear! This will run its course and we'll be rid of it. Men that cannot perform their duties will be replaced by those who can until this be put off. We'll reorganize the watches to satisfy the requirements - lighten the load of the day's toil until all things be sound!"

Redford kept his eyes fixed on James and nodded his head. A reassurance filled him and he regained some optimism although he scratched his arms and head more frequently.

"We shall overcome this, Redford. Have no doubts."

"Well enough...well enough, James."

"Get a few literate men to the doctor's books and search for some explanation and treatment. I'll see about a nearby port for medical aid if the condition worsens," James said. Redford turned and left the captain's cabin with a nod of comfort, closing the door behind him.

James turned his back to the door, faced the windows, and sat on top of the desk. A grim stronghold of fear overshadowed him as he covered his mouth with a handkerchief and violently coughed into it.

Just before dark, that cold evening, Joseph and several others were aloft on the main topgallant yard, furling the sail for the night. The men working around him coughed continually and Joseph glanced at them from the corners of his eyes in alarm. He became increasingly fearful as he finished his work, but remained silent.

At two o'clock in the morning, Kwame, Aengus Murphy, Alen Reid, Zareb, Cormac O'Kelly, Vincent Moreau and most all the other men coughed continuously in their sleep. Joseph lay there, wide-cyed in fear, gripping the sides of his bunk with white knuckles; a cough from here, then a cough from there, all around the room. Some of the men began to moan softly in their sleep as if in pain. In the midst of it all, no man was awakened by it other than Joseph. He had enough and decided he had to react. There was something abnormally wrong with the crew and it terrified him. He quietly turned and put his feet to the floor, took up his coat and put on his clothes and hat. He opened a narrow utility storage door and found a single candle inside among the items. He placed it in his coat pocket and crept to the ladder. Scotty Watson moaned loudly and startled him. His heart pounded in his chest in fright and he knew he would not again return to his bed. As he passed by, Scotty leaned over his bottom bunk in his sleep and vomited on the floor. No other men stirred and Joseph rushed to the deck in confusion.

He ran in fear to the wall of the tryworks and leaned against it to catch his breath and try to think of what to do. He recognized John Morgan near the wheel, sitting on the step of the galley with his head in his hands. John coughed violently and paid the wheel no mind. He rubbed himself all over with his fingernails, scratching his entire body and his crawling scalp.

Joseph immediately turned and ran to the starboard bow whaleboat. At the base of the bulwarks was a small cask of water and a cask of hardbread stores for whale sightings. Also beside them was a canvas bag that held a compass and other survival items to sustain several men twenty-four hours at sea. Joseph hesitated, not knowing what to do. The air was cold and the sea was black. He took the ropes from the davits into his hands and looked forward the bow into darkness and then aft to John Morgan. Staring at the boat in front of him, he struggled to make the decision, risking an even greater possibility of death. He quickly determined not to leave the ship out of a great fear and let go of the ropes. Turning aft towards the wheel, he moved closer in compassion and loneliness and John's pains became clearer.

"John," he said with a sad smile.

John looked up, startled, but then was relieved to see him.

"Hello, Joseph," he said with a nervous smile. "Seems I'm not doing so well am I?"

Joseph came near, but not enough to touch him in his fear. He took a deep breath and looked down in sadness.

"Unable to sleep?" John asked while coughing. Joseph looked John in the eyes and nodded with a sad face. "You know, when I was ill my mother used to sing to me. She had a rocking chair that we both fit in nicely on the porch and her voice in the cool winds always brought me immediate health."

"I'm not going to sing to you, John, if that's what you're after!" Joseph said with a smile and both of them laughed out, but John's was labored.

"When we get to port I may find a doctor's nurse that will be stricken with it in her compassion of duty to my gain," John said as both of them laughed again. "And when she does, I'll think of you."

As they both laughed again, John added, "But only for a moment!"

After their joking, there was a moment of quiet and they looked to the ground in both cheered spirits and fear. Joseph looked long upon John in sadness.

"I never said thank you for being a first-rate confidant to me...one as a brother," Joseph said. "You've been a pillar to me in all these months. And I wanted you to know it."

John kept his optimistic demeanor and held a smile on his face.

"Only here at sea can an American and an Englishman be such devoted friends," John said. He began to laugh, but his strained coughing immediately replaced it. "I can say the same for you, Joseph. When all is finished, maybe we will meet again someday and can do all those things that we dream up...together."

"I would like that."

Joseph gained one final smile on his face and then became more sincere than he could ever remember as his heart sank with the weight of the world.

"I pray for your quick and full recovery, John."

"It is nothing. I'll be relieved in an hour and on my way to a warmer bed. That will certainly benefit me the most," he answered without his smile and a more pained look in his eyes.

Joseph turned to his side and looked to John again.

"A good night to you, my friend."

"And the same, Joseph."

Joseph stepped away slowly with great sorrow and hoped with an immeasurable burden for John. He finally turned and made his way to the bow, out of John's sight, and took hold of the whaleboat supply bag. He hung it around his neck, positioned the two small casks at the bulwarks under his arms, and stared out into the dark night. He turned and quietly descended the blubber room hatchway ladder.

Joseph stepped in the darkness to a tiny storage closet room that was hidden and rarely used in a narrow corridor beneath a steep set of stairs. He locked and barricaded himself inside and began to feel around through his supplies. He pulled a tinderbox kit from the canvas bag and made a quick light for his candle. The tiny space glowed dimly and he examined the inside of the closet with extreme anxiety. He laid his head against the wall and closed his eyes to gain a few hours of sleep while the night was still. He heard nothing more from that place than the creaking of the ship.

In the morning, Joseph woke to Alistair's screams not far away in the hold. It was frightening, but he had no other place to hide.

"Aaaaaaahhhh!! Let me out of here, you pigs!! Aaaaaahhhh!!!" he screeched in agony.

One small crack in the woodwork allowed a very small amount of white sunlight into Joseph's closet and he realized the sun was up.

"Give me some food!" Alistair screamed. "Bring me food! Aaaaaaahhh!! Help me! Somebody help me!! They're going to kill me in here! I starve!!!"

Joseph immediately became unnerved by Alistair's crying out with both pity and fear. He was tempted to sneak out to feed him a break of hardbread, but did not trust him and did want to risk having the lunatic know of his presence. While Alistair stopped to breathe and let his strained throat rest from screaming, he listened and could hear some movement around the ship with muffled voices. There were several banging sounds and a few shouts. Joseph was afraid to move and only listened. Someone above his closet coughed so intensely that they began to gag and vomit. Joseph's heart began to race within as he was increasingly filled with dread.

Yelling, moaning, coughing, banging, crashing items being dropped or thrown and people arguing continuously penetrated the walls of the blubber room storage closet over time. In the next several days, Alistair had been completely neglected and screamed out constantly when he had the strength.

Joseph greatly feared him and covered his ears with his hands to stop the sound of his vulgar threats and his torment. He ate the hardbread when it was quiet and drank his water - too afraid to come out. The candle grew shorter. He knew something was terribly wrong, but was too afraid to know what to do about it.

$\mathcal{T}$hree days passed and by candlelight Joseph found his supply of hardbread down to nothing but small crumbs. He was terrified of going abroad on the ship and did not even consider moving. As he sat still in the dark, the sound of someone falling down the stairs over him beat upon the right wall. An unrecognizable voice moaned and cried out, but the words were unintelligible. Joseph sat upright in fright and put his feet against the door. Through the walls, he could hear the man stand up and hobble down the corridor, dragging one leg as he walked. The door handle to Joseph's hiding place began to shake and tried to turn, but stopped. He carefully moved without making a sound and put his ear to the door to listen. Just on the other side, a heavy breath pierced the air of the hallway and pressed upon the door. It entered his ear for a long moment and he was afraid.

Fists immediately began to beat against his door in a fit of rage and shouting, but with no understandable words. Joseph fell back against the opposite wall, put his feet against the door and held it there with all of his strength as it was nearly smashed in. He had no plan if the man were to prevail and discover him there. He tried to think of a way to escape without becoming ill or being killed in some other way, but his time was up. He did not know what he would do. Alistair cried out to the man that stood in the hall to turn him loose with both violent threats and desperate pleas.

The beating abruptly stopped as heavy scrapes slid down the door to the floor with groans mingled with gagging.

Joseph waited a long time and listened. His heart pounded out of control in real fear. He held his breath for what felt like an hour and hesitated to come up with anything for his escape. He put his head to the door and listened, but heard no one except Alistair's continuous screaming threats below. Something was very wrong above them and he waited for the sound of new voices – the sound of land or another ship. It would not be much longer before he would be forced to come out. There in the darkness, he trembled and put his hands over his ears in mounting desperation.

Chapter 8
In the Flashes of Lightning

$\mathfrak{J}$oseph was asleep with his head against the wall in the night, two days later, when a loud crash jolted him wide-awake. The ship began to toss violently in a sudden storm that threw him against his side. Not far off, Alistair screamed for his life within the iron shackles of his cage.

"Let me out of here!! You rotten swine! I'll cut your eyes out of your heads! I'll gouge 'em out of your pig skulls! Aaaaahh!! Let me out!!"

Joseph covered his ears again, petrified of Alistair's screeching voice. His screaming had gone on for so many days that he could hear it in his sleep. He could hear it even when it was silent in his room inside his head. The ship began to creak and moan under its weight as it leaned hard side-to-side. Loose items fell to the decks above and Joseph heard things crashing around him on the lower deck and down below in the hold.

The ship was caught in the middle of a terrible cyclone. The Fortune had all sails fully loosed in the

223

rigging which was not normal under the conditions. It leaned far in one direction and then rode straight up a giant surge. It splashed down on the other side and the brutal wind began to tear the sails from the masts. Ropes snapped along with the top yard poles and there were no men aloft to resist it. The rain blew in at an angle over the gunwales with great force and the Larboard Boat ripped away from its davits and was shattered against the seas.

Bastiaan Rasmussen, who was covered in black sores and crazed, ran to the Starboard Boat and jumped in. He let it down, cut it loose in the water, and rowed out into the darkness as hard as he could. He quickly disappeared into the blowing mists and the dips and peaks of the giant swells.

Joseph trembled and held himself up with one hand on each side of the closet to keep from being broken against the walls. The ship began to crack and the sounds of large beams of wood splintering roared through the baffles.

"We're all going to die!!!" Alistair screamed in agony and terror. "Let me out of this death trap!! Aaaaaaaah!!! Aaaaaaahh!!!"

Joseph feared the ship was going to sink. He removed the barricade from the door and turned the handle to get out, but it would not open. He stood back and rammed his shoulder against it with his body repeatedly, but it would not budge. He kicked it as hard as he could from inside and still could not get out.

"I hear you!" Alistair cried. "I hear you there! What are you doing?!! Get me out of here! Where are you?!! I hear you, you bastard!! Let me go or I'll rip your bowels from your belly! I'll slice out your tongue! I can hear you! …I hear you!!"

An extremely strong wind blasted over and through the ship. It created a low hollow pitch that warned any person aboard of what was coming as the multiple cracks of wood grew louder in Joseph's ears.

On the main deck, the wind shrieked through the rigging and masts with the sounds of a hundred screaming ghosts. The main mast instantly cracked fifteen feet from its base, being with filled sails to the masthead. It split with a powerful boom and fell over to starboard side as a reed broken near the bottom. The wheel spun out of control on the tiller and swung from side to side with no one there to correct it.

Joseph's heartbeat began to ring out in his ears and all other sounds faded beneath it; Alistair's screams, the wind, the waves, and the crashes upon the decks above and below - pound, pound, pound in his ears, louder and louder. He beat against the door with his fists. He smashed himself against it to break it open to no avail.

A massive wave threw the ship entirely out of the water and it plummeted back down. It smacked into the ocean and the water dove over the gunwales like a tidal wave. Joseph was thrown down to the floor. He stood again and beat against the door with his entire body, trying not to go down with the ship. The Fortune dropped again and he fell back against the wall to the floor.

The ship lunged forward as it suddenly ran aground with a loud grinding boom. The keel of the ship cracked and split and the sound was as a deafening blast of thunder. The frame of the door became askew with a piercing crack as the hull was crushed. Joseph was thrown against the door and fell back onto the right sidewall with pain. He realized the ship no longer moved on the sea and leaned slightly forward as gravity laid him against the bottom of the sidewall. Alistair became silent at the moment of the crash and Joseph did not hear him again.

He slammed himself against the door repeatedly and it opened only enough to let in air. He could hear water gushing into the hold like a waterfall and knew he had to get out fast. He put his feet on the wall behind him, pushed as hard as he could, and got the door open about twelve inches. He pressed his head out, looked down, and saw a body lying over with the legs up against the opposite wall of the corridor - knees locked, holding the door shut. He rammed the door again and the corpse fell completely over to the left, onto the face. Joseph pushed it to the side with the door and forced his way out of the tiny gap. The wind ripped through the rigging above and booms of thunder shook the hull. In streaks of light that beamed through the hatchways, Joseph could see black sores on the arms of the body which was rotted and gruesome. He turned and flew up the stairs that rose over him as the entire ship threatened to break in two.

He quickly got to the deck and hung onto the bulwarks which were smashed and strewn with ropes and blocks that tried to hinder his passing. The downpour instantly soaked him through as he ran past the main mast on the larboard side to the bow. The Fortune leaned forward in a sandbar deep in the ocean. The fore royal and topgallant masts snapped off over his head with a resounding burst and the ropes shot in all directions like the lethal whips of the Devil's armies. In the flashes of lightning, he could see palm trees on a shoreline about a quarter of a mile from the bow of the ship, lying over in the wind. Joseph climbed over the side of the bulwarks and hung onto the cathead for the starboard anchor. The last whaleboat aboard, the Waist, positioned amidships, ripped off the supports, flew around to the back of the ship in a whirlwind, and shattered into a thousand pieces against the mizzen mast. The shards sailed over Joseph's head like a hundred wooden stakes as he dove into the raging tidal wave that came up to take him.

The swells of the ocean were tremendous and nothing like Joseph had ever seen. He swam hard for land, rising up one side and going down another. Lightning stretched horizontally across the skies and thunder vibrated the waters around him. Joseph was thrown to the beach and the wind blew him forward to his face in the sand. He stood and ran into the tree line in the drowning rain and near constant flashes of blinding white light. Trees snapped and fell in front of him and he dove beneath the pile for a makeshift shelter from the onslaught of the storm. In the distance, he could hear the Fortune creaking and grinding in the winds, sure to be crushed into driftwood.

Crawling down into a shallow embankment under the giant leaves, he gasped for breath, violently trembling with biting fear.

In the morning, the beach was hot with a burning tropical sun. Joseph was awakened by a loud and long call of some exotic jungle bird that he had not heard before. His clothing was wet and he was completely covered in sand. A mosquito buzzed around his ear and he swiped at it as he sat up straight and looked at his surroundings. The cold weather dressings were still upon him; wearing a wool button up coat and long pants. He was alive and had survived the storm. He crawled on his hands and knees to the edge of the trees, lying low to see the ship.

The Fortune was still there and appeared somewhat sound, run aground a quarter mile from the shore. Joseph sat silently, looking around, and heard nothing but the waves rolling in and birds deep in the foliage behind him. He got to his knees, removed his coat, and placed it under the palm leaves out of sight. He stood to his feet and stepped out onto the sand, warily watching everything around him. After making his way to the water, he turned to his left and saw that the beach eventually curved inwards to the left. On his right, it did the same - nothing to see from there but ocean. Joseph looked back at the jungle behind him and then turned around to face the ship in the ocean. The solid ground felt good beneath his feet. The sand was strange under his shoes and did not move. He paused for a moment, watching the Fortune and then began to walk to it in the water. He moved out to his waist and then began to swim. As he got to the starboard side of the ship, he grabbed hold of ropes that draped down over the hull from the fallen masts and climbed up.

The ship was eerily silent. Joseph moved very slowly across the deck, still wearing his shoes, and attempted to keep from causing the beams to creak under his weight. Everything was destroyed and to his dismay, found that all of the whaleboats were gone. The waves far below splashed up against the quiet hull in a soft and peaceful gesture as if they had never attempted anything hostile towards it. Joseph turned to see Rawley Chapman, dead, lying on his side between casks. The man's mouth gaped open in an expression of terror and the body was covered with infected dark sores. Joseph looked on, horrified, and quickly backed away to the forecastle hatch in fear. He stared at the dark opening at his feet, but hesitated to look inside. Spying aft, across the deck on both sides, he saw no stows of hardbread for the whaleboats. Everything in sight of value was gone.

He slowly crept down the forecastle ladder and stopped halfway. The room was filled with dead bodies, all in the same state as Rawley Chapman's with decay and contamination. He quickly climbed out for fear of being infected and held his breath as he trembled. It was worse than he imagined and wondered how or why he was spared.

To keep from being noticed by Alistair below, Joseph stepped softly upon the beams. There were more dead men that littered the odd corners of the deck and he quickly moved past them, watery-eyed in dismay and sadness, to the galley and went in.

He threw open the cupboards and pulled out the drawers. He unlocked crates and pushed the hanging hook-pots aside, but found nothing that he could eat. All of the stores of fruit and salt beef were gone. Everything that had been tucked away for the officers was missing. He stared at the wall, wondering, and thought to go into the hold. It was against his wishes, but it seemed to be his only hope for food. He was at war within himself. The moral obligations to tend to the lunatic and keep him alive weighed upon his shoulders like two anvils. It was dragging him down and his thoughts were continuously bent on seeing if Alistair had survived the wreck or was half sunk in seawater gasping for breath. He was afraid of him and knew that he was the Devil himself. The eyes of that creature were enough to send a chill down any man's back and Joseph had seen them in their potently operating and wicked form. A putrid smell infiltrated his nostrils and twisted his stomach as he thought upon those windows into Hell. He spun to his right and found the boy, Samuel, lying dead against the wall behind him. Joseph covered his face in horror and ran quickly from the galley door.

He carefully and very nervously stepped down the staircase into the blubber room on the second deck. Each step was a mustering of all his courage. It was good that the lunatic was not screaming out and he sweat from his forehead in the thought of rousing the beast from a deathly slumber. He listened and heard nothing but waves splashing against the outside of the hull that would sometimes creak. Taking some turns through the corridors and wreckage, he stopped for a moment to listen, but there were still no sounds of life. Dead crewmen lay on the floors ahead where they collapsed and their strange disease crawled over their faces and their exposed flesh. He kept his face covered by an arm and did not look them in the eyes. He went to the main hatchway where casks were lowered into the hold and very reluctantly got on the ladder to climb down. His legs had turned to stone and fought him for control. It was a conscious effort to descend into the bowels of Hades where his tormentor would be waiting with curses that only Godless demons would dare utter on the earth.

Joseph searched from his position and could not see where Alistair might be caged because the casks of the hold were scattered and some were destroyed. Water covered the floor causing many of them to float freely. He put his feet down into it and waded forward, searching for the food stores. Many of the casks were broken apart and some of them were only missing their lids. The hold was completely destroyed and the water rose to Joseph's waist in the tilted floor. He moved very slowly, not knowing if Alistair was still alive, but desperately hoped he was not. He tried to find any food stores from his end without troubling the water at all, but felt that they could be behind the most distant bulkheads. He anxiously took a deep breath and waded forward to approach from behind a tall heap of heavy whale oil casks that were stacked to the ceiling. He knew that by the sound of Alistair's screams before that he might have to pass by his cage to go that way.

At the corner of the high stacks, he halted, carefully placing his hand upon them to stabilize his movement. He inched his face to the very edge while great drops of sweat ran down his face. He peered around the corner with just one eye.

Alistair's cage sat atop a bolstered table, empty. The black padlock on the door was unlatched and the crude iron shackles dangled open from their chains.

Chapter 9
The Canopy Bed

oseph jumped back in horror, darted to the nearest ladder at the booby hatch, and climbed out as fast as he could. He ran to the booby hatch ladder in the blubber room while pulling his knife from his pant-waist, secured at his back. From there, he hurried to the weather deck above, dashed to the companion stairs, threw open the door, and ran down into the captain's cabin in only swift seconds.

He flew to the captain's musket and flintlock pistol rack at the back of the room and found it empty. The powder casks, shot, and all the firing components were gone as well. In a panic on his way out, he turned and saw James Fletcher's body on the floor by the bed just like the others; his face twisted from a painful agonizing death. Joseph rushed up the stairs to the main deck and burst out of the stairway door. He hurriedly slid the knife back into his waistband and jumped over the side of the ship, grabbing hold of the rigging that hung to the water as he fell. As he slid down into the ocean, the rope broke loose in his hands and went with him. He kept it in his grip and swam hard to land while watching the shoreline. He drifted to the right and went further down, away from everything that lay in open view of the ship.

Joseph arrived on the beach around a bend and darted into the cover of the jungle, dragging a fifty-foot piece of rope behind him. He immediately lay down in the foliage and looked to the Fortune through the cover of trees that surrounded him. Watching in fear for the lunatic with rapid breaths, he remembered his knife and felt for it in his pant-waist, realizing that it was gone - lost in the sea.

After dusk that evening, while only a small amount of sunlight remained, Joseph covered himself with smooth giant leaves that he had plucked from the stems nearby. He laid his head to them and suffered from thirst as the sound of the waves rolled in behind. Not knowing what to do, he lay motionless and stared through the canopy above to a pink and yellow sky.

On the morning of the following day, the sun beat down with intense heat. Joseph dripped with sweat as he slept. His lips were dry and severely cracked by the wind that blew the saltwater mist and sand over them and his face, neck, and arms were disfigured with fresh insect bites. Mosquitoes covered him and drank his blood when he lay still.

Joseph's eyes popped open and he was fevered. He swatted the little devils away and slowly sat upright, rubbing his neck and face with a terrible itching. There were lumps that covered his body. Holding his hands out, he discovered that bites were even between his fingers. In a panic, he stood and ran to the ocean, falling into it and splashing himself to drive away the biting insects and the itching. Fearing the lunatic's gaze, he spun and looked behind to the beach and tree line in fear. He quickly regained sound judgment and returned to the jungle to hide.

Being in a weakened state without food or water, he slowly dragged himself into the trees, choking and coughing. He knelt to catch his breath and placed his hand against a large tree trunk. He collapsed to his knees at its roots with labored breathing and then twisted onto his back halfway onto a faintly trodden path of dirt. Holding his trembling hands to his face to look at the bites again, he drifted out of consciousness.

𝕿wo days passed. Joseph opened his eyes and discovered a dark-skinned woman caring for him. His face and neck had been covered in green-brown clay and he lay securely in a canoe-like thatched wood hammock-bed. His shirt and shoes had been removed, cleaned, and placed beside him. He was beneath a cluster of large trees on the edge of a village that was busy with many primitive people.

They were dressed in colored feathers and thick woven leaves with strange piercings in their flesh. Upon many, a peculiar display of bright colors was painted on their bodies. Their dwellings were domed huts, like wigwams, made of flexible bark and large jagged leaves. Joseph noticed several fires burning in the distance as half of the people of the village stood in a circle to look at him. They spoke to one another in some unknown language. His caregiver put a wooden bowl of water to his mouth and he drank. Some type of medicinal leaves floated upon the surface of it and it was bittersweet. His vision became increasingly clouded and he drifted away again from their unusual faces.

$\mathcal{A}$nother two days passed. The native woman smeared medicinal clay all over him again in the night by the light of a torch. The sickness and perspiring had not forsaken him as she pulled a mosquito covering over that was made of very fine strands of root fibers. Dangling from its edges was an insect repelling plant. Joseph moaned softly in a fever as she stood, took hold of a thick vine that hung down beside her from the treetop, and pulled on it. The hammock bed that held him rose thirty feet above the ground to the canopy. She gave the vine a twist around a hook below and it kept him there. With her flickering torch, she turned away and entered the door of the nearest hut and closed the animal skin covering behind her.

A loud call of an unknown jungle creature echoed from the treetops in the night.

Joseph slept in the hammock-bed high in the canopy, hid away from wild beasts, quarantined, in his weakened state. In the early morning hours, yet another two days after, he heard in his sleep a blood-curdling scream of a woman echo in his mind. He jumped awake inside the insect covering and the hammock-bed swung side to side from his movements. He lay still for a moment, thinking that he had been in a dream. He reached up and touched the inside of the covering in confusion, pulling it from over him and squinted in the light of day. His face was caked with cracked mud and he touched it with wonder, having no memory of its cause. He peered out and realized that he was high in the air at the edge of a native village. There was no stirring and a few smoldering fires lingered from the night before. Joseph leaned over and saw the vine rope hooked in a pin on the side of his hammock. He released it and pulled which let him slowly to the ground.

As the bed touched down, he got his leg over the side and managed to stand. He surveyed the area in complete amazement. There were many clay pots and bowls made of wood that lay about. Many decorations of colorful feathers and strange bird heads were fixed upon everything. He walked forward without his shoes through the middle of the place in total silence, but saw no one. He heard no one. It was all oddly still and even though he was an alien to that place, for some reason felt that it was unusual. The door to a hut nearby was open and as he approached, found no one inside. The one near it was empty as well. He immediately ran into four others and discovered that everyone in the village was gone.

Joseph wrinkled his brow and stood dumbfounded, wondering what it could mean. If he were not raised into the canopy by a hammock-bed, he would not have believed he ever really saw those people. The recovery of his shoes and shirt entered his mind and stepping backwards, away from the hut, he made his way back for them. A large basin of water sat in the open and he washed his face and body of the clay. It fell away in big chunks and took some time. His skin was nearly healed and felt tender and soft. He drank and became still for a moment to think. The lunatic invaded his mind again and in fear, took hold of an empty wood pitcher, threw its strap around his shoulder, and gathered up his clothing. He charged into the hut that stood nearest his bed and found a black stone blade knife against the doorway within. Its edge was as sharp as a razor and it was heavy in his hand. It appeared to be made from some other place in the world and the natives must have traded for it. The handle was solid and fit well into the hand - tightly wrapped in red and yellow string which made it appealing to the eye. Its threatening form at the end of his arm instilled security and relief. He took it with encouragement and departed for the invading trees.

The worn hard-sole shoes slipped onto his feet with ease as if they were lost without his design and he welcomed them. The jungle floor was rugged and dangerous, carrying all manner of insects and serpents, he was sure, and the jagged rock beneath it would try to wound him. He stripped off the insect net covering from the hammock-bed and slung its awkward bulk around his neck. The village made no objection to his departure in its silent day slumber and he cautiously backed away into the thick jungle alone.

Traveling in a straight line, he carefully listened for any movement in the foliage around him, always keeping his eyes attentive to the sun's path. He was completely lost without the captain's sextant and had nothing more than the common reasoning that he was somewhere near the equator by the heat. For the time being, he would find his way without its assistance and hoped that it would be of no consequence. He wanted to put it all behind him and not look back – and not go back.

The sound of trickling water pulled him away from his intended path. It led him to a small stream of fresh water that was cool to the touch. As he knelt to the ground, he filled the wood pitcher to drink and poured it over his face and down his back. Keeping on the lookout, he stood and continued on, wondering if he would ever eat solid food again.

Later in the evening, near what Joseph perceived to be the six o'clock hour, he heard the ocean in the distance and quickly came upon a beach, although it was not the same shore he had seen before. He gazed over the water as the sun readied itself to set on his left side. No land made itself visible in any other direction and his heart sank. He slumped down with his back against a tree, knowing that he was on the northern edge of what he now believed was a small island. The native people came into his thoughts again and he wondered where they were and why they had left him alone with nothing. In hopes of finding food, he turned back into the cover of the trees, aiming in a new direction.

Near dark, the jungle had become ominous. It seemed to metamorphose into an alternate personality like an angry man whose suppressed feelings emerge with strong drink. The shadows crept in like ghostly fingers and to Joseph, seemed that the paths had ill will towards him for being there. It was unnerving to be naked in such a place and his ignorance of what lurked in the darkness made him almost helpless. It was harder to see in the failing light as he traveled increasingly deeper and every nightmare of a story he had ever learned quickly became material. He was in fear, but was not completely afraid. His defense was only simple - the words of his mouth and seemingly small and ineffective, they were powerful. He would keep them secret and safe within and they were there as a reserve of arrows for an archer's bow when he had need of them. He wondered if it would be enough.

A set of enormous tree trunks came upon him in the shadows and he sat between the large protruding lateral roots of one of them. With the sharp-edged beams exiting from his back like the giant arms of an octopus, he felt secure, hidden among them. He covered himself in the insect net that cloaked his presence, lay motionless against the tree, and listened nervously to the strange night sounds. The waxing crescent moon slowly appeared through the moving leaves of the jungle canopy like an elevated prowler peeping on the movement below. Joseph gripped the stone blade knife in his sweating hand.

$\mathcal{E}$arly the next morning, the loud calls of the canopy woke him and he remained completely still. The tree had eyes and they could only be seen in close proximity. He scanned the jungle foliage through the strips of organic netting that hid him completely, but saw no threats. Whooping calls echoed from valleys and hilltops and seemed to exude from the rocks themselves. In all the noise of insects and their predatory birds, he detected not a single movement on the ground floor. The night reminded him again of home in England where he was not carefully rocked to sleep by the pitch and roll of the great cradle. He felt more alert in that regard, but he was becoming increasingly weakened by his starvation. The thought of it dragged him achingly forward and in the quiet still, knew he was alone. He slowly pulled the covering from his face and a tree across from him immediately captured his attention in the new sun. At its base, in between the deep grooves of its roots, was a triangle-shaped area in the bark that appeared to be rotted away. As he approached, it appeared to be hollow. He put his fingers into small cracks around the crumbling edges and broke away a large triangular chunk of the base between two tall roots. Joseph stuck his head inside and discovered that a large area of the tree's trunk was hollow up to five feet high. With a nearby stick, he smacked around inside to see if there were any reptiles or insects hidden within that he should worry about. He deemed it a worthy place to hide and placed his things inside until something else could relocate him.

Crawling inside, Joseph laid the bark door cover against the hole and found that he had plenty of room to live and sleep. He felt secure for the time being and knew that it would have to work. His stomach growled again and he took a swig of his water, which then began to make him sick because of it. With the stone blade knife firmly grasped in hand, he crawled out in search of food, being now many days without. He moved slowly, always in fear of coming upon the lunatic, pondering the creature's fate - wondering if the thing was dead or alive.

During the next few hours, Joseph traveled down into ravines and up on rocky hillsides. Everything was concealed in dense growth and seemed to merely poke through it to be noticed. It was heavy, but not difficult to negotiate. He found that although most times he could not see his feet because of the broad leaves that brushed against his body, his steps were not usually hindered and his steps were not uneven. He slowly made his way through twisted vines and mangled tree roots where large flying insects buzzed past his ears. He kept the net dangling from his neck and was not bothered beyond already being there. He found a stream and followed it at a distance and after some time, became thirsty and made his way to it for a fresh drink.

He knelt and cupped the water to his mouth. He splashed it over his face and neck to wash away the heat and sweat. For a moment, he sat on the rock and did not know what to do. As he examined his surroundings, he assumed the water flow originated from somewhere other than before because of the distance. He thought of the Fortune and her stows that sat sealed and unspoiled in the hold to eventually rot. Like a golden idol that lay at the bottom of the sea to seduce men to their drowning deaths, he was tortured by its promises of both life and death - but for the dead that corrupted her decks and corridors and being shot through with a lead ball, was tempted to go back to molest her. The struggle was tremendous and he could not remember a moment in life so closely pressed against reason and insanity. The thought to go and have another look triggered a motion in his leg to bring him again to his feet when there was movement ahead of him.

A small monkey poked out from beneath long thin plant leaves that draped in heaps over a horizontal cleft in the rock, which lay on the other side of the stream in front of him. Joseph sat up straight in surprise, noticing the monkey held a tiny banana in his teeth. The little creature sat down, peeled, and ate it while taking no notice of the spy in his midst. Another unwary member of his group approached from beneath the same leaves and another climbed down from a tree and went in. Joseph stood and made himself seen. The troop took first notice of him and ran away into the trees with signaling chirps and squeaks. He drew near to the cleft, pulled the overhanging leaves to the side, and found a shallow wedge in the rock where the monkeys had been dropping bananas. The creatures reappeared among the limbs and leaves above him with screeching warnings and he turned and saw that they were climbing around big clusters of tiny green Sugar Bananas. A little smile appeared on his face as his hope was revived. His belly ached for the sensation of chewing something with flavor and he quickly turned and knelt. He reached into the cleft of rock and snatched up several of those ripened and quickly peeled one and shoved it into his mouth. As he chewed, his cheeks bulged out and he moaned in sheer joy. The fruit was sweet like it had been dipped in honey and rolled in cane sugar. The experience was one a man would never forget. He had traded a mouthful of bitter acid for what the ancient mythological gods would go to war for the control of earth over. It was a gift from heaven and the tiny seemingly unimportant man beneath it knew it. His life for that moment was spared and spared sweetly and he was overcome with emotion. With his mouth full, he looked to the sky and spoke in a soft garbled voice as he always did when it was provided.

"Thank you, God."

He peeled another and crammed it into his mouth followed by another. The monkeys above squealed and squawked at him and threw a fit. He was destroying their cache and they could do nothing about it but voice their outrage. He peeled another and devoured it in one bite. He leaned over the stream and swallowed a handful of water to wash it down. This time the water was mingled with sugar and went down pleasantly. Then, he peeled two at a time and ate a bite of each with one in each hand. Finally, after fourteen of them, he lay with his back against the rock and his face towards the sky and laughed quietly to himself - his mouth bulging with squashed bananas. The troop was in dismay and watched him, literally hanging onto the edges of their trees. They made no sounds and inspected their supply that hung richly beneath them to calculate the loss and if they could recover. Joseph turned to them and smiled.

"You got plenty more! I didn't eat 'em all! Have no fear! There's enough for you and me both! I'll share 'em with you!" he laughed.

The monkeys looked at him, puzzled, it seemed, and Joseph could not help but to laugh again.

In an hour's time, Joseph had fastened his stone knife to a long stick with cords of vine and raised it to the clusters of green bananas. He cut them off with much effort, catching them as they fell and delivered them to his hiding place where they were heaped along the wall. The mosquito covering was spread and hung above the opening on jagged pieces of the interior and made for a good entry for air without the threat of insects or disclosure. As he leaned back against the wall in the moment of still where he had finished his short term goal, Joseph was filled with sadness and determination. He allowed a little light from outside to come through a crack in the doorway.

𝔄 hot morning, several days following, led Joseph out even further to investigate the extended territory. He searched for food, a way to escape, or someone to help him. He moved slowly, keeping his senses keen on any movement or sounds in the jungle. It was sometimes hard to see in any direction for a distance greater than forty feet and he tried to use that to his advantage. Making his way further from his hideout into the unknown, he traveled northwest with his spear in hand.

After spending the greater part of the morning and afternoon in exploration, he approached an opening in the thick foliage where the sky could be clearly seen. The place was not very large, only two hundred feet across, and one side rose up against a rock ledge. Joseph paused for a moment, looked it over, and quickly moved through it along his right side. As he went, he kept his eyes upwards to the sky and took a deep breath of the circulating air in the open area. The smell of the ocean was refreshing to him and almost caused his guard to be temporarily interrupted. He immediately stopped at a troublesome sight that had entered from a curve in the right tree line. Two wide posts made of tree trunks, covered in large spikes protruding from all sides, stood forty feet in front of him. They were as big a round as barrels and rose to at least twenty feet before they were lopped off. Each one was like an evil brother to the other and they held their place firmly fifteen feet apart. He was immediately afraid and confused by them as if he stood before a great and terrible totem that could strike terror into the heart of the most sinister trespasser. It was enough to send him back into the cover of the jungle and pass carefully another way, but it was too late.

In an instant, a trap was sprung under his feet with the sound of a snapping twig. A thin, but resilient rope tightened around Joseph's right ankle above his shoe and a giant bent tree began to straighten up a short distance away from him with a loud whoosh through the leaves. Joseph was quickly jerked from his feet, dragged twenty feet over the ground, and taken upside-down into the air as the tree stood fully up, pulling on a system of rope that ran through holes that had been bored through adjacent limbs and trunks for leverage. It shook the canopy of the jungle like a magnificent beast. Hundreds of birds in the surrounding branches soared upwards, squawking in a cluster and making a great tumult. Their sound frightened him and he knew the master of the device was signaled. Immediately, he was ten feet in the air and swung forward, straight for the spiked totems that seemed to eagerly reach out to lethally puncture him. He pointed his spear ahead to defend himself upside-down and quickly pushed off from the pillar that tried first, lunging himself to one side and barely missing being impaled upon its long and treacherous arms. He swung out in an uncontrolled spin and fell back again towards them. He turned himself hard to the side and brushed past the points, which shred his shirt across his chest. He swayed as a pendulum and the blood rushed to his head. As he tried to sever the line on his foot with the spear, he swirled back around to the spikes again. Joseph, once more on his spin, managed to stab the spear into the pillar and push himself away. As he did, it snapped in two at the exact center. The end in his hand was instantly ripped away by leverage between two spikes and the spearhead end stayed thrust in the pillar itself. With this, he was swung wide in a chaotic spiral around them, but his hands were empty.

At that moment, a young fifteen year old native boy discovered him from the tree line. He was hidden from view and nearly too afraid to move. His eyes were extremely wide in fear, but with great apprehension and necessity, quickly ran into the open to Joseph. He shouted with fear in his language and trembled so greatly that he could barely stand.

Joseph saw the boy coming below and reached his arms towards him as he came around in his swing.

"Help me!! Please!! Hurry!!!" he cried desperately. The boy ran and raised his hands high to him, but Joseph spun past too high and too fast and missed him.

In the return swing to the pillars, Joseph prepared himself to be impaled. He lunged his body and arms to direct himself to the broken spear that stuck out from the spikes at an equal length. Without any time to think about what he was doing, he contorted to force himself into facing them. In an instant, he took hold of the broken spear handle between the spikes and pushed himself away again - this time, pulling it out and taking it with him. He rotated around in the circular pattern again, spinning away from the pillars on the backside. He turned the spear around in his hands and pointed the broken end downwards with the knife tip in his hands.

On the next pass, the boy could reach and laid hold of the very end of the spear stick. He ran along with Joseph below and slowed him down. As he did, the blade broke apart from the stick in Joseph's hands, being split and weakened by the impacts.

Joseph bent forward and upwards with the blade and struggled to reach his ankle. The rope was so tight that he was sure his foot would be sliced off. In the excruciating pain of the grip, he pulled himself up by holding his thigh with both hands. He managed to inch closer to the rope as he grunted under his own opposing weight.

The boy stood under Joseph and raised the spear handle-piece, thinking he could re-attach the knife and better reach the rope. He was terrified of being exposed in the open as they were and knew that in only a moment he would be free to return into hiding.

As Joseph relaxed, straightened himself, and reached down for the stick, there was a shot. The boy's brains splattered on the leaves behind them and his body dropped to the ground. Joseph looked in the direction of the shot and saw the lunatic, Alistair Smith, charging towards him from the tree line. Joseph immediately got to his ankle with the knife and began to slice away at it. Another shot was fired and the bark on a tree directly behind Joseph split off. Joseph sliced through the rope with careless madness, cutting himself several times, and fell to the ground with a thud in the thick foliage. He got to his feet and ran into the jungle as the lunatic came behind him. Another shot was fired at his head and bark flew off near his face as he turned away into the trees.

Joseph ran for his life. He jumped over rocks, went down the sides of ledges, passed through ravines, and ripped through the thick leaves of the jungle plants as fast as he could go. He ran aimlessly, trying to get away. He paid no attention to where he was or where he was going and heard the lunatic coming steadily behind him.

Joseph could hear his threats in his mind; that screeching voice that promised to cut his guts out; those screams of vile inception that was the voice from the stinking tunnels of Hell. They were not the inventions of man, but of those cursed monsters that had defied God and sought to defile any who would revere Him with life. In his stride, Joseph could see the lunatic standing over him with a blade, slicing off his body parts, peeling away the flesh from his torso and forcing him to eat himself just as he had sworn. In blind terror, he ran hard and swift and came to a long double-row of trees. As they came into sight, he planned to purposely fall onto his blade and send it up into his own neck and head with force as he hit the ground.

The space between them was near twenty-five feet wide, which was clear and covered only in short grasses. As he sprinted between them, he saw the bodies of the native people of the island tied to the trunks facing outwards. Their hands were bound around the trees behind them and their feet were tied in the same way. A twisted rope of vine kept their heads upright against the tree trunks, wrapped around their foreheads. The men, women, and children of the entire village had been killed and strung up in this way - a bloody and terrible sight to any living eyes.

Joseph looked upon their faces in complete horror as he ran. His eyes widened in fear as he came upon the filleted corpse of the woman who had taken care of him in the tree hammock-bed. He stopped running for just a moment in disbelief and stared at her - the one who had saved his life. His eyes produced the tears of his dread as he panted. His face and head twitched involuntarily as he stared upon the bodies. He took one last look at her and stepped away. A whistling ball of shot struck the body and splattered him with black blood. The sound rang out a split-second afterwards from the distant trees behind him. He turned and flew down a path into thicker jungle ahead, but was afraid he would fall.

He ran with intense desperation and came out of the jungle at the rocky stream that flowed past the banana trees; a place that he knew. He did not slow and dashed towards the water and jumped a four-foot ledge, down over the top of the cleft in the rock. The surrounding monkeys screeched in fright and scattered into the canopy to hide. He quickly turned and pulled the leaves aside that covered the fissure. He laid himself flat on his back and slid in sideways, wedging himself in with barely enough room for his entire body. To fit it under the rock ledge above, he turned his head to the right. It was very tight and he barely managed it. He laid still and silent, struggling to not make a sound of panting breath. There was a small opening in the leaves that lay over his face and he could partially see out from beneath them with both eyes.

The lunatic immediately jumped down from the ledge over him, inches from Joseph's face, ran forward fifteen feet, and stopped with his back to him, breathing heavily. He was naked. Draped over his back and shoulders were six muskets hanging by their leather straps and he held a pistol in each hand. On another strap, he held a gunpowder pouch with a supply of shot. He was covered in dirt and sweat like a wild animal and his appearance was that of a madman. It made no sense to Joseph and heightened his fear. Alistair scanned the area, hunting, listening, but the nature of his face was not viewable.

Joseph lay completely still and tried to hold his breath as the lunatic stood completely quiet just a few feet away. At that moment, a large brown tarantula crept out from behind Joseph's head and very slowly crawled over his face. Joseph clenched his eyes and mouth shut, gritted his teeth in great fear and tried not to move or even twitch. He felt every hairy leg touch down on his face as it dragged its large pulsating abdomen across his left ear, then the bridge of his nose to his right eye. Joseph dripped great drops of sweat and tried to control his trembling and his fear.

The lunatic paced the rock, searching, and went out of view, running away to Joseph's left and passing by his feet. There was no sound from him and the spider crawled away into the cover and was gone. Joseph gasped and his face was red from the heat and restricting the involuntary muscles in his chest from breathing. He heard nothing more and waited for what seemed to be five minutes. From amidst the silence of the jungle, Alistair shouted from the distance.

"Joseph! Joseph!! How is it that you live?! It would have been better for you to have died!! I'll make good on my promises, Joseph! You more than the others, you fool!!"

Joseph heard no more but the sound of the trickling rainwater of the stream rolling over the jagged rocks. His face reflected his despair and his lips quivered. He fought against his nerves to keep from weeping in grief. His eyes became watery and he wiped his face with a trembling hand, but he did not cry.

Chapter 10
The Banana Trees

$\mathfrak{J}$oseph was trapped inside the tiny dark closet in the hold of the ship. A low growl that seemed to come from an enormous animal seeped through the walls from outside. The sounds were from the lunatic and they grew deep and monstrous. They elevated in volume and mutated into roars in lower-than-human tones. Joseph covered his ears in paralyzing fright. Beneath the growls, the screams of the crewmen, as if they were being eaten alive by some beast, were mingled within. Then, Miss Evendale sat nervously in her carriage, traveling through the autumn countryside and leaving London with great urgency. She continued to anxiously stare through her windows to see if anyone followed her. The carriage turned right at a fork in the road, down a lane that was nearly grown over with tall brown grass and dead weeds. It ran alongside an empty bare forest. She took no notice of the route taken by the driver and they went further from any road that would allow anyone to come near them. The carriage halted and shook as the driver climbed down from his seat. She watched through her window and her hands began to tremble. She wondered why they had stopped. The door opened and Alistair Smith stood glaring at her with a frightening look of rage. She screamed out and covered her face with her arms. He grabbed her by the hair and dragged her out the door to the ground. She screamed as he got on top of her and began to strangle her to death with his hands. Over a loud crescendo of undefined noise that emanated from beyond the trees, his voice resonated.

"You should have loved me!!" he screamed in a deep and terrifying voice.

Something ripped and its jagged modulation shook Joseph awake in a panicked sweat. As he sat upright in the darkness, away from the wall, he heard someone or something stepping through the foliage outside of his hiding place. The light of a fire outlined the cracks in his doorway as heavy steps stopped just a few feet away outside. Joseph held his breath and took hold of his stone-blade knife in a tight grip. Someone's breathing penetrated the tiny cracks and Joseph began to tremble. It moved once again and the steps traveled away into the subdued deadness of the jungle, carrying the light with it. Joseph froze in alarm and made no sound for hours. It appeared that a hiding place had once again saved him, but he wondered if it was a deceptive illusion. Maybe it was his prison or his own self-made snare that held him while his enemy waited for him to try to emerge outside. The thought weighed heavy on his mind as if a strong man shook him and as the hours rolled away, grew more brute and terrible. His visions of vicious terror played over for him and represented instances of the madman waiting with an aimed musket to shower the interior with his brains. He knew that his life would be cut short in blood if he would only simply poke his head out of his door. Joseph wanted to run. He wanted it to end, but there was nowhere to go. The visions kept him there within his dark and lonely walls, but the ones that had erected themselves within were far more harrowing.

The sun finally rose to its place. To Joseph it felt as though the old master had given up on the ways of men and would not follow his promised course. After all, why would he? The whole debacle was sickening and life did not deserve to live upon the face of the earth. He half expected the darkness to remain over all corners in honor of the ways of his grand hell on his tiny island. The jungle buzzed with chirping birds and the canopy calls of the monkeys who held no heedfulness towards the unraveling universe and he wanted to be ignorant, or so he perceived, as they. Joseph sat in his dark hiding place, nervously waiting for the night to come and no longer desired the sun or his treachery. He stared at the door, fighting the most historic and monumental battle of all in complete still and complete silence.

When the moon took his turn hovering over the jungle, he remained mostly veiled in shredded clouds. The night creatures crept from their dens of wood and stone to make their calls and for many hours of the night, had their reign upon the jungle without him. Still, Joseph sat as a stone in the same position of the day before and dared not to venture out. His eyes were fixed upon the open door and his bones ached from their torment. He would have to choose whether it was his time to die where he lay or his time to die outside of the hideout. There was no movement from the shadows of the jungle in front of him and it was everything to believe that they were not alive.

"Go out..." he said to himself. He searched the moonlit jungle ahead. "Go out."

He summoned courage or madness and finally crept from his tree before sunrise. He carried a container of water on his neck and a cluster of ripened bananas tied around his shoulder with a thin vine. The mosquito covering went with him as well towards the Fortune and he always stepped with caution. A walking stick poked the ground of his path and parted the cumbersome shroud for the threat of the jungle never ceased to make itself known.

When the sun rose again, Joseph arrived at the beach where he could see the Fortune. Her beauty had been marred and was now nothing more than a graveyard for the cursed. It made him sad to look upon her, but somehow she seemed to call to him. He hunkered down among the broad green leaves, hiding himself under the mosquito covering while keeping a clear view of the ship. He watched it continuously throughout the long day to be sure it harbored no breathing soul aboard. In the sandy soil at his face, he drew triangles with a tiny twig. They meant something of worth and in a multitude of their angles they showed him what it was - a triangle within a triangle - a greater one alongside a smaller and another turned within that - a triple triangle with a double - a quadruple triangle on a curve.

Joseph remained still as the day drew on and carefully took a drink of water. He put a tiny banana to his mouth and ate, never taking his eyes off the beach or the ship. He swatted a bug away from his face and the ship was silent.

At dark, Joseph had seen no trace of the lunatic. He threw off his covering, stood stooping, and ran to the incoming tide. The outline of the Fortune was somewhat visible against the sparkling water's dim reflection of the First Quarter moon. He waded into the ocean, nervously looking back to the island behind him. He felt naked, exposed even in the dark with his back vulnerable. It gave him a shiver as he quickly began to swim and dove over the waves that rolled towards him. His thoughts told him to warn them to turn back and go another way. He welcomed the physical movement and the exertion that was required. He had barely moved a muscle in days and it had been working against his mind.

At the side of the battered ship, Joseph climbed the rigging that hung down into the water from the broken main mast. He ascended to the edge of the gunwales and carefully raised his head just enough to see over. The ship creaked softly in the wind and Joseph heard nothing else. It made him tremble. He climbed aboard and took a deep breath, not wanting to come across any of the dead at night...or the living.

Joseph crept along the main deck to the cooper's box and to his dismay, found that none of the tools were inside. He stepped aft to the racks that hung under the boat bridge where whaleboats had previously sat on skids above. There, lying across them were bundles of the cooper's lumber - staves to make up fresh casks. Joseph took one of the large bundles into his arms and backed away from the doorways of the decks. He was afraid in the night and hurried to get away. As he threw his right leg over the bulwarks where he faced the bow, the starboard anchor, tied to the cathead, caught his eye. He paused for a moment and brought his leg back over onto the deck. He looked aft to the broken main mast and beyond to the cracked and leaning mizzen mast. He stopped and gazed upwards as if suddenly possessed by an intricate dream. The wind blew softly over the torn mainsail canvas and it rippled in return. The jeer and sheet blocks of the lower main yardarm grabbed his attention with subtle movement and the wheels of his mind began to turn.

On the evening that followed, before sunset, Joseph carefully stepped out from his hiding place and covered it. He needed daylight to work, even if it was fleeting, and attempted to utilize it. From a few escaping steps, he scattered leaves over the threshold of the doorway to conceal his footprints. Nearby, he uncovered the bundle of staves taken from the ship, which was hidden with the broadest leaves. The long piece of rope was also disguised beside it in the undergrowth. Joseph threw the cordage over his head, lifted the lumber onto one shoulder, and stood peering into the void.

In forty-five minutes, Joseph had passed slowly and quietly through the twists and turns of the jungle and found a place fit for a gauntlet; a spot where he could be in an offensive and defensive position to try and kill the lunatic if he should come near. From a low crouch to the ground, the area could be scouted in front of him where another stream of water ran over rock. It was stronger than the one he usually drank from and traveled faster. Behind this and further away, the rock rose to a mound of ledges. To his right, the stream veered to the left and traveled straight down a steep hill, over a set of falls and out of view. To the right of the stream, there was a passage between two rock ledges that stood waist high - a possible pinch-point. Joseph went between them and sat against one on its opposing side. He lifted his eyes from there and could see the rising mound just fifty feet away, overlooking the spot. Joseph pulled his stone knife from his pant-waist, grabbed up several solid durable sticks, and began to sharpen them into spikes.

He worked for an hour and wiped the sweat from

his face with his dirty sleeve. The sun made his path to beyond the hillside as he wanted to retire and left Joseph with the memory in dusk. His beneficiary laid a wood spike in a pile with ten others and peeled one of his tiny bananas. He pushed the whole thing into his mouth and took up his rope as he chewed. He stared at the lifeless thing in his hand for a moment, trying to realize what would resurrect its power.

"Running Bowline Knot. Running Bowline Knot..." he whispered to himself.

Joseph took its end in his right hand and laid it over itself in his left hand. He paused again.

"Take the end 'round the standing part, pull the bight under the right hand.... Cross..."

He struggled to remember. He squinted his eyes in a state of severe meditative concentration as they were fixed upon the rope end.

"Through the bight..." He paused. "Make the Single Bowline Knot...here…and it's done." A tiny smile wrote itself on his face and he nodded his head slightly with surety. "And it's done."

He stared upon the creation and the projection it imbued made *him* even shudder. It was a nasty business and unsavory, but it was blood that he wanted and much of it so that it would run upon the rocks and the trees, flow into the rivers and paint the living things to their eyes - to permeate the waters of the seas and kill the fish that were in them. Blood had not before been mingled with lust, but now it was all that he wanted to see. It was all that he wanted to taste.

He laid the knot aside and took up two of his sharpened spikes. They were dreadful to behold, even in their idleness, and Joseph knew that their power would be terrible. He gripped them both tightly in his fists and pulsated the muscles in his arms with quivers to strike. It was imaginary, his motions of ramming them and then twisting them into the guts through the ribs of his foe, but the look in his eyes did not believe it. He broke free of his fantasy and softly tapped them against the bundle of lumber, staring at the peril of their pointed tips...deep in his polluted thoughts.

Five days had passed and Joseph continued to dwell in the solitude of his tree. It was peaceful within, he could admit, but for the consciousness of the lingering spirit of death that lurked without. The doorway was open and he watched the rain fall upon the thick leaves in the afternoon. The patter that had removed all other sounds of the island in its magnitude had a soothing effect on his soul. For the moment, he had forgotten his dilemma and rested in the sounds of running water. It was a reminder of how it resonated against the unfurled mainsail and the distant ones above it when the weather was in that way. When the temperature was right it could pacify the entire crew to sleep on their feet. Its presence brought him peace and he imagined the levels of freshwater rising in the island streams. He took the time for repose when it was come and hoped that it would do his mind some good.

He picked up a tiny banana and peeled it, almost

unknowingly, and brought it to his mouth. He came out of his stare and looked down to the fruit in his hand. He looked along the floor of his hideout where he had six other small bunches of them ripening. The semblance of paradise was quickly blown away as a vapor and their first allure and sweetness went away with it. He threw it to the ground, finally disgusted with his invariable diet. As the thing bounced against the wall and rested still against the dwindling heap, he was immediately reminded of the Israelites who murmured against God because of the manna. He was sorry and in his inner rebuke, nodded his head in correction.

In the underbrush in front of him, a bird of paradise appeared and put on an elaborate and pleasing display of color and sound to attract a mate. No one noticed and he flew away. Joseph sighed and looked to the ground as he wondered what he would do to escape.

Another six days and nights went their way without incident and the seventh found Joseph gazing to the night sky that peeked through tiny spaces in the cover above. It rested calmly around the earth without a single complaint. In all the nights that Joseph had looked up to it in his life, he could not recall a moment of frustration arising out of it. It never had given off a single instance of ill will or discord within itself and he wondered what it was that ruled its world. He knew that The Creator held it in

His Hand, but just as any poet or writer or scientist or philosopher or old man or young man had done in all the ages, he pondered its mysteries deeply time and again. Joseph knew that knowing the truth and the secrets behind the greatest enigma of all time created even more and greater enigmas. The idea that Heaven was God's throne and the earth His footstool was the most prominent imagery of Him in power that he could imagine. The night was busy with the sounds of the jungle as he sat on the ground outside of his hiding place in such a small square of life. The higher he looked up, the less important he became. Inside his tree there was only a single banana remaining of his provisions. A shrill cry reverberated through the trees from some unknown distant animal and Joseph turned in alarm. He listened for any identifiable movements in the jungle, but they did not make themselves accountable. He readied himself to retreat into the security of his miniature home when his attention was drawn to the large moon that had stopped in a small opening in the canopy directly above him. He stared upwards and its light illuminated his face.

"The Lord is my shepherd. I shall not want. He maketh me to lie down in green pastures. He leadeth me beside the still waters. He restoreth my soul. He leadeth me in the paths of righteousness for His Name's sake. Yea, though I walk through the valley of the shadow of death, I will fear no evil for Thou art with me. Thy rod and Thy staff they comfort me. Thou preparest a table before me in the presence of mine enemies. Thou anointest my head with oil. My cup runneth over. Surely goodness and mercy shall follow me all the days of my life and I will dwell in the house of The Lord forever," he said quietly. He kept his face toward the moon and encouraged himself again with the Holy Scriptures.

Late that night when the sky had settled, Joseph lay low in the cover of the jungle plants and watched the banana trees in the open area under the moonlight. He saw no movement in the shadows and rose to his feet after much exhaustive study. He quickly crossed the smooth surface of rock by the stream with his spear in hand.

Swiftly climbing a banana tree, he cut off bunches with the knife point that was raised high over his head. He clung to the tree by his legs wrapped around with his feet locked at his ankles, twenty feet from the ground. The scaly trunk naturally leaned somewhat forward and he was able to lay his abdomen against a crooked dip. The jungle was always in his focus as he worked, being high above the ground and in the open. The clusters fell to the rock below and some split apart while a shape took form in the darkness on his left.

Joseph's heart nearly stopped and immediately pounded wildly in his chest. He began to tremble and it sent a light tremor into the draping leaves above. In Joseph's widening eyes, the shape took the form of a man, but he was unsure if it was a man or just the ambiguous and beguiling shadows having their wicked fun with him in the jungle growth. The creature gave him tunnel vision as if he was an owl and the life or lack of it around it had fled away into darkness. It was a darkness within a darkness but it was defined in edges of living panic. From where Joseph was, he felt that it was staring directly into his eyes. Never before in his existence had he realized a more gripping and frightful image. The shape made itself within the negative void of the existing lines and somehow that seemed impossible.

He froze in fear with his arms extended upwards, holding his spear. Frog calls buzzed in his ears like screams of warning. For a moment, time slowed down to a halt and the invisible minutes that passed made sure to step slowly to watch. Joseph's legs and arms began to grow weary as he held them in an awkward position. Pain seeped into his muscles in drips like the brown colors of tea in a boiling brew, but he dared not move. He blinked hard and stared into the dark tunnel, but was unsure of what he saw.

The shadow moved forward from its lines in the jungle onto the rocky ground of the stream. Under the moonlight, almost directly in front of him at a distance of about eighty feet, it stepped lightly without a sound and revealed its nature. It was a man. Joseph's heart beat with accelerating rhythms that hindered his hearing and thwarted his sharpened thought. The man moved forward and features formed into his cheekbones under the fine paint brush of the moon. Joseph realized that it was the lunatic, slowly waving a musket gun as he drew closer. Joseph was entirely exposed, hanging on the side of a tree, just above him. The lunatic came near and his steps were felt in tremors as when Satan plants his feet upon the outer edges of the Holy Kingdom and stopped, studying the defense of shadows as if he were their judge. Joseph felt that he was looking directly at him and the concealment of the night was a betraying informer. Beads of sweat carved a course down the twitching skin of his face and their gift of moonlit sparkling had an ulterior motive like the Devil's diamonds.

The lunatic lowered his weapon and quickly turned to his left to face the stream. He crouched to his hands and knees, put his mouth to the water, and lapped it up with his back to Joseph who watched overhead. Trembling in great fear, Joseph quickly ran the spear down his hands to its center and spun the blade downwards, towards the lunatic below. He drew back his quivering right hand that held it, making the decision to quickly throw it into his back.

At that moment, something large fell through the branches behind them and hit the ground with a thud. The lunatic turned rapidly, stood, and drew a musket to his shoulder. Joseph flinched and froze in his position as the lunatic ran forward past him into the trees. Joseph instantly slid himself down about nine feet and as he did, the lunatic immediately returned, but much closer than before. Joseph halted his movements again and followed him with his eyes. He feared to even draw breath in the confidence of being detected.

The lunatic knelt to the ground, facing Joseph, and noticed the scattered clusters of bananas over the rock. He took them into his hands and discovered they had been cut clean with a sharp edge. Joseph slowly readied himself to raise the spear again over his head to throw or to run. He suspected he would have only two seconds after movement to release it on a strict course before the lunatic could draw and fire. There was not a single degree of error available in his aim. It was too risky and it was too much to require of him for the consequence. He would only try if he had no other choice, but his moment was now and he found that he was afraid.

The trees around him creaked as they swayed in a new breeze. That demon, keeping his head down, slowly backed away from the banana trees. He stepped into the stream backwards and crossed over into the broad leafy canvas of the jungle's edge. Joseph watched him fade dark into the welcoming shadow as the sweat flowed down his face and dripped heavily from his jaw. His moment had passed, but it had passed too quickly and too soon. There was no turning back and the fear restrained his arms like thick iron shackles so that he could not do as he wished; so that he would not be seen. The lunatic, with damnable honor, reached out his arms and put on a great royal robe of black shadow that signified his rule over the hellish night. Joseph believed that he sank down into the cover of growth at the edge of the rock, seemingly on a hidden dark throne, knowing that someone was somewhere in the trees above him.

Joseph trembled. He never removed his stare from straight ahead across the water and was frozen in a fear of violent soul-stealing death. He knew the lunatic was watching for movement in the trees. The moon overhead refused to move with him and the calls of the night creatures throughout the entire island made warnings both near and far of an impending evil. Joseph understood their expression and was remorseful for not understanding their words.

He knew that it would hurt him. The wind blew and rustled the palm leaves overhead, but there was no life in the jungle across the water. Joseph's body became increasingly weary against the tree. He shuddered, fearing that he clung helplessly in the sights of a smoothbore long gun that would end his life. He kept his gaze ahead as the moon joined him...and waited.

Three hours passed this way in the night and the Full Moon had moved behind the distant tree line in his wane. Joseph, just as alert as he was at the beginning, stared long and hard into the leaves ahead. He knew that he was being watched and his first movements would give away his position. The moonlight had become less intense and he wanted to inch his way down into the shadows...but could not.

At six o'clock in the morning, the birds of the jungle began to make their calls as Joseph attempted to outlast the lunatic's attrition. His pale face and reddened eyes revealed his state of exhaustion and the wear that the night had on his nerves. Still, Joseph clung to the tree trunk with his ankles crossed under his body, resting one on another against it. His reasoning was that if he was seen reaching the ground the lunatic could easily shoot him before or during a ground pursuit. More time...he wanted just a little more time.

Joseph quickly flashed his eyes to the banana clusters in the surrounding trees overhead. The monkeys had not yet made their appearance. He wondered if it was perhaps because of him. He wondered if it was perhaps for him.

At what seemed by the sun's position to be five o'clock that evening, Joseph clung to the same position like a living statue. Nothing in the plants across the tiny stream had moved. The day was passing and his stomach growled and wrenched on the hour. He was getting accustomed to the pain of hunger and waited for it to subside and forget about it. Flying insects landed on him and flew off. They buzzed around his ears and greatly tempted him. Harmless ants crawled over his hands and body in lines as if he were not there. Finally, his grip began to yield to the manifesting numbness of his body. Over time, he had performed untraceable exercises of tightening every muscle of his body in waves to circulate blood flow. He would flex his biceps, triceps, pectorals, thighs, buttocks, shoulders and calves gently over and over to keep from blacking out, but it was not enough. He was sleepy and as he stared forward, went into a daze and lost his focus. Without warning, he instantly slipped down the tree three feet before he had time to think into an opening devoid of leaf cover.

The shot cracked from the lunatic's position and the ball ripped through the tree under Joseph's head. Joseph fell off to the ground as the scaly bark burst outward where his face had been. He landed on his back without dropping the spear and immediately rolled to his feet although he could not feel them and ran hard with an extremely painful limp.

Immediately, the lunatic burst from the jungle cover where Joseph suspected him like a blast from a cannon. He leapt over the stream in stride and charged him, holding a curved club, carved from a chunk of wood, over his head. He carried the muskets tightly cinched against his naked body and trailed only a few seconds behind his prey.

Joseph ran against the pain as best he could. His legs were weighed down with iron; encased in stone. Regardless, he ran swiftly and passed over the jungle terrain as a hunted deer, but could not feel the ground pounding onto his feet. The blurred figure maneuvering the jungle behind him stayed close enough to fire a pistol. Joseph looked back for a split-second, never breaking his stride and turned up a hill among the dense trees.

The lunatic tripped on vines in the heavy brush and went down on his face, but quickly recovered, guns and all, in one rolling motion, giving his target just two extra seconds of lead over the hilltop.

Joseph successfully made his way into the open where he had prepared a defense - the gauntlet – but felt that it was in vain; it was too late and he would be shot dead at any second. He darted towards the pinch-point in the rock ledges with everything in him and mentally prepared himself to meet his Maker out of schedule in full sprint. The lunatic was no more than twenty-five feet behind as Joseph bounded over the space between the rock.

The lunatic, to refuse Joseph the luxury of dying quickly by his hand, drew back his club and threw it like a tomahawk as he stepped into the delicate crunch of a fragile trigger. Joseph turned to his left, ready to follow the heavy stream at the top of the hill and glanced back behind him. From a trench in the ground that had been hidden beneath a single layer of broad leaves, a trap snapped up like the large bite of a Great White shark; the bowed frame made of the cooper's staves set with rows of long wood spikes like deadly teeth. As the points instantly entered into the lunatic's thighs at the front and back, drawing his attention away, the spinning club struck Joseph on the side of the head and knocked him unconscious.

Alistair screamed out in agony as he lunged forward upon the spikes in his momentum and drove them completely in to the frame that held them. He bent over at his waist and was held there firmly by his legs. The muskets that dangled from his neck in the front and back prevented the teeth from entering his organs, but his legs were penetrated entirely through on both sides.

Joseph fell limp, face first, into the rushing white water and was pushed down over the stair of rock into a shallow pool far below.

The lunatic screamed with terrible agony and got a pistol into his hand. He gritted his teeth in rage and pain and his eyes watered from it. He waved the gun side to side to fire at anything that moved and tried to turn and look behind him. As he did, the muscle in his legs twisted against the embedded spikes and he cried out in his torment. Saliva streamed down from his mouth. He let his pistol go to hang down from a strap at his hip and took hold of the frame of the jaw. He forced it open with all of his strength while gritting his teeth with a scream. Blood flowed from multiple giant puncture holes as he arduously struggled to free himself. He pushed the mouth open far enough in the front to strike down against a spike that was deep in his thigh with the hard stock of a musket. He snapped one off and fought to keep them from reentering the wounds in the front, but had to pay for it with added pressure in the back. He contorted himself with a raised hand and broke four more blood-soaked spikes from the same line. He leaned forward, sliding himself off of the ones in the back that were deep in his buttocks and thighs like meat from a fork. As he attempted to roll out, a ratcheting and tightening system that maintained severe pressure with kinetic energy by rope, snapped it closed again with irrepressible force. The damage was doubled and the long points unbiasedly found new flesh to puncture into. A ragged and awful wail sliced the air from the madman's mouth and he took hold of the pistol that questioned its senseless absence. The living triangles of rope worked in accord as potential energy from a line that ran away in a shallow trench beneath a meager leaf cover to a smartly resisting palm head. Alistair fired into its workings, the smooth pegs of triangles at his thigh and split the rope in one place amidst a flash and spray of burning powder. The surreptitious tree that made his havoc returned to his former opposite lean softly with miniscule movement. The lunatic gritted his teeth and screamed as he fell forward on the unraveling mechanism, over the front jaw of the trap to the ground.

He convulsed in agony, groaning and grunting, and then carefully crawled up the side of the rock ledge to his feet. His blood followed and smeared upon the rocks behind him. He took hold of another primed pistol, turned, and aimed to the upper rock ledge where Joseph was supposed to be in position to slay him. No one rose to beset him and he violently trembled in both rage and pain.

Joseph's inanimate body floated face up in a large shallow and very slow moving pool at the base of the rocky ledge waterfall. Blood flowed from a head wound into the water around him. He floated in plain view for some time and a slight whirlpool pulled him around a mud bar grown up with tall grasses.

At that moment, the lunatic jumped to the muddy bank of the pool and remained low, holding his stomach and clenching the flintlock pistol in his shaking hand. With his other supporting his weight on the ground, he remained still as he crouched there, bleeding in the mud, but hissed and grunted in voices of pain. He looked forward, down the stream and over the trees beside him as Joseph quietly floated behind the grassy bar in the water to his left…out of view.

Chapter 11
Under An Orange Sky

$\mathfrak{T}$he tiny current pushed Joseph under low-hanging leafy branches and grasses that leaned over the ledges of the far bank to the water. The lunatic went down to his knees in the mud and turned to look in Joseph's direction, but missed the sight of him. He labored to his feet and limped off quickly over the uneven ledges into the jungle.

Joseph came to rest as his head touched the smooth sediment that had heaped beneath the dark shade of shelter. His eyelids twitched in small shafts of sunlight that beamed down from a single clear opening along the rocky embankment above. The water continued to cascade over the ledges not far from him, but he was partially submerged over his ears to his cheekbones and heard nothing.

At eight o'clock that evening, Joseph had not moved. He lay motionless in the pool near the base of the waterfall in partial concealment. An eight-foot snake slithered upon the surface of the water and crossed over his knees on its way upstream. As its tail whipped past, Joseph gasped with a shout and sat upright through the grasses in the water, not knowing where he was. His body shook in fear and he touched his head wound with his hand. It was only lightly bloodied, but pounded with a painful headache. He crawled from the mire and the drooping branches with a loud careless groan and stood slowly in the water. He straightened up by placing his hands on his lower back and moaned aloud from the ruthless ache in his body. He unexpectedly remembered what had happened in a flash of information and bowed down to the water alongside the high bank and peered out. He inched forward, climbed from the water, and crouched low to the ground among the leaves. The lunatic had sprung the trap. He could see it in his mind. It had succeeded. He could remember. He made a sour face and reached to the back of his neck. A large black leech was attached to his flesh at his hairline and he quickly slung it off to the ground. His fingertips were red from it. He stared at them as his blood was mingled with the water that dripped from his arm. He knew that it would all end that way - in blood.

He moved forward and upwards to his attack position that overlooked the trap, above on the hill. The sun was setting and after so much time, he did not know what to expect. The ideas of what he would see filled him with anxiety and he reached forth his hand to fill it. Lying on his stomach against the rock, he wriggled upwards to its ledge to a heap of sharpened bamboo spears that he had placed there to kill the lunatic. He took one into his open right hand. His eyes moved just far enough upon the ledge to see in the setting sun the trap had been sprung, but was empty. It had been successful in that it caused a cruel affliction to his enemy, but had failed to kill him on its own; or so it appeared. Joseph was unsure by the standing stakes that were red with evil blood. The demon was mortal and bled out his life as all do and a deep hope that he would suffer in misery to death under some rock permeated him to the pores of his skin. He slumped back down below the ledge and turned onto his back in despair. He would not be so lucky. The lunatic could not be killed and would not merely die. If only he were there to finish him; to pierce him through with a hundred pikes; to hold his severed head on a spear and gouge out his damned eyes. He was unnerved and disappointed unto deep depression. He rubbed his mouth and chin with his hand, distraught at how things nearly transpired; frustrated that this malevolent deceiver got away. He tightly clutched a long bamboo spear from the bundle and quietly backed away into the jungle, nervous and shaken.

As dusk approached, Joseph moved slowly in soreness through the alternating heavy and light density of foliage. He was becoming more comfortable in the dangerous atmosphere with natural things and now had become more accustomed to the unnatural things as well. He traveled a new way, limping and using the bamboo spear like a cane and crutch when he could. He traveled down into a ravine, like a flash-flood riverbed, and followed it upwards to the side of a hillock, rising to the base of a very large elaborately multibranched tree. As he rose on its opposing side, he paused to catch his breath. He stretched himself slowly and could feel the muscles within in organized refuting over his bones. He leaned backwards to give relief to his demanding vertebrae and looked upwards into the canopy. There, directly above him, was the silhouette of a boat sitting upright in the very top of the tree. Joseph paid it no mind and stooped to the ground, placing both hands on his knees to catch his breath. He realized that he should be puzzled over what he just saw and it finally became reflected on his face. He stood upright and gazed straight up again. A real smile appeared amidst his aching head and he snorted in disbelief. He looked to the ground, shaking his head with a strengthened smile and then up again to a boat in the treetop.

Joseph, being a nimble climber from his time aloft, slowly got himself sixty feet from the ground to the treetop on the uppermost branches. He broke free from the canopy and could see the jungle spreading out all around. The ocean's sounds drifted to him in clarity at that height and he turned himself around towards the setting sun. He smiled softly, squinting his eyes upon it as he watched the red sphere disappear on the horizon far away; remembering those peaceful moments from the crow's nest. He sighed again in a lonely sadness yet felt some gift of encouragement and then turned to a sight he never imagined he would see.

To his amazement, he looked upon a whaleboat from the Fortune in excellent condition. Again, he snorted and shook his head in disbelief. Inside the boat laid a twisted mess of whale-line rope in a great heap, submerged in stagnant rainwater. Joseph put his hands on the gunwales and pulled it downwards towards him. The boat was unstable enough to tip and the water poured out over the tree's arms to the ground. Joseph grabbed hold of the whale-line and began to coil it around his arm and shoulder. He hauled to the end, but whale-line from the main tub still remained in a great twisted heap. He threw the rope over the boat at its waist and slowly climbed beneath to retrieve it. He tied a knot, threw the rope over a limb, and began to let it down as awkward as it was - as best he could.

As the boat traveled through the limbs every fifteen feet, Joseph made his way down over it until it reached the ground; sometimes sideways, sometimes pointing straight downwards, but always quietly. He jumped to the dirt alongside the boat, which had flipped upside down, and rechecked his surroundings. He dug his hands under it and turned it over. Held in the bottom of the boat, tightly strapped in by rope, was a human leg and foot, severed at the hip. It was decayed, but still Joseph noticed the familiar black sores upon the flesh. He jumped back and covered his face with his arm in disgust and fright.

"God, have mercy…" he mumbled softly into his sleeve.

He took hold of a thick broken branch lying nearby and poked at the leg to get it free. Working it out from under the ropes with one hand, he flipped it over the side of the boat onto the ground while keeping his other arm over his nose and mouth. He stepped a few feet away and cleared a place of ground to bury it and to hide it. He gouged away at the earth with a stick and put the leg there at the base of the tree, keeping his face covered from the smell.

Joseph pulled out the remaining line that was coiled throughout the inside of the whaleboat. As he did, he found that everything, including the mast and sail was still braced inside and intact. Amazed again, he smiled, staring at a miracle. He moved to the front of the boat, took hold of his towline, and began to drag it slowly through the growing shadows of the jungle ahead.

After a few days, Joseph lay still in his hideout in the heat of the day. By then, he had the makings of a beard and his appearance had greatly changed. He looked along the wall where the bananas had usually sat in storage, but on that day there were none. He had not eaten in two days and knew that the search for a new issuance of nourishment was impossible. He wrapped his arms around his waist and hunched over as his empty stomach turned in knots. He became increasingly disturbed at the thought of returning to the banana trees.

Through an opening, Joseph saw the waning crescent moon among the countless stars in another clear night. It had been yet another three days without food and he tried not to focus on the numbers. He paused for a moment as he crouched low, making his way to a new secluded place in the freshwater stream. He found his way there in the dimly lit night and put his hand into it. It flowed only at a small trickle as if the water supply threatened to run dry into a shallow pool the size of a punch bowl. He lapped it up from his cupped hand, lying prostrate on the ground and dreamed that it was a river of honey. He wanted to chew it to remind him of meat and potatoes. There had been no rain in a week. His appearance became more disheveled than any other time before as he hungered. His skin poked pale through his loosening clothes. He could not hunt well at all in the darkness for fruits or berries and feared to go abroad in daylight. He took in enough water which woke his belly to gripe at him and looked up again at the night sky from the ground. He was beginning to slip and felt like a thin empty shell. He was a lonely ghost cursed to be invisible to haunt the hills and valleys of a lost and silent world. There were none who were spared of his companions and their souls were snatched away like his into oblivion. It was more painful to his life expectations than to his wasting condition. These were the things that stole his dreams and left him in want for every good thing. He was no longer living, but existing - and he was failing even in that.

He dipped his water container into the pool, stood, and returned to the dark paths that brought him there.

$\mathfrak{T}$he rains had not come and the temperatures of the island rose to wretched levels in the days following. Nothing stirred in the growth. Nothing shook the leafy plants on the hillsides. In pressing survival, the despondent man left his hiding place in early morning as the sun lifted again with a promise to cook him well if he were to exit his body and leave it idle. Joseph crept low to the ground on his knees and did not raise himself any higher. He was an animal and crawled upon the earth as one in search of food. He was humbled as Babylonian King Nebuchadnezzar and in his heart, like Job, wondered why. The insects would occasionally cling to him and eventually go their way, but he no longer regarded the bites of the others. In his slow drudgery, he was stealthy. It put him in the animal world and they above made no observation of his intrusion. In dull and muted human senses, he worked his way to a sweet smell of flowers. It became stronger and for the growth that pressed hard upon him, he could not see anything out of the ordinary, but the forced focus of green blinders. It grew in strength and hit him in imposing waves to where it seemed to permanently cling within his nostrils in layers.

When the last bit of leaf matter parted to him, there, on strange short gray trunks that stood three feet tall were pink flowers. The peculiar trunks were like that of soft woody trees and held many rings of design to which each oozed with a type of golden sap. They were deadly lures to ants for some reason and hundreds, maybe thousands of them were swallowed in it. Joseph reached his finger and caught a glob of the gooey ant mixture before it fell to the ground in its weight and looked at it. He brought it to his nose. Its scent was the pure essence of floral perfume and it ran down his finger like unrefined honey.

He began to breathe with puffs of anxiety and readied himself, staring on in burdensome contemplation. He quickly smeared the clump onto his tongue and mashed it around inside his mouth, preparing for bitter poisonous recompense. The flavor was as it suggested by display and smell and not deceptive…much to his relief. It had notes of sugar cane mingled with honeydew; rose petal and beet molasses and the added prolonged richness benefit of ants. To Joseph it was divine and he wanted a spoon. In the undergrowth, he had found an answer for his number one problem of that day and he was grateful. He chewed the lumps and swallowed them carefully with the odd sense that one feels when eating large clumps of insects, but it would have to do. If he ever dreamed of living another week on the earth or seeing another human being again it would certainly suffice. His choice was first buttered oxen or broiled mutton and goat's milk with red grapes and cheese curds with baked pheasant, pork loin in chicken egg soup or peppered turkey dropped over lamb sausage and as he smeared the sap into his mouth from his hand, he, for a moment, did not remember those things.

Their yield was exhausted and Joseph resorted to licking the smooth gray trunks for the last fading remnants as a dog at oozing sores or a drunkard against the wall of a busted barrel. There were only five representations of the species and he feared he would not see another cluster of them like it anywhere that he was able to pass. With his knife, he carefully slashed a portion away into its light yellow meat, but there was no more of the golden prize to exude that way. He was temporarily revived and with the life that he had gained, moved slowly on to return into the impatiently waiting dark.

Joseph's beard had grown full. He returned to his hidden drinking water cache in the night and found that it had nearly run dry. He lay prostrate, dipped his hand into it, and realized that only his fingertips had gotten wet. He brought a single handful of water to his mouth and looked again to the sky. A waxing crescent moon appeared to him on a clear canvas. There were no welcomed threats of cloud and it seemed that they had also finally abandoned him. He was nearly ready to give up and risk what was left of his life to venture out for food. He began to lose hope as he stared long at the moon which had followed him there across the ocean from England. With deep breaths, he stared motionless at the night sky and it was his only sky. He wondered what they were doing back home. He wondered what wars or rumors of wars had brought out their ugly heads for all to see. He did not care. Sitting there in a place where quiet was so heavy and influential that it rang in the hearer's ears, it was easy to think upon mankind in a detached objective way. He was no longer part of it; no longer a functioning person with any use or purpose at all. He could feel his soul pushing and pulling upon his chest to force air in and out of his body and he wanted him to be free of it. He felt trapped within a trap within a trap. It was enough and was tired. The meaning had been drained out of the bottom. His mind had finally wearied him of thought and he did not want to figure it out anymore or know the answers. It was an awful way to die; the soul first before the body and he wondered if it had finally crept up on him. He would sleep and if it were to be so, he would wake again and feel himself around on the earth like a blind dog.

That night at two o'clock in the morning, Joseph once more found sleep against the wall of his hideout in his usual upright position. His head was forward against his chest in nearly complete darkness. His soft breathing was clear in the quiet of the tree. In that silent moment where things had been predetermined, predestinated, and set in their right place, something quickly crawled over his arms and legs and roused him to wake. He jumped and sat still in limbo of half sleep and legitimate confinement as giant cockroaches, centipedes, and other fast multi-legged creatures of the insect kingdom wiggled in through the cracks in his door and ran over his body to the ceiling. He cried out and frantically brushed them off as screeching sounds of the jungle animals penetrated his walls. He dove for the exit in fright, quickly pulled down the mosquito covering from the door, and pried it open. When it fell open, dozens of insects ran in from the edges and coated the walls before he could escape.

Joseph crawled out, brushed the ones that had fallen on his back from scraping the doorway, and darted twenty feet from his tree in panic. The animals of the island roared and screeched with confounding dread. The sound was foreign and unknown and the alarm blared in his ears. A dark heavy smoke rolled slowly in on his left and an invisible swarm of birds began to fly over him with squawking from the darkness. The jungle was on fire.

Joseph ran into the gray-black wall of carbon vapor to see what was happening. The monkeys, birds, and reptiles of the jungle retreated towards him wildly over carpets of fleeing insects. As he stood stunned, a long green snake zipped between his feet before he had time to jump out of its way. Joseph's face glowed red in the light of a roaring and crackling inferno that spanned the entire island, north to south. He was enveloped in smoke and it took his breath. Terror-stricken, he covered his face with his arm and backed away, coughing, and fled the way he came.

He sprinted as fast as he could in the dark, down through the ravines and over the rock ledges in the swelling smoke. The fire excelled quickly and burned everything close behind him in a booming wall of heat. Joseph ran hard and passed through the jungle towards the sea, darting left and right through the heavy cover and terrain that tried to make him its prisoner.

He made an enormous curve, bringing himself near the southernmost edge of the flames. Well illuminated by the approaching fire, he stopped and began to pull away foliage that concealed the whaleboat. It was uncovered within a cloud of smoke and he took hold of the towline tied to the bow to save it. He dragged it through the trees with all of his strength, running as hard as he could for the water. The sand of the beach touched his feet and he saw the Fortune at sea, flashing yellow in the flicker of immense fire. Lizards, snakes, and insects fled from the jungle to the shore and lingered in the shallows, forced to drown themselves because of the intense heat.

Joseph quickly pulled the boat to the sea and jumped inside, hiding in the shadows made by the line of trees between him and the flames. He grabbed up two oars, set them into the oarlocks, and paddled swiftly towards the Fortune for asylum. The whaleboat rose up against the incoming tide and Joseph swung out to his left, into the strongest light of the fires to master it. He paddled hard in complete awe, seeing that the entire island burned at once. Several birds, cockatiels and green parrots, fluttered into his boat with terrified screeches and tried to find footing as others passed overhead to the ship behind him.

He broke free from the push of the tide when, suddenly, a chunk of the gunwale of the boat shattered into pieces. Joseph jumped and his passengers flinched as the sound of gunfire cracked from the distant beach in front of him. The lunatic stood at the edge of the tide aiming a second musket and fired again. Splinters of wood blew up into Joseph's face as the shot shattered the loggerhead that lay at the rear of the boat.

Coming alongside the Fortune quickly, Joseph paddled lying down along the centerboard. He had only fractions of seconds to retreat and feared another shot would penetrate his boat and hit its mark. He sat up briefly to see the lunatic dive head first into the ocean towards him before he circled around the ship and out of view. Joseph hurriedly tied a short whale-line from the boat to a piece of split back stay rigging that draped down into the water from the Fortune's broken mizzen mast. He clambered up the side of the ship along the chains to the channels, to the lanyards on the starboard side until he scaled the bulwarks' summit of the weather deck.

He ran to the Fortune's bow as the entire island was ablaze before him. He frantically searched the reflections and shadows that writhed on the surface of the sea, which glowed orange and yellow, for his enemy. He dashed to the larboard side and then to the starboard, but saw nothing. The fire raged in the distance and the howls of the animals continued to echo over the water. Great flocks of colored birds took refuge aloft on the torn rigging and skewed angles of the fallen yards. They cried and fluttered from all directions as they lit onto the deckhouses and gunwales around him. Joseph, wide-eyed in terror, backed away from the bow and quickly glanced over the decks for an effective weapon or cover. He knew that if he would attempt to only hide, he would be eventually discovered and killed. He turned away, sprinted aft along the starboard side, and saw the decomposing corpse of Rawley Chapman again, amidships, wedged between the casks. Joseph quickly kneeled to him, avoiding the look of his twisted face and ran his hand along the back of the dead man's cold hard waist where it pressed against the deck. There, he found his eight-inch knife held inside its scabbard. Joseph drew it out and held it to his eyes; the blade glimmering in reflection of the fires over the bows.

He crouched low and crept out again to the bow of the ship, waiting for the lunatic to show himself. He carefully looked over the larboard side again from bow to stern, but saw nothing clinging to her hull. He dashed to the starboard side doing the same, but found nothing. Joseph ran aft towards the wheel to secure the stern with the knife held forward.

Alistair, who was naked and carried no musket guns, crawled up from the ocean quickly, clinging to the bobstays and bowsprit shrouds on the larboard bow. He held fast with his left hand grasping Fortuna's Wheel - her face stirring in crimson, her eyes alive in the flashing fire. There, against the side of the ship, his pistol, dry and ready, waited for his hand. He pulled it free from a rope that stretched tightly under the gunwales and double-cocked the hammer.

Joseph crouched low and hurried forward again on the starboard side of the tryworks. Fear had gripped him in his uncertainty. As he first came into full view of the bow, he saw the lunatic taking aim from over the side and instantly ducked backwards against the tryworks' wood overdeck wall. The pistol cracked from the gunwales and the ball passed through the wall and through Joseph's left arm. Joseph cried out, turned the corner, and charged him in an attempt to prevent the lunatic from having time to fire another.

Alistair had a reserve stashed at his hand and pulled it free. He attempted to get over the bulwarks at the bow to deck, but Joseph was on top of him in an instant, swinging the knife. Alistair was unable to fire for his pistol hand momentarily held him to the ship in his climb. He dodged Joseph's first lunge at his face by a fraction of an inch and yanked him overboard, head first by the throat. Joseph got his free hand into the lunatic's hair and pulled him down with him and they fell head first against the side of the ship. Both men, tangled upside-down in the fore lower shrouds that were ripped from the foremast, struggled hand to hand, face to face over the ocean.

Joseph bled from his wound, but fought fiercely for his life. Alistair tried to shake him loose to turn the gun at close proximity, but Joseph's grip did not relent. Alistair clenched Joseph's right hand with his left, over top of the knife, and landed blows to Joseph's head and shoulder with the handle of the pistol. He tried to turn the muzzle into him again, but Joseph resisted with his elbow on the corresponding arm. The lunatic attempted to land another, but missed, striking the side of the ship near Joseph's face and the gun went off. The powder ignited and flared with yellow sparks and burnt their arms along with the side of the ship. Tiny droplets of showering fire like falling stars were drowned the ocean. The shot grazed the hull and created a shallow rut in the timbers as it cut an inch into the surface with a burst of splinters and struck the water below.

Joseph dealt a blow directly into Alistair's right eye, knocking his head backward. He smeared his left hand down across the devil's cheekbone and got his fingers under his jaw. As he did, he turned the knife with great effort around from facing upwards, away from his enemy, down towards him. Both of them grunted and gritted their teeth as they executed great physical strength in the race to keep their feet wrapped in the ratlines above them.

Alistair cried out and dropped the pistol into the ocean, fearing he would fall without his right hand as Joseph pulled up and dug his fingers under his jaw. The knife, forced downwards at the same time, put Alistair's left arm in an awkward and vulnerable position. He growled and roared like a wild beast as he pounded Joseph's head with his fist and got his loose hand around Joseph's throat. Before he could squeeze, Joseph lunged and sliced across his forearm with the edge of the knife. For a split-second it freed Joseph's knife hand. Alistair was cut deep enough to be frightened and his blood squirted out in a single open spurt to the water. Joseph drew back to stick him in the neck with the blade and came down with it. Alistair swung back on the shrouds, out of the way of the stab, and twisted Joseph around, escaping his grip on his face.

Alistair, in a flash, pulled himself right side up on the swinging ratlines and quickly scaled the side of the ship to the main deck. As he went, he planted his foot on Joseph's hip and thrust off him as Joseph curled upwards to catch his ankle.

Joseph immediately followed, but remained a few seconds behind. He kept the knife in his right hand and hurried upwards to the weather deck, but Alistair had disappeared from view. He slid aft to his right as he ascended the ropes, attempting to appear on deck from another place. He took hold of a loose rope that stretched down from the bulwarks and swung on it over the ocean. He grabbed hold of a few fragments of the busted lower main shrouds that draped down like the set he had dangled upside-down from before. He got his left hand onto it and raised his knife hand up near the top edge of the bulwarks when a chain beat down over the edge and struck his right hand. Joseph cried out and dropped the knife into the ocean. It burned with pain. Again, Alistair drew back the large iron chain and beat down against the side of the ship, trying to crack Joseph's skull. Joseph fell backwards and nearly lost his grip as he attempted to avoid the onslaught. He hung by one arm, his left hand, wrapped tightly in the ratlines, amidships. Again, the lunatic, who was out of view, dragged the chain to the main deck causing it to rattle against the timbers of the gunwales. He swung it down again like a heavy whip. It whistled through the air, flogged the side of the ship like a battering ram and Joseph swayed to one side, barely missed. The chain rattled again, grinding upwards like the ratcheting of a drawbridge as Joseph looked down between his feet that dangled without support, high above the ocean. Swaying side to side far below between his legs was a single line of shroud with a Dead Eye turned on its end. It stretched behind his back and Joseph managed to wrap his free hand in a loop at its center.

Alistair was wide-eyed and gritted his teeth as he drew back the heavy chain again, ready to hone in the fatal blow. He twirled the giant links around his side and behind his right shoulder in one motion. He heaved it forward over his head to strike as the Dead Eye on the end of a rope whipped up over the bulwarks diagonally with the momentum of a released spin and struck him in the chest. He fell backwards onto the deck, dropping the chain, and gasped for air. It nearly collided with his head and would have broken it.

Joseph immediately slung his leg over onto the main deck at the sound of Alistair's fall and turned aft, towards the main mast, just inches from the lunatic. Alistair reached up for Joseph's legs as he passed, but missed him by only centimeters. He quickly crawled forward on his hands and knees like a spider to the starboard bulwarks as Joseph turned his back and ran. He looked back as he did and ducked to the side as a broad hatchet spun past his head and stuck deep into the main mast.

Alistair came running directly behind it and tackled Joseph at the fife-rails that surrounded its base. He tried to strangle him and beat his head onto the deck.

They bludgeoned each other with the bones of their fists and tried to gouge out eyes. Joseph clenched his own wrist for support as he lied on his back and cracked the lunatic over the face with his elbow. Alistair drew back a hand and punched Joseph's forehead, banging it onto the deck. He reared back to inflict it again when Joseph landed his elbow into Alistair's side. He followed the move by catching Alistair under his jaw with his right hand and throwing him over to the right, sliding out from beneath him.

Joseph eyed the axe handle sticking out of the crippled mast and tried to reach for it. Alistair dove onto Joseph again and bent him back as both managed to their feet, going for his throat. They wrestled against fife-rails and the pins began to dig deeply into Joseph's back. He worked his hand free and his fingertips rubbed against the hatchet handle as he reached back as far as he could. Alistair noticed and lunged forward. He grabbed hold of Joseph's forearm five inches from his wrist, nearly able to reach the hatchet from his position.

Joseph, nearly overpowered, headbutted Alistair on the bridge of his nose, broke it, and knocked him back. It burst with blood as Joseph jerked the broad hatchet from the tight grip of the mast. Alistair gritted his teeth and screamed into Joseph's face as Joseph came down swinging the blade. Alistair caught Joseph's axe hand and pushed him away as Joseph leaned forward into the strike. The blade sank into the side of a cask that was strapped to the bulwarks among several others. Joseph pulled it out as Alistair got his hands on the axe handle with him and whale oil spewed onto the deck from the hole.

It spilled rapidly down the main deck in a broad river to the bows as the ship leaned forward on the seabed below. Joseph raised the blade again and forced it downwards onto Alistair, but he resisted and forced him back. The swing landed into the top edge of a second cask and the iron hoop along its head created a spark against the blade. The staves were rent open. The oil gushed onto the deck from the second hole and burst into flames.

The fire immediately traveled the path to the bows in the oil and the entire front of the Fortune went up in flames. The oil ignited as it flowed from the busted casks and the fire quickly grew in size. Flames dripped from the spaces between the temporary bulwarks at the Flensing Stage into the ocean below.

The tied whaleboat was pushed forward, towards the ship's bows, in the incoming tide and knocked against the hull. As the men continued to struggle, the burning oil flowed into the belly of the boat upon the ribs from the bulwarks above and specks of fire began to rise up from it.

Alistair punched Joseph across the side of the jaw with his right hand and knocked him back with his left clenched onto Joseph's axe hand. The men twisted and turned away from the flames that spouted up around them. The lunatic slammed Joseph's back into the tryworks' starboard side, pushing with his right forearm under Joseph's neck. Joseph choked and landed his left fist onto the lunatic's cheekbone, both still struggling for the blade. Joseph maintained his grip on the hatchet and sent his left knee into the lunatic's ribs. He repeated with more force and pushed him away with his upper body, causing Alistair to lose his footing against him.

The fire grew and spread over the ship. Some of the rigging and standing rigging began to catch fire as the fore part of the Fortune started to burn.

Joseph pushed himself from the tryworks' brick

and the men, both out of breath, continued to fight as they moved aft on the deck. Alistair kept his grip on Joseph's axe hand and Joseph tried to pull it free.

Alistair attempted to push Joseph to the ground to get the upper hand and both ended up pressed against the bulwarks at the cutting-in stage, amidships, on the starboard side. Joseph stood aft and Alistair before, against the bulwarks. The hatchet blade gleamed in the light of fires as it was raised above them, hungry for more, over the side of the ship and over the sea. Alistair began to overtake him and bent him backwards over the gunwales. He pressed his right hand against Joseph's throat with great strength and laid him down.

In one final moment of opportunity before certain death, Joseph slid his left hand across his chest under Alistair's strangling arm and drove his left elbow straightforward into Alistair's face. He expended such force with his arm and shoulder that he broke out Alistair's front teeth and knocked him backwards.

The lunatic let go of his grip on Joseph's axe hand and fell to the ground, but immediately scrambled to his feet to retaliate before Joseph could react. His look was crazed and of total madness. He crouched low like an animal anticipating a deadly pounce on its prey. Joseph stood ready in the flickering fires in only a short moment of sizing between them. The lunatic lunged at him, taking hold of the bulwarks with his left hand for leverage.

Joseph, in an immense rage with flaring wild eyes, swung the broad hatchet down and chopped off Alistair's left arm at the elbow against the gunwales. The blade sank deep into the timber and firmly stuck as the forearm with its hand and fingers fell over the side into the ocean. As Joseph prepared to take two hands to pull the hatchet free, the lunatic cried out with a long and terrible scream. He stumbled and fell onto his back, staring in horror at his severed arm. His blood gushed out and sizzled in the fires of the deck as he stood, turned, and ran away towards the bows.

Joseph immediately let loose of the haft and rushed for the wheel. He reached up under the boat bridge and took hold of a harpoon that he had placed there.

It was a thing of unnatural beauty; one of Mister Stearne's makings and there were none other its equal in all history of time. It was straighter than Thomas Alexander's mythological Trident and under the dancing light of demons, radiated brighter in absolute power. No living man had laid eyes upon one ever before or after. The conjuror forged it in razor sharp flawless terror and turned it upon the wheel of bitter cruelty. It would sing as the most wicked of hated goddesses when thrown and fracture a valiant path through the battling air - holding sure as islands of volcanoes under any magnitude of pressure with a delicate pin. It promised its champion beforehand to slay all and could bewitch children to kill with its touch. It would slide through any entanglement of meat or matter as if the substance had been softened like heated butter and not stray from its projected straight-line path in definitive execution. Here, it was held forever fast under any known measure of earthly weight for the coming ages and eternities with one of Mister Digby's masterful knots; the infinite model for all nautical bonds before and after to a line that extended upwards from beneath the boat bridge, aloft. The dead would have their retribution at only the sight of it and Joseph wielded it with terrible sovereignty.

He came out and stood in the open, alongside the starboard bulwarks' cutting-in stage with the beaming iron raised in supreme balance over his shoulder. It made itself weightless in his hand and tried to lift away ahead of his motion.

Just as the lunatic neared the bows to dive over into the sea, Joseph threw the harpoon to its splendor of complete perfection over the deck into his back. The two-flued iron point passed eagerly through organs and flesh, ripped through Alistair's chest, and jutted out from between his ribs beside his sternum.

Alistair fell forward onto his face with a screeching gasp. He rolled onto his hands and knees amidst the fires and slowly crawled towards the bows - pulling against the point sticking out of his bare chest with his fingers.

Joseph laid hold of the broad hatchet with both hands and pulled it free. He raised it over his head, turned, and looked again upon his tormentor. He swung down onto a taut rope that ran aft over the gunwales from belaying pins to the broken main mast. The line snapped and the starboard anchor swung forward from the darkness over the sea from the mizzen mast as rope began to quickly pay out around blocks in the rigging both high and low. Blocks moved and buzzed as ropes unreeved rapidly through them. The anchor swung towards the bows from a yardarm of the main mast over top and past the burning whaleboat below with a hundred loud creaks. As it made a full swing forwards by gravity, it stopped and dropped straight down towards the sea. The line of rope leading from the harpoon over the starboard side instantly became taut and jerked Alistair backwards, dragging him with great speed across the burning oil of the deck. He smashed through the bulwarks at the cutting-in stage and Joseph ran to the broken wall and looked over the side after him. Their eyes met as the massive anchor plunged into the ocean beneath them. Alistair screamed all the way down as he was dragged backwards with the anchor to the bottom of the sea.

Joseph stared into the deep as the lunatic disappeared into the black waters; taken back to where he came from. Joseph was stunned and unable to move. He could see in his mind's eye the villain on an uninterrupted decent that passed through the sea floor in darkness and continued on into the illuminated heat and unquenchable fires of Hell.

He struggled for his breath and blinked his eyes quickly, twitching from shock and exhaustion, unable to hear the speaking world around him. He stood listening and heard Alistair's faint screams as his flesh began to melt off in the bowels of the earth. His senses returned to the natural world and the fires that blazed on the ship crackled and sizzled in his ears. He immediately turned to everything in a panic and threw open a storage box near the main hatch. Inside, laid torn fragments of spare canvas. He seized a corner, dragged out a piece about ten square feet in size, and rolled it over his shoulder.

He darted to the stern of the ship and climbed up

onto the hurricane house. He jumped into the sea and swam to the surface. He pulled himself into the whaleboat and beat out the flames with the wet canvas. The boat was lightly charred in places, but sound. Joseph wrapped the heavy cloth around his neck and climbed the side of the Fortune to the burning deck.

He stepped over the bulwarks and fiercely beat down the flames, moving quickly from aft to forward. The oily sole sizzled and steamed in objection from his assault, but it ultimately heeded. Every last bit of strength that he had left was exerted and he pounded out the fires to nothing but smoke and steam.

He breathed heavily and suffered from enormous thirst and became weak as he dropped the canvas to the deck. Leaning forward to rest his hands on his knees, he looked to his gunshot wound which had been submerged in salt water and ceased bleeding heavily. He turned and looked over the bows as the island was one complete blaze. He felt faint and fell forward onto the steaming hot canvas, delirious from the fight.

"His Mercy endureth forever," Joseph said in a whisper with his last bit of strength. He heard the screeches of the island animals fade and all went black.

Chapter 12
The Wind Blows

*J*oseph woke to the sound of waves and the gentle banging of the whaleboat against the side of the ship. It was cleven-thirty in the morning under an overcast sky. He lay on his stomach on top of the bunched canvas in the same position as when he had collapsed. He made a grimaced face as he opened his eyes and raised his head. He reached into his mouth and pulled out a tooth, a second molar from his lower jaw. He almost paid it no mind, but rubbed his jaw from the pain. He slowly got onto his knees and tried to raise his wounded arm. There was not much more to do with it but groan in pain.

He stood with demanding labor and turned to face the island. It smoldered and was nearly all reduced to ash. Few trees did remain in view from where he was, but they were charred skeletal structures of what they once were. Joseph limped to the starboard side and looked over. His whaleboat was intact, tied off to the dangling rigging.

He pushed the boat from the ocean onto the shore

with a limp. There was grief over the loss of the island like a dead friend and it made him solemn. He stood in awe, not knowing what to make of it or what to do next. Hot ashes and smoldering tree stumps covered his path inland and he quietly took it in. He stopped and crouched down, touching a burned palm leaf with his dirty black hands. Something moved in the distance in front of him.

A tiny monkey like one from the banana trees stood watching him from the ground just forty feet away in the open among the smoking ashes. A very small smile grew on one side of Joseph's face, being happy to see him. The monkey turned his back and carefully walked away, further into the island between the red coals that almost totally covered the ground. Joseph did not move and watched him go, but the monkey returned and waited for him. Joseph squinted as he looked upon the monkey with the sudden feeling that he wanted something. He rose and hobbled forward across the gray desolate landscape.

The monkey spun around and walked on, leading the way into what was left of the jungle. He jumped over sticks and hot coals that were scattered across the ground, occasionally looking back. Joseph followed, some forty feet behind, and noticed there were no sounds anymore; the animals were all gone. It made him sad and he felt that too much had been sacrificed for his freedom. After some time of managing hillocks, ravines, and fallen trees that were in the processes of burning away in the middle of desirable paths, he realized they were heading towards a place that he knew well.

The monkey led Joseph slowly on to the cleft in the rock, climbed up the withered overhanging foliage that covered it, and sat upon the top edge. The plants remained unburned, clinging to life by the protection of the surrounding rock and to Joseph's dismay the water had all run and been burned dry. He came near and crouched with his knees to the ground and pulled the grasses to the side with his right hand. There, like another miracle, was an unspoiled cache of bananas and mangos piled from back to front. Joseph laughed out, but only softly in relief. He turned to his right, looked at the monkey, and nodded.

"My name is Joseph," he said with a big smile.

The monkey scratched his arm, jumped down, and walked away behind him over the rock. Joseph reached out and picked up a ripe mango. It was smooth and vividly picturesque. He stared at it in his hand and could not remember the last time he had even seen one. He breathed deeply in anticipation, nodded his head as he closed his eyes, and took a bite – skin and all. He chewed slowly, keeping his eyes closed to absorb the moment. The sensation of solid food mashed between his teeth had faded. It felt good and strange even though his jaw was incredibly sore and the space for the absent tooth throbbed. The fruit tasted better than anything he had ever tasted before; the flavors so vibrant as if they were color. Of all the puddings and cakes and treacle tarts with clotted cream that he had experienced in the better days of his childhood, there was nothing to compare. His lips quivered as he nearly wept with happiness for it. A clicking sound came from behind and Joseph opened his eyes and turned. The monkey screeched and chattered, turned, and continued over the side of another ledge. Joseph, still chewing the precious mango, stood and followed him.

He went on in wonderment as the monkey led him along familiar paths. The jungle was mostly ash and they passed through paths of concealing smoke. It grew dense and Joseph could not see the monkey in front of him anymore. He stopped and covered his mouth with his arm to breathe. A swift breeze blew over him and it dissipated to reveal nine trees standing untouched by the fire. Joseph stood in awe. They formed a cross - five trees long and five trees wide; his hideout tree being the second one from the top where the perpendicular line crossed. He walked around it in amazement, admiring and contemplating the formation as the monkey sat still and watched him.

Joseph came to his hideout tree and knelt at the doorway. He looked up from the ground along the great trunk to the sky as he placed his right hand upon it. His face beamed with a great smile and his nerves were healed in a moment of peace. He no longer felt totally alone. He looked on again through new eyes that had been replenished with hope and the gray ash that surrounded him did not seem to be so gray. The colorless clouds moved slowly together above them to their preordained mixture and made preparations.

The monkey looked to Joseph and then his eyes flashed upwards to the open sky. Drops of rain began to fall. At first they came slowly, but then fell heavily upon them and upon the smoldering ashes. Joseph's smile grew even bigger as they splashed onto his upturned face with an open mouth to drink it.

The place of the villagers had been destroyed. Their huts no longer stood, but traces of them lay in heaps among the soot and embers. The rain continued to douse all evidence of fire and in the clearing of mud and pavements of stone steps, their relics could be distinguished. Joseph picked through the remains in steam and lifted beams and threw aside burned structural carvings. There was nothing of any more worth or value in the aftermath. He turned to go his way and forfeit any idea of finding another living soul when something under a smoking plank caught his eye. He kicked over the debris and found an orange Egyptian alabaster box that had been burned out of a large wood case that held it. It was large itself; maybe fifteen inches square and did not fit in with the black landscape. In the pouring rain, Joseph knelt to it and raised the heavy stone lid away with both hands.

The sight that lay within literally brightened his face when it became exposed to the cheerless light. Looking back at him was the large emerald eyes of a golden skull. It was unbelievable. It was incredible. It was the size and shape of an actual human skull and was flawless in its luster and workmanship. It made Joseph want to weep for its eerie beauty and for that it made him afraid. He gently pushed his fingers into the spaces and lifted it. The gold was solid and took some effort to carry. Joseph snorted in disbelief and trembled with amazement. The eyes of the face were finely sculpted gems that flashed with green fire and seemed to wake at his touch. The jewel of the island had revealed itself to him and he could never in one hundred lifetimes ever put a price upon it. He supposed it to be a god of the ancient world and how it had found itself here under the burning hut would forever be left to his speculation and dreams. He loved the thing for its material allure and knew that armies would slay each other over it. It turned in his hand with great esteem. It came with a measure of sadness because of its immortality and he wished for the peoples to be standing there before him to present it as a blessing of duty; but they were gone. In consideration of what was happening, he realized that they were. He looked into its eyes and into his own reflection in its brilliant surface and when he saw himself, nodded.

The moon returned full again that night in a clear sky. Waves rolled onto the beach sands softly just as they always had for millions of years, shimmering with white light. Joseph stooped and took bananas and mangos from the ground and placed them into his whaleboat. It was filled to its fullest potential with small casks of oil and water, baskets of food, and other supplies. Beside his safely salvaged guitar was Augustin's whale tooth Scrimshaw of the Fortune in her glory - a memento to remind him and his agreement. Near those was a bundle of letters written by the crew to their loved ones and on the top was Captain Grey's loving correspondence to Annabelle, his wife. A flickering whale oil lantern lit his view where he stood against the boat on the sand. He reached into his pocket and pulled out the half-shilling coin and turned it in his hand. He was still and smiled only slightly in melancholy as he looked upon it. He slid it back into his pocket, leaned into the boat, and pulled a small cask from one corner. He tapped it open, took a drink of water, and closed it again. His arm was wrapped tightly with a piece of sailcloth, fixed to constitute a clean healing. The monkey stood watching him on the sand and Joseph turned and looked upon the island for the last time.

"Come on," he said as he turned to his new friend.

The monkey stood and looked at him.

"You're coming with me, little fellow."

The monkey ran quickly and jumped into the boat. He climbed among the items and nestled himself into the mosquito netting.

"I'll call you...John."

Joseph got a tiny smile on one side of his face as he pushed the boat into the ocean from the shore. As he drifted away from the charred ruins of the island, well lit in moonlight, Joseph took up the lantern and placed it upon a makeshift pole that protruded from the loggerhead post-hole behind him. He reached forward and picked up a large brass compass taken from the ship and set it on top of the supplies that were stowed around him.

He placed two oars in the locks and rowed a couple of hard strokes to drift the boat out to sea. As he prepared to take them in, something caught his eye from the Fortune which lay silent upon his left. A dim blue-green glow of light quickly outlined the shapes of men standing along the starboard side of the ship. Joseph's eyes widened in fear and he turned and dunked the light into the ocean, putting it out.

There, in the darkness of the starry sky, ghosts of the dead, the crewmen of the Fortune, appeared, standing side by side in a blue-green glow. Some stood behind others as all were there, even her captain, to watch him go. They were still and silent with longing looks upon their faces.

Joseph stood in his boat as he drifted past them and tears began to stream down his face. Drifting further, in view of the stern, he saw John with his hand raised to him. Joseph wept and reached out and waved goodbye as the glowing spirits softly faded away and disappeared into darkness. He stared on as the ship went black – only a dark silhouette against the moonlit night.

Joseph turned his back to it and sat, weeping aloud. He brought the oars aboard and set them along the inside edges of the boat, placed the boat's mast into the step, and wiped his face of tears as he raised the sail with a rope.

Behind him, a giant angel, glowing only dimly in a white robe with a broad golden belt and long flowing hair, stood in the ocean between him and the Fortune. He rose thirty feet above the surface of the water, which came to his upper thighs below his waist.

The angel leaned forward, took a deep breath, and blew.

The canvas sail that draped down against the mast in front of Joseph caught a soft wind and opened full, pushing the tiny boat forward into the darkness of a starlit open sea.

The End

From the author:

Thank you for buying a copy of *The Whaler Fortune*. If you have enjoyed this book, please tell someone about it by leaving a book review online where you purchased it to encourage other readers. I thank you for it. Be sure to go further with me and read *Revenge of the Wolf* – my new Victorian England Mystery/Suspense/Thriller that will make your palms sweat and keep you up all night until the very end.

Joseph's song, *Homeland*, is available as a single on iTunes and Amazon mp3. It was written and performed by me. Search: Wyatt Michael – Homeland.

This story took me a total of two years to write because of research on the subject. My goal was to write a "high-seas adventure" maritime thriller and I am very happy with the fight-for-life struggle that was produced. I have always had a fascination with the sea and the tall ships, although it was more of a fear. I think we are fascinated with what we fear. The men that went to sea for years at a time with no communication with those on land, who risked starvation, storms, drowning, disease, death, and a hard life of extreme physical affliction were totally insane in my opinion. These are the things of great stories, great films, and dreams of the artistic imagination. I hope you enjoy this as much as I have and see the underlying theme of this story.

~ Wyatt Michael

About the Author:

Wyatt Michael is a musician, singer, songwriter, suspense/thriller novelist, artist, and screenwriter. He owns Michael & Company Pictures, a film production company that he writes for. Wyatt learned to play the saxophone in 1984 with his school symphonic band. He held First Chair position for five years until he quit to learn guitar in 1989. Throughout his teens and early twenties, his music was showcased on many radio stations from Ohio to California (before internet radio was an idea). Later, he and his co-writer Samuel Atkinson built a recording studio and taught themselves how to use it. Over the next six years, his band, Only Makebelieve, recorded and finally released *Message From A Mockingbird*, an Alternative Pop masterpiece album that received rave reviews from critics all over the world. The group set out on a tour and promoted the album, which also ran on national college radio. Through stressful job situations - working nights in dark factories for years on end and driving semis across ice-covered mountains, Wyatt created a mental way of escape - writing stories. He began to write film scripts and his friends found them to be worthy of the screen. After getting a feel for the new creative form, Wyatt took on the daunting endeavor: The Whaler Fortune - his first novel. The Whaler, Fortune is a Biblical Psalms 91:11 story. Of all the stories Wyatt has written, this one most reflects him personally; hence "Joseph Michael" and his talents/woes.

www.ingramcontent.com/pod-product-compliance
Lightning Source LLC
Chambersburg PA
CBHW020725210626
46807CB00016B/29

* 9 7 8 0 6 9 2 2 6 0 9 2 0 *